D1362716

Sins of the Father

David Harrison

CREME DE LA CRIME

First published in 2006
by Crème de la Crime.
Crème de la Crime Ltd, PO Box 523, Chesterfield,
Derbyshire S40 9AT

www.cremedelacrime.com

Copyright © 2006 David Harrison

The moral right of David Harrison to be identified as the author
of this work has been asserted by him in accordance with the
Copyright, Designs and Patents Act, 1988.

All rights reserved. No part of this publication may be reproduced
or transmitted in any form by any means, electronic or mechanical,
including photocopying, recording or any information storage and
retrieval system, without prior permission in writing from the
publisher nor be otherwise circulated in any form of binding or cover
other than that in which it is published.

All the characters directly involved in this narrative are fictitious, and
any resemblance to real persons, living or dead, is coincidental. Great
care has been taken to ensure that no offence is caused to members of
the entertainment industry who are mentioned by name .

Typesetting by Yvette Warren
Cover design by Yvette Warren
Front cover image: Peter Roman.

Printed and bound in England by Biddles Ltd, www.biddles.co.uk

ISBN 0-9547634-9-1

A CIP catalogue reference for this book is available from the
British Library

About the author

David Harrison is a writer and consultant. He lives with his family in Brighton.

www.david-harrison.info

Acknowledgements

For their help and advice with research, I am indebted to Tony Deakin, Rod Lambert, Rebecca Rankin, Amanda Sorrill and Superintendent Steve Voice. Any errors or liberties taken are entirely my responsibility.

For encouragement and support over many years, I'd like to thank my parents, Ann and John Harrison, as well as Lucy Deakin, Kate Rosling and Claire Burrell. Most of all, love and thanks to my wife, Niki, for putting up with so much, and to James and Emily for their understanding. Lastly, a huge thank you to Lynne for making it happen.

For Kathleen Harrison, 1911–1995

Sins of the Father

October 1968

He was playing a happy camper when the blackmailer re-appeared. It was early morning in a field in Buckinghamshire, the air cold and crisp, the mud painted green in a mockery of summer. The distant croak of ravens sounded as forlorn as he felt.

A collective sigh of relief as the take ended: no one fluffed, no one corpsed, Sid's lascivious cackle perfectly on cue. Now a mass lighting of cigarettes, overcoats hustled on, hot tea and bacon sarnies eagerly awaited. Braying laughter from Kenny at his own filthy anecdote.

There was the usual small crowd, die-hards from the nearest village clutching autograph books, stamping feet and blowing steam like horses waiting for the off. As Eddie peeled away from the other actors they raised a small cheer. He acknowledged them with a wave, but his shoulders were set towards the man in the shabby brown raincoat: Leslie Jones, dogsbody and extortionist.

"What are you doing here?"

"Saw your Roller coming in. Latest model, isn't it?"

A couple of teenagers were suddenly next to them, nudging each other. Eddie wanted to tell them to fuck off, but he took their books, scribbled his name and turned away. He advanced on Leslie, who retreated a couple of steps.

"You got what you wanted."

"Set my sights too low, I reckon."

The first time Eddie had paid up – only a hundred quid – and told himself he'd got off lightly. He should have known better.

"What d'you think the papers would make of it, eh?"

Leslie said. "The booze and drugs and those young girls. And the ceremony? That was your idea, wasn't it?"

Eddie must have flinched, for Leslie was grinning with feral delight. "With you doing so well right now, I thought we'd make it a thousand."

"You're joking."

"I leave that to you, Eddie."

"And this is it? No more."

"You'll have my word, won't you?" But the eyes were taunting: believe that and you'll believe anything.

Eddie stayed quiet over breakfast, keeping out of the fray. Sid and Kenny were winding each other up as usual. After this he had a couple of days free, thank God, and Mary was coming up. He'd suggested leaving the baby with her mother but she wouldn't hear of it.

After brooding for a couple of hours he made a phone call from the office. "Bookie," he told the production assistant who kindly made herself scarce. He really had thought about calling his bookie, perhaps try to win his way out of trouble, but he knew it never worked.

If he paid up, the bastard would be back for more. His face had said as much.

No. That wasn't the answer.

One thing about a showbusiness career, you made friends with all sorts of interesting people. That's what had got him into this mess; now it would have to get him out.

There were two of them, big men with unpleasant faces. Not the kind you'd want to meet in a dark alley, but it wasn't an invitation Leslie could refuse.

After a warm-up with bare fists, they asked if he'd told anyone else or kept any proof. He said no. They went to work with a cosh and a knuckle-duster, concentrating on the ribs, the kidneys, the shoulders. Then they asked him again. Still no, so they smashed his left knee to a pulp. He was gone for a time, and when he came back he swore it was all in his head, safest place to keep anything.

The one in charge nodded. We believe you.

For a moment Leslie felt blessed relief. They could see him thanking the Lord it was over.

But it wasn't over. They stuffed him into the boot of their Ford Zephyr, drove to a quiet bridge in Norbury and dropped him into the path of the 22:09 to Victoria.

Ted rang later that night: problem solved. At first Eddie was shocked, but then he asked himself, what else had he been expecting? These people didn't mess around.

He could relax at last. His career was safe, his family were safe, and that's what he really cared about. His understanding wife, his little baby son.

Nicky would never have to know.

Nobody would know what he'd done.

August 1972

Summer holidays. A crappy fortnight in Cromer for the third year running.

"Show some gratitude, you little bitch!" her mum had snapped. "They don't have to do it."

They. Uncle Vince and Auntie Gwen, Mum's sister. Dolled up like a tart but just as sour inside. They ran a B & B, and Gwen never failed to point out how much the rooms could be earning at the height of the season. "Still, you wouldn't have a holiday otherwise, would you?" she chirped.

Vince drove to Croydon in his flash Triumph to collect them. Hilda spent the whole way up complaining about her daughter. "I dunno what to do with her, honestly I don't."

"She's at that age, though. What is she now, fourteen?"

"Thirteen. Just a phase, her teachers reckon. But I wonder."

"Just a phase," Vince echoed, casting a sly look over his shoulder that made her want to curl up tight. Plenty of those glances in Mum's direction, too: the old bag lapping it up. She tried to imagine being a man and wanting to kiss her mother's thin disapproving lips, or put his thing inside her. Disgusting.

Billy was sick as usual, just past Brentwood. They parked up for half an hour and left the doors open to clear the smell. No one was cross with him, of course, not poor Billy. Nine years old and he still couldn't read more than *Janet and John*.

He wasn't simple, she was supposed to tell people. Just a bit slow. But so friendly, so trusting and kind. It didn't matter that she was stronger, faster and much smarter. Everyone loved Billy. Billy was special.

Worst of all, the idiot adored her. The more she tried scaring him away, pinching and slapping him when nobody was looking, the more he trailed after her, lapping up the abuse.

Vince had a song stuck in his head, *Son of my Father* by Chicory Tip. All he sang was the title, over and over. He probably hadn't given any thought to the words, but she hated him for it all the same. Just as she hated the sticky perfumy cuddle from Gwen when they arrived, and the mothballs-and-gravy smell of the guesthouse. Only a mug would pay two quid a night for this.

It took Vince three days to make his first move, sidling into the attic room where the bed smelled of mildew and you could hear seagulls dragging their claws on the roof. She shut her eyes and kept her breathing steady, faking sleep while he bent over and kissed her as delicately as he could manage, filling her mouth with his beery breath.

The next night he pressed his lips against hers and held them there, while she felt bile rising in her throat and thought she might have to spew it in his face. Somehow she controlled it, told herself that if she didn't react it wasn't happening. She could hear Billy snoring on the mattress beside her bed, lost in innocent dreams.

Then he lifted the blanket, his fingers scuttling over her chest and across her stomach. Just as he delved between her legs, Gwen barked his name from the floor below. Vince jumped as if he'd been shot. Her eyes sprang open and for a second they just stared at each other. Then he was gone.

By now the weather had improved, warm enough for the beach. She was a strong swimmer, went twice a week to the baths in Croydon. One of the lifeguards had told her she was good enough to swim competitively, but she had no interest in that. It wasn't about other people.

6

In the shallows Billy screeched with delight as the waves swept in, like the sea had come to play with him. Sometimes he'd let her guide him in up to his chest and try floating while gripping her shoulders. "Swimming!" he'd cry. "Look at me swimming!"

Gradually he became more confident, not trying to scramble out when a wave caught him in the face. And all at once the idea was there. This would show them.

They'd come down early, Vince and Gwen still clearing up after breakfast. Mum had popped to the kiosk for some fags. No one else about.

She helped Billy float out and then, immune to his giggling excitement, she thought instead of her uncle's greasy touch as she turned her back to the shore, placed a hand on each of his shoulders and pushed down hard.

His eyes never left hers, even when he gulped some water. He looked surprised, but it was a kind of cheerful surprise because he thought she was just fooling. He trusted her too much to think otherwise.

Then he started to panic, kicking his legs, clawing at her arms. Why couldn't he just accept it? She pushed harder, using all her strength to keep him under. His hair caressed her wrist like seaweed. A stream of bubbles rose to the surface and suddenly she wasn't pushing any more. He'd fallen away. He'd gone.

She shut her eyes and swam out, a fast and furious crawl, holding her breath. Fifteen strokes, sixteen, eighteen. Make it to twenty, you can do it. Twenty-one: lungs bursting. Twenty-two: getting light-headed, what Billy must have felt, nothing mattered any more. Twenty-three: give in to it and you'd be at peace. You could be with Dad too.

Twenty-four: and up she came. A frantic gulp of air, lungs burning, head spinning. A tingling in her belly like when she touched herself sometimes in the bath.

Son of my father. Reunited. She felt jealous, more than anything. Nobody to help her take that journey.

Daddy's treasure. Daddy's princess. Alone.

It took a minute to recover, then she turned and swam for the shore. Looking up, she spotted Mum on her way back and started to scream.

Part One

1

It was an innocent enough question, but it had her sweating. Looking round the room as though the answer lay on the shelves of DVDs, or behind the rear projection TV.

"You don't remember the weather?" Nick repeated.

"Not… um… not really."

"It wasn't raining, I suppose? You'd remember that."

Lauren Doyle nodded. Yes she'd remember that, not yes it was raining. Her hands were fidgeting so she sat on them, wriggling her thighs comfortable. Up till then she'd been cheerful, chatty, throwing in details he hadn't asked for. Leaning forward in her V-neck sweater, making sure he saw plenty of cleavage.

He changed tack, dismissing her confusion as un-important. "The men in the other car would have been injured, you think?"

"Oh yeah. It was a hell of a whack."

"So I see. Now, this vehicle of yours. The Escort."

"What about it?"

He strung it out, saw the tension drawing her towards him. The killer question was often a silly one.

"Does it have four gears, or five?"

She burst into tears. The door flew open and Lauren's husband Kevin stormed into the room, fists clenched. Nick started to rise but his briefcase was on his lap. Doyle grabbed his shirt and hauled him up, scattering papers everywhere. A squat, bullish man, he seemed undeterred by Nick's height advantage.

"What's your game, all these stupid fucking questions?"

"Kev! I said we shouldn't of —"

"Shut it, babe. I'm doing the talking from now on."

"OK, then," said Nick. His face was only a couple of inches from Doyle's. He could smell onions and too much aftershave. "Let me go and we can discuss —" Doyle pulled him closer still, their noses almost touching, then shoved him back. Nick hit the sofa and rolled on to the floor.

"Don't hurt him. We'll just get —"

"I said shut it!"

Nick tried to speak but Doyle kicked him in the stomach. "Get out."

"Mr Doyle, this isn't going to —"

"Get the fuck out!"

Nick got up on his hands and knees and began gathering his paperwork. Doyle stood over him, big Reebok trainers just itching to kick again. The first actual assault since he'd gone freelance, Nick thought. A milestone of sorts.

There was an envelope half under the sofa that didn't belong to the case. Then he remembered and plucked it out. The letter from Franks. The letter about Dad. Wouldn't want to leave that here.

No one said a word while he tidied his file. He shut his briefcase and walked out as hastily as his dignity would allow. Doyle followed him to the door, so close that Nick could feel the man's breath on the back of his neck.

"My principals will be in touch," he said.

"Bunch of fucking shysters."

The door slammed when he'd barely cleared the threshold. He stretched and shook the tension out of his shoulders the way Dad used to do. Nodded to himself.

"I think that went quite well."

It's just a breathing space. It doesn't have to be permanent.

Sarah had been telling herself this for ten minutes, while

the suitcase sat on the bed next to her, waiting without reproach. When the phone rang she was jolted back to the here and now, to the decision she must take.

Had taken.

She stared at the phone. She knew it was Nick, and she knew she wouldn't be able to explain. Perhaps it was better not to try.

The window was open and she could hear some children passing the house, shouting and laughing; there was a rumble of skateboards. The phone went on ringing, a tantalising beat of silence between each tone.

If she told him, he'd act surprised, baffled, as though he had no idea things were this bad. Then he'd say something flippant and probably make her laugh. Even when she was crying he could make her laugh. Even when she hated him.

And if he made her laugh, she'd waver. And then she'd agree to stay, and he would promise to talk about it but somehow he wouldn't, and the whole miserable saga would continue.

The answering service cut in, and there was silence for a few moments. Then the phone rang again: he had redialed.

She pressed her hand to her mouth and stared at the phone as if waiting for a small animal to die.

She was out. It was safe to go home.

Nick snorted. Not funny. He considered calling her mobile, but she might think he was checking up on her. And he was hardly in a position to do that.

He was parked in a lay-by on the A27, sipping coffee from a mobile catering van. The car was vibrating slightly from the rush of late afternoon traffic. Light aircraft buzzed overhead, travelling to and from Shoreham airport.

He examined his face in the driving mirror for signs of injury; there was a mark on his chin where he'd hit the floor. Nick was just under six feet tall, with a slim build and, at thirty-seven, only the beginnings of a paunch. His dark hair was cut short and so far bore no traces of grey. He had warm brown eyes and a slightly lop-sided smile that charmed almost everyone who saw it – Kevin Doyle being a recent exception.

The encounter had left him bruised but exhilarated. His suspicions had been confirmed when he arrived at the Doyles' house in Sompting and saw there was plenty of money in evidence: a brand new BMW 3-series coupé on the drive for starters. So how come Lauren had been driving a ten-year-old Ford Escort, bought and insured only a month before the accident?

The car she'd rear-ended was a Renault Espace containing five people, all of whom had lodged claims for whiplash injuries. Allowing for the vehicle damage, compensation for injury and legal costs, the claim had a reserve of £35,000. He still had a lot of work ahead to prove it was fraudulent, but at least now he knew he was on the right track.

When he'd finished writing up his notes on the interview, he took out the letter from Howard Franks. The gist was the same as the others, but the tone was becoming harder. Franks intended to proceed with his biography of Eddie Randall, regardless of the family's objections. *It will make uncomfortable reading,* the letter warned. *I urge you to co-operate with me. At least then you'll be prepared for what's to come.*

Nick resisted the impulse to throw it away. His sister, Diana, had convinced him that ignoring Franks was no longer an option. They were supposed to be discussing it tonight.

Perhaps he and Sarah should pay her a visit, he thought. Maybe go to the pub for an hour or so. That way they might pass a whole evening without fighting.

Yeah, and a pig might take off from Shoreham.

The phone stopped ringing, and in that moment she knew she'd go through with it. The Randall charisma had been denied a chance to work its magic.

She went back upstairs feeling lighter of heart. Now to finish packing and get out before he came home.

In the bedroom the phone rang again, and this time she snatched it up. She had anger behind her now. She'd be able to tell him how it really was.

"Sarah?"

"Oh, Alex. I thought —"

"Yes?"

"Doesn't matter."

"Are you all right? Are you crying?"

She touched her cheek; evidently she was. She sniffed and rubbed her nose with the edge of her palm.

"Sarah, tell me what's wrong."

"I don't love him any more. Sometimes I feel like I hate him. So why is it so difficult to leave?"

"Leave? You mean you're walking out on Nick?"

She looked at the suitcase, almost filled, and nodded. Thank God it was Alex. It gave her a chance to tell someone, and in so doing tell herself.

"A breathing space."

"Ah." Alex was nothing if not perceptive. In the last few weeks her wisdom had been about the only thing holding Sarah together.

"In theory this should be an easy decision, but now that

I'm about to do it…" She gave a little laugh and thought: Poor woman. Dumping all this on her.

"It's quite natural to feel scared," Alex said. "This is a chapter closing. Even though it's an unhappy one, you'll still grieve at its passing."

"Do you think so?" Could she hear doubt in her voice? Was she wavering already?

"Where are you staying?" said Alex.

"The Parkside in Eastbourne. Just two nights, to start with."

"Do you want some company?"

"Someone to get slaughtered with? Maybe. Can I call you if I do?"

"Of course."

"Thanks, Alex. For everything. You've opened my eyes."

"Don't mention it. Look, I shouldn't delay you."

"OK. I'll be in touch."

She finished packing and dragged the case downstairs, all the time expecting to hear Nick's car on the drive. She had nothing rehearsed if he came face to face with her, but that didn't worry her now. Two days away, some time to herself, and then maybe she'd invite him to meet somewhere and talk. Nothing ruled in or out.

It was just after four in the afternoon when she stepped outside. At the end of the road she could see Hove promenade, the beach-huts standing like crenellations, the sea beyond as flat and green as a child's drawing. The air smelt warm and scented with barley from an offshore breeze. Traffic thundered past on the main road and seagulls cried their sad echoey cries. Everything so settled, so normal, it seemed ludicrous to think she might never come here again.

✳

After making the call Alex found her hands were trembling with excitement. This wasn't at all what she'd expected. Hoped for, maybe. But she certainly hadn't imagined making an impact so soon.

Sarah was leaving Nick. Walking out on him. And Alex was to have some of the credit. It meant that certain aspects of her plan would have to be re-thought, but it was undoubtedly a positive development.

She pondered for a while. She had a few hours to spare. If she used them wisely, she could perhaps consolidate her position. The moment of maximum vulnerability, either you exploited it or you lost it forever.

Alex was an exploiter. An exploiter *par excellence.*

And many other things besides.

2

When Nick drew up outside his house there was no sign of Sarah's Peugeot, and all the front windows were shut. He unlocked the front door, wondering if she'd gone to the gym. Perhaps she'd assumed he would be late home, or then again perhaps she hadn't. However much they might deny it, they were both still trying to avoid one another when they could.

He checked the answerphone for messages, then dialled 1471 for the last caller. Number withheld. He rang his sister.

"I don't suppose you've spoken to Sarah?"

"Not since the weekend. Why?"

"No reason. Is it OK if we come over tonight?"

"Sure. Do you want dinner?"

"Best not. Sarah might have something planned."

He rang off, aware of the hint of disapproval in Diana's farewell. She thought Nick was an idiot, jeopardising his marriage the way he'd done. "If Pat ever cheated on me, I'd cut his goolies off," she'd told him.

He went upstairs, pulling off his shirt and tie. There was an ugly bruise where Kevin Doyle's foot had connected. In the old days, when he was office-bound, he thought it was bad enough taking an earful of abuse over the phone. The threat of physical assault hadn't been part of the equation when he decided to go freelance as a claims investigator.

Still, he had been seeking a reaction and he'd got one, so he could hardly complain.

In the bedroom he stepped out of his trousers and then stopped. Something looked different. He surveyed the room slowly and didn't get it until the second time round.

Normally there were two suitcases stored on top of the wardrobe. Now there was only one.

He pulled the doors open. He wouldn't have classed himself as an expert on his wife's clothes, but an awful lot seemed to be missing. He picked up the phone and called her mobile, expecting it to be switched off. Instead he got a ringing tone, almost inaudible over the beating of his heart.

"Hello?"

"Sarah. Where are you?"

"I'm… I've decided to get away."

He sat down heavily on the bed, felt his stomach settle a couple of seconds later. "You're leaving me?"

No answer. He could hear her breathing rapidly, nervously.

"Are you coming back?"

"I don't know."

"Where are you going to stay?"

"A hotel. Don't ask me where. And don't call me, please. Give me some time."

"What about your job?" Sarah worked for an American bank, based in Brighton.

"I rang in sick. If I have to, I'll take some leave or something."

"Sarah, come on. Come home and talk about this."

"I've been waiting three months for you to do that. It's too late. I have to think it through myself. Make my own decision."

He said forlornly, "Is there someone else?"

"What? You bastard! You're the one that screws around, not me!"

The call ended abruptly. Trust him to ask the one question guaranteed to push her over the edge. He re-dialled but the phone was switched off. He cursed himself and lay back on the bed, wondering if he'd lost her forever.

Kevin Doyle's temper was quick to ignite, slow to subside. While it smouldered, no one around him was safe. Today there was only Lauren, and she knew the pattern all too well. After he threw the insurance investigator out he raged for ten minutes, telling her how fucking useless she was, telling her she'd fucked everything up. She cowered and cringed and apologised, but it didn't stop him lashing out, a fast open-handed blow to the cheek that lifted her off her feet.

She collapsed and lay still, crying without a sound. If he heard her snivelling he'd want to hit her again, he'd want to kick her and kick her until the anger was out of his system. But the tiny part of his brain that urged caution managed to take control.

He spun away and checked his phone for messages. Lauren climbed to her feet.

"I'm really sorry, Kev. Honest. I just never expected him to…"

"Nah." He thought of how long he'd spent rehearsing her, all the details about the accident, what the other driver said and did. Never thought the bastard would trap her over the number of gears. Something like that could have caught him out, never mind Lauren.

He felt his mood softening, and she must have seen it too. She embraced him from behind, nuzzling her head against his shoulder. He could feel the weight of her tits pressed against his back, making his groin tingle. They always had great sex after a fight, Lauren eager to please. Anything he wanted. Tempting.

But there was also Roger Knight, waiting to know how the interview went. Roger had been dubious about using

Lauren, but Kevin assured him she'd do OK.

Lauren kissed his neck and said, "What d'you think he'll say?"

"He'll say 'I fucking told you so'. He'll say that's why he's the ideas man, and I'm just the guy who does the fucking work."

"You ain't scared of him, though."

"Course I ain't," he growled, and felt her flinch. "But he's got the set-up, hasn't he?" The power and the money, but he couldn't say as much to Lauren.

She said, "I was thinking, though. It's not like this bloke's got any proof."

"He'll *look* for proof. And we could've done without that."

She clicked her tongue and held him tight, perhaps so he wouldn't hit her again. "What're you gonna do?"

"I dunno. Stop him making the connection." Waiting for her next question: *how?* And finding an answer: *kill him.*

But that was a bit drastic, wasn't it? At this stage?

Maybe. Maybe not.

"Babe?" Her hand moved down, slipping easily inside his jogging pants, stroking him the way he liked.

"I've gotta ring him." But he didn't push her away.

"Afterwards…"

He thought about it, and then nodded. "Put an outfit on. I'll be there in a minute."

She giggled with what could have been genuine pleasure, gave his cock a friendly squeeze and made herself scarce. Kevin watched her go, adjusted his trousers and then dialled the number.

Roger Knight was already in a bad mood. Trapped on the phone to his ex-wife, he heard the crunch of gravel that announced Caitlin's return. Better if he could conclude their business before she came in, otherwise he'd be facing difficult questions about his conciliatory approach to Lynn's demands.

Not that he was particularly happy about them. The trouble was, Lynn held all the aces: Sally, Bridget and Tim, aged fifteen, thirteen and ten. Three wonderful kids living six hundred miles away in Aberdeen and growing more distant by the day. Regular access visits had been agreed by both sides and ratified by the court, but as any divorced parent knows, there are a hundred sneaky ways visits can be sabotaged.

If Caitlin privately disapproved of his apparent weakness, Kevin Doyle would have one answer: kill the bitch, or at least scare the living hell out of her. But that wasn't Roger's style. Besides, if the kids ever suspected him of dirty tactics he'd lose them forever.

"Any of them about?" he asked.

"Bridget's horse-riding and Tim's in the garden with a couple of his mates. I think Sally's on her computer."

"Will you call her for me?"

A pause. Then she said, "Not answering. Probably has her headphones on."

The front door opened and Caitlin came in, flushed with excitement, strands of blonde hair falling across her face.

"I've got to go, Lynn," he said. "I'll send you a cheque."

Caitlin's smile vanished as she registered the weariness in his voice. He put the phone down and she said, "What is it this time?"

"The holiday. She doesn't think they'll have enough spending money."

"It's bloody all-inclusive."

He shrugged and looked away.

"How much?" she asked, more gently now.

"Five hundred." He met her eyes, expecting a harsh reaction, but instead there was a grudging smile. "It's only money."

"You're too soft on them," Caitlin said, but he could tell she wasn't cross any more. They embraced and kissed, then kissed again.

"How did the audition go?" he asked.

"Great! I'm through to the next stage. Unofficially."

"Well done. Do you want to eat out tonight to celebrate?"

"No. I want to stay in and celebrate." There was a sparkle in her eyes that made him laugh.

"I'm a middle-aged man. I don't know if I can stand the pace."

"Course you can. Anyway, I'll go on top. You just have to lie there."

They were heading towards the living room when the phone rang again. Hoping that Lynn had mentioned the call to Sally, he grabbed up the receiver and a gruff voice said, "It's me."

Roger's face fell and he almost groaned. Caitlin caught the look and frowned. He mouthed, "Doyle," and she mimed vomiting, then went into the living room and shut the door behind her.

"What is it, Kevin?"

"There's a problem with the claim."

"What do you mean?"

"The fucking investigator from the insurance company."

"You told me Lauren could handle it."

"She could have, but this guy knew it was a fucking con. He tripped her up."

"How badly?"

"She didn't admit to nothing, but I had to go in and sort it out."

Roger sighed. That sounded too much like a Doyle euphemism.

"Tell me you didn't hit him?"

"It was no more than a tap. I fucking had to. Then I threw him out."

"I'm sure that allayed his suspicions."

"Yeah yeah. I don't need any more grief. The thing is, he's gonna be sniffing all round us now. We need to sort out what we're gonna do."

"I think it's better if you leave that to me, don't you?" He could hear Kevin snorting furiously. Nobody else could get away with talking to him like that. "Come to my office tomorrow morning and we'll discuss it calmly. OK?"

Kevin put the phone down without another word. Roger tutted, then entered the living room. Caitlin came in from the kitchen, dangling two bottles of Budweiser by their necks.

"How was Neanderthal Man?"

"Extinct, if I had my way."

Sarah wasn't keen on the idea of drinking alone, but after an hour in her room, brooding on the conversation with Nick, she realised it was a choice between getting out and going insane. Lately home had felt like a prison cell. There was little point in exchanging that for another in the hotel.

The bar seemed to be full of flabby, tired-looking reps, and they all turned to watch her enter. Careful not to catch anyone's eye, she ordered a Coke and chose a table by the window. At the bus stop across the road three teenage girls in skimpy outfits were huddled together, giggling at something on a mobile phone. Sarah thought of her own clubbing days, tarted up to the nines to look older than she was. Now she'd have to do the opposite.

She didn't consciously register the black Focus when it turned into the car park, but a couple of minutes later, when she turned and found Alex walking towards her, she realised she had been thinking of her friend. She rose from her seat and the two women embraced, Alex pecking her cheek as they broke away.

"I wanted to see for myself if you were OK. You don't mind?"

"Of course not."

Alex shrugged off her handbag and examined the room. "Nice place," she said wryly.

"Mmm. I'm unscathed so far." A quick glance confirmed that every man in the room had taken notice of her friend's arrival. That wasn't particularly surprising. Alex was a tall and athletic woman with long auburn hair and sharp blue eyes. Her well-tailored trousers and close-fitting top made the most of her swimmer's physique: long legs, taut stomach, broad shoulders and firm bust.

"They look like hungry sharks," Alex said quietly as she sat down.

"They are now you're here."

As if on a cue, a young man in a Pierre Cardin suit sauntered past and nodded. "Ladies."

Smirking, they watched him make for the bar, where he sent them a lazy over-the-shoulder glance.

"How very suave!" Alex said.

"He can't be more than twenty-five."

"So what? Don't you fancy a toy boy?"

Sarah shrugged. It was going to take some getting used to, the idea that she was available.

"Not tonight, eh?" Alex reading her mind again.

"No."

"Have you eaten yet?"

"Don't really feel like that, either."

"We could just get a bottle of wine and take it up to the room?"

"Good idea."

The Romeo at the bar turned and grinned as they approached. Sarah asked for a chardonnay and two glasses.

"Found somewhere better to go?" he asked.

Alex put her arm through Sarah's and leaned close. "Something like that," she purred.

"Why not stay for a while?"

"I don't think so."

"Put this on the room, can you?" Sarah said to the barman.

"Or maybe I should tag along with you?"

Nothing if not persistent. Alex ignored him until Sarah had signed the bill and they were ready to go. Then she faced him and said, "To be honest, you're not what we go for." And she darted the tip of her tongue into Sarah's ear.

Romeo went red and turned away.

"Sorry about that," Alex said when they reached the lobby. "Sometimes you have to shock."

"Certainly shocked me."

"It was worth it, wasn't it? I think I heard the clunk of his jaw dropping."

Sarah laughed. Suddenly she felt exhilarated. The boundaries were dropping away, and if anyone could offer a few pointers to a more exciting life, it was Alex.

Diana opened the door and read it all his face.

"What happened?"

"Sarah's gone. She's left me."

Nick stepped inside and they hugged. His sister leaned

back as if assessing him, then slapped his face.

"Ow! What was that for?"

"Throwing away your marriage. I could throttle you."

Nick rubbed his cheek. "Thanks for the sympathy."

"Just being my brother doesn't entitle you to sympathy."

"All right, but don't hit me again. I've had enough of that for one day."

He followed her through to the kitchen. Diana lived in a detached three-bedroom house in Seaford. In the extended breakfast room her husband Patrick was feeding yoghurt to their baby daughter, Chloe. Their four-year-old son Ryan was in the living room, singing along to the Bob the Builder theme tune.

Patrick raised the messy plastic spoon in greeting. He was a tall black man with a slight build and a soft-spoken, public school manner. He wore tiny rimless glasses which lent him an air of studious charm. He was a partner in a firm of estate agents but, Nick often joked, still managed to be a likeable human being.

"Sarah's walked out on him," Diana announced, her plump arms folded across her chest. "And you can't really blame her, can you?"

Patrick raised his eyebrows in a gesture that said, "Uh-oh." Nick grinned and put his arm around his sister.

"She loves me really."

"Someone has to," Diana said. "Do you want a coffee?"

"Cheers."

Nick chatted with his brother-in-law for a minute or two, and then Patrick wiped up the remains of the yoghurt and lifted Chloe out of her highchair. "Come on, let's see what havoc your brother's creating. Leave these two to talk."

"Thanks, Pat," said Nick.

"And no fighting!" Patrick admonished as he left the

room.

Nick grinned and sat down at the kitchen table. Spotting an errant dollop of yoghurt, he scooped it up with his finger and ate it, then grimaced.

"Serves you right," Diana said as she set a mug of coffee in front of him. "I suppose you'll be wanting dinner now?"

"Not really hungry."

"I can't tempt you with these, then?" She picked up the cake tin from the unit, opened the lid and wafted the aroma of newly baked buns in his face.

"Well, maybe just a couple."

She handed him the tin, then fetched a plate and sat down opposite him. "What will you do?"

"She said she wants some time to think. I have to respect that."

"But you've also got to think about it. Do you really want the marriage to succeed? Are you willing to have children, if that's what Sarah wants?"

Nick frowned. "You didn't know this was on the cards, did you?"

"Absolutely not."

"You're doing a pretty good job of siding with her now."

"It's not about sides, Nick. The fact is, I've always thought Sarah was the right person for you. I hate to see you screwing up your life for the sake of..."

"Yeah, OK." He didn't need it spelling out. "Anyway, the idea was to discuss these letters from Franks."

He thought she'd accuse him of dodging the issue, but she merely sighed and fetched the envelope from a kitchen drawer. They exchanged letters like two presidents signing a non-aggression pact.

Diana's was slightly different in tone, less confrontational than the one Nick had received. Evidently Howard Franks felt Diana was susceptible to persuasion.

I have for many years held your father in the highest regard as an actor. It is precisely because I feel his talent has been overlooked that I embarked upon this project. However, it is my duty as a biographer to explore all aspects of my subject's life, and that must include the unsavoury side.

Eddie Randall was by no means the first celebrity to succumb to the temptations of the flesh. His weakness for alcohol and gambling is already in the public domain: your late mother herself referred to it in the Sunday Times *interview shortly after his death in 1976.*

It's possible that you and your brother know nothing of your father's secret life. I would implore you to give me your full co-operation, and in return I will share the information as I uncover it.

If I were to abandon this project now, I would be failing in my duty as a writer. And if I do not write this book someone else will, possibly someone who lacks my experience, my empathy and my integrity.

Nick threw the letter down and gave a disgusted snort. "He wouldn't recognise integrity if it asked for his autograph."

Diana's eyes were glistening with tears. "But he's right, though. And he's got something really bad, hasn't he?"

Nick took a moment to reply. He wanted to offer some reassurance, tell her it was just a tactical manoeuvre, a bluff, but he knew it wouldn't sound convincing.

"I think so," he said. "And whether or not we co-operate, we have to find out what it is."

3

Whether it was the newfound sense of freedom and independence, or perhaps just the wine, Sarah found herself weary from laughter. For more than two hours she and Alex had talked and joked about any number of trivial subjects, never straying near the dangerous territory of the real world. Instead they discussed soap operas, bitched about celebrities and generally acted like two teenagers on a sleepover.

Suddenly it was ten o'clock, and Sarah realised she was exhausted. She got up from the bed and stretched. "I feel shattered. Do you mind if we call it a night?"

Alex rose, a funny half-smile on her face. Sarah beckoned her for a farewell hug and the two women embraced. Then Sarah felt lips brushing against her ear, her neck. Startled, she looked up and Alex kissed her. The sensation of the other woman's tongue in her mouth felt both outrageous and wonderful, and Sarah found herself responding. A few times she'd caught Alex regarding her strangely and wondered if she was bisexual, but she hadn't liked to ask.

It was a surprise to both of them when Sarah pushed her away.

"I can't do this."

"Let's go to bed."

Sarah laughed nervously. "No. I'm really sorry. I'm just not… I only walked out on him a few hours ago."

"I understand. It has to be your decision."

"Look, I'm really flattered."

"It's OK." Alex shrugged, apparently unconcerned. She picked up her bag and turned towards the door.

Sarah cringed. "Now I feel dreadful. I hope this won't damage our friendship."

"Not a chance." Alex smiled. "I promise."

"I'll see you in the morning."

As soon as the door closed, Sarah sank on to the bed and raised a hand to her mouth, gently touching her lips. There was a heaviness in her stomach, a kind of sick feeling, but whether it was repulsion or excitement she couldn't tell.

You're free now, she reminded herself. You can do anything you want.

"Anything," she whispered.

It was past ten o'clock when Howard Franks considered his work for the day was finished. He saved everything to disk and then spent twenty minutes surfing the internet for references to his own name. Tonight he found one new item, a review of his biography of a hell-raising Formula One driver. It described his writing as 'appropriately over-wrought' and 'steeped in cliché, some of it frighteningly apt.' Deciding that the overall tone was one of grudging approval, he resolved not to let it spoil his mood. After all, it had been a very productive day.

Slowly but surely – another apt cliché – his portrait of Eddie Randall was taking on depth and colour and tone. Darkness and light. With the kind of information he was unearthing he was virtually guaranteed a lucrative tabloid serialisation.

The book launch would be accompanied by the usual round of TV and radio interviews, the part of the job he loved most of all. Over the years he'd raised his own profile to the extent that, modesty aside, he was better known than some of his subjects. That was certainly the case with Eddie Randall at the moment, but it would soon change once Howard's PR machine got to work.

If only Randall had done more to establish his profile in the States. He'd had supporting roles in a couple of American movies, but nothing earth-shattering. By that stage of his career he was taking any work he could get to keep the bookies at bay. A trophy second wife and a young family to support, but still drinking and partying as hard as ever, despite the warning of a minor heart attack in 1968.

A very significant event, as far as Franks was concerned. Eddie had been admitted to the Royal Sussex County Hospital in December and released after five days with a warning to modify his lifestyle. A picture in the Brighton *Evening Argus* showed him mugging for the cameras, surrounded by adoring nurses.

And now Franks knew that the small-time conman, Leslie Jones, had died just two months before, while Randall was working on a guest role in one of the *Carry On* films. It looked increasingly as though this phase of Eddie's life would warrant a whole section of the book, and perhaps the lead excerpt in any newspaper serialisation.

He studied his watch, a Cartier Roadster that had set him back nearly £3000. Lindsay was running late as usual. Completely unreliable. He was tempted to continue surfing, but made himself get up. Time to open a bottle of wine.

Having refused his sister's offer of supper, Nick drove home soon after nine o'clock, brooding over the letters from Howard Franks. In Wish Road the house was dark and already had a sad, neglected look to it.

So Sarah hadn't had a change of heart. Hadn't lost her nerve and come home, unpacked her suitcase and agreed to give him another chance. And why should she? As Diana had made clear, he didn't deserve it.

Reluctant to enter the house, he lingered on the driveway and turned towards the sea, glittering in the light of a rising moon. He thought back to the warm June day when they'd moved in, eight years ago. It had been the middle of a heatwave, and on their second night they heard thunder rumbling far out at sea. They walked barefoot across the road, sat on the beach and watched an electrical storm rage on the horizon. How privileged they had felt. How content.

He sighed. "No one to blame but yourself," he muttered.

Indoors, he checked for messages and tried Sarah's mobile again. Then he searched the freezer and found a box of microwave chips. Setting the timer, he wondered if this was a symbolic moment: the resumption of his bachelor lifestyle, complete with stodgy fast food and too much beer.

"Maybe," he said, popping a tin of Carlsberg.

He took the chips and the beer into the living room and sank on to the couch. With cable it took about ten minutes to examine all the TV channels on offer. He settled on News 24, the volume so low it was barely audible, then realised he was only seeking the illusion of company.

The chips were hot but tasteless, and fell heavily into his stomach. He shut his eyes and remembered that he had a couple of reports to write. And the reply to Franks that he and Diana had agreed on. Suddenly he felt too tired to think, let alone move.

Where was Sarah now? There must be dozens of hotels in Brighton alone, not to mention all the other towns along this stretch of coast. If he wanted to track her down, he had no idea where to start.

He contemplated another duty: ringing her parents.

Gerry and Lisa Clarke had moved to France six years ago, shortly after Nick and Sarah married. He still remembered the disdain with which retired consultant Gerry had introduced Nick to one of his golfing buddies: "Eddie Randall's son. You know, he was *that actor*." Lisa was slightly warmer, but only when her husband wasn't around.

He fetched another beer, opened his briefcase and got as far as shuffling papers for a few minutes. He read Franks's letter again, and then he selected a videotape and slipped it into the machine.

End of the Peer was a dated but sharply observed comedy of class from the wonderful Boulting Brothers, filmed in 1959 and released the following year. What Nick liked about these films was their sheer Englishness, the thrill of seeing those streets and buildings of half a century ago, black and white, familiar but different, a world you could almost touch and yet was gone forever.

It boasted the usual fine cast of comic talent: Ian Carmichael, Terry-Thomas, Dennis Price and the ubiquitous Irene Handl. Although Nick couldn't recall meeting any of them, he'd watched them so many times over the years that they now seemed part of the family. His link to Dad.

And here he is, twenty-one minutes in, playing a cheeky working class pub landlord in an unnamed suburb of London. An establishing shot of Eddie in the car park, wrestling a beer barrel into the cellar, and then we cut inside, probably to a studio at Shepperton some weeks later. Behind the bar, young and muscular in shirt-sleeves, tanned from his decidedly un-working class summer on the Riviera, Eddie is soon flirting with the Rank starlet playing a frightfully posh secretary, to the chagrin of her boyfriend, upper class Carmichael.

Nick muted the volume and found himself unable to

take his eyes off his father. 1959, Eddie would have been, what, forty-one? Only four years older than Nick was now. How come he looked so young, so vital, when Nick felt so old and tired?

The camera cut to Ian Carmichael, and Nick found himself lip-synching, "Do you mind…?"

Back to Dad: "I'll talk to 'er any way I like. Now 'oppit!" And a lazy smile at the starlet whose name Nick always had to check in the credits. A glint in Dad's eye that might not have been exclusive to the character. Did you employ your charms on her? Did she keep you amused in the breaks between filming?

Had she gone running to Howard Franks with a tale to tell?

"Oh Dad," he whispered sadly. "What did you do?"

It was nearly midnight when a flash of headlights between the curtains heralded Lindsay's arrival, but by then Howard's sense of exhilaration had slipped away. She should have been here hours ago, when he was still fresh and excited. He'd devoted a lot of thought to the kind of sex they would have, but when he got up to answer the door there was barely a stir from his groin.

Howard lived in a three storey, late Victorian terraced house in Highgate, on the edge of Queen's Wood. It had four bedrooms, a games room and gymnasium, and a lap pool in the long rear garden. A few years ago he'd had the whole place refurbished by an interior designer who had since become a mainstay on a BBC makeover show. Although he tried not to keep track of such things, its value had now passed the million pound mark.

Paranoid as any sensible wealthy Londoner should be, he checked the tiny monitor in the hall: Lindsay blowing a sarcastic kiss at the lens. He considered leaving her out there, make her wait for a change, but she was just as likely to turn around and go. A little more headstrong than he normally preferred, this one, but there were compensations.

"I wondered if you'd gone to bed," she said, stepping past him without so much as a peck on the cheek.

"Getting my beauty sleep?" he said.

"You said it, honey." Putting her sexy American drawl to work.

He followed her into the living room and watched her throw her jacket over the back of a chair, knowing it irritated him when things weren't in their proper place. She was wearing a high-necked lambswool sweater and the sort of indecently tight jeans that normally did nothing to flatter a woman of her age.

She caught him leering and grinned. As always when they first greeted one another, he was conscious of her height advantage. He was a neat, dapper man who paid considerable attention to his appearance, but there was little he could do about his stature: five feet six inches.

"Come and sit down," he said, leading her to a sofa. "I've been waiting for you."

"Why didn't you call?"

He shrugged. He hadn't wanted to appear needy.

"Mm." She opened her arms to him and they kissed. He thought he tasted alcohol on her tongue, but it might have been the wine he'd had earlier. A fleeting thought that perhaps she was cheating on him, but then he pushed it away. His hands moved around her waist, but she took one and pressed it between her legs, where he could feel the heat even through the thick denim.

"You're not the only one who's been waiting," she said, thrusting herself against him. They kissed again, and he could feel her fumbling with his trousers. She unzipped his fly and he felt his body go tense. A moment later he heard her surprise: "Oh!"

"I'm tired, that's all. Busy day." He knew it should turn him on when she took the lead, and yet somehow he always felt a bit… intimidated. And he wasn't a young man any more, not that he would admit it. He'd told Lindsay he was forty-eight, though in fact he was fifty-three. "It doesn't happen often," he added, somewhat lamely.

"Don't worry." She gave him a quick kiss, then jumped to her feet. "Mind if I throw a sandwich together?"

By the time he'd restored his dignity and joined her in the kitchen, she was spreading butter on to three slices of granary bread. Somehow she seemed to combine a normal appetite with a superb figure, something that few of Howard's other girlfriends ever managed. And at thirty-nine, Lindsay was actually the oldest partner he'd ever had, perhaps a sign that he was finally ready for a long-term relationship.

Her unabashed enthusiasm for sex certainly helped, as did her vow never to have children. "I heard my body clock start and I threw it across the room," she had told him.

He watched her slicing a tomato with expert precision. She'd worked in restaurants while travelling the world in her early twenties. Both her parents had worked in the movie industry, and her childhood had been divided between New York state, California and Hertfordshire. Ten years ago she'd elected to live in England, and she was now practice manager for a large firm of commercial lawyers based in the City. They'd been seeing each other for nearly three months, but in that time he'd not even been invited to her flat. All she would say is that it compared very poorly with his own house.

"Good day?" he asked, when it became clear that she wasn't about to initiate a conversation.

"I'd say so. You?"

"The book's coming on a treat," he said, brightening up. "I really think I'm on to something, thanks to you."

She shrugged. "Don't mention it." Her mother had worked at the studios in Borehamwood where Eddie Randall made half a dozen features. She'd had a brief romance with him in the late sixties, and later told her daughter about some of his more unpalatable proclivities. Lindsay had contacted Howard after reading a newspaper article about his proposed biography. His request for an interview had been followed by dinner at the Ivy, and then a thrilling sexual encounter in the back seat of his Lexus.

While Lindsay constructed her double-decker cheese salad sandwich, Howard outlined the approach he intended to take with the book.

"The mob angle should really rack up the sales," he told her gleefully. "I'm going to claim that Eddie got into bed with some serious villains."

"You mean the ones that took out this Larry Jones guy?"

"Leslie. Yes. He was killed in October '68, and you know what's wonderful?"

"What?" she asked flatly, not looking up from the sandwich.

"Randall had a heart attack in December, two months later. Isn't that perfect?"

"You think the two things are linked?"

"I haven't a clue, but it'll seem like it by the time I'm finished. *Under the burden of almost unimaginable guilt, Eddie Randall wishes himself dead and almost succeeds.*"

Lindsay began to speak but he raised his hand for silence while he committed the sentence to memory.

"And what if his family take you to court?" she said through gritted teeth.

"More publicity. More sales. Anyway, I've given them every chance to tell me their side of the story."

"They don't seem too interested so far."

"Oh, they'll come round. I only need one of them to break."

She looked at him sharply, and he met her disapproval with a brazen smile.

"You think you can break one of them?"

"My dear, I was a tabloid journalist for fifteen years. It's practically second nature."

4

Having lain awake half the night, Nick was sound asleep when the alarm went off at seven. He was sprawled almost sideways across the double bed, a leg draped over one side, a hand gripping the mattress on the other. And it hadn't been a dream. She was gone.

He rolled on to his back and rubbed his eyes. A Springsteen song was running through his head: *You're Missing*.

The face in the bathroom mirror looked a little more middle-aged than it had the day before, and again he thought of Dad in *End of the Peer*, full of vitality, only forty-one. All Nick saw were bags under his eyes and lines taking hold on his forehead. He forced a smile, narrowing his eyes until the ghost of his father appeared.

Eddie Randall had been fifty-eight when he died. It was the famously hot summer of 1976, a few days after Wimbledon, where Eddie had watched Bjorn Borg take the men's title. They were preparing to set off for a holiday in the South of France, and nine-year-old Nick had a clear memory of his father struggling to lift a suitcase into the boot of their Rolls Royce. "No need to be going away, it's so bloody hot here," he'd said. Mopping his brow, he'd gone inside to fetch another case and collapsed in the hall.

Nick's world had fallen apart overnight. The tabloids raked up stories of gambling and rampant womanising, while his mother – Eddie's second wife – discovered that they'd been living on fresh air for the past two years. She was forced to sell the large house in Alfriston, while Nick and his sister were taken from their exclusive private school in Seaford and sent to the local comprehensive – to the delight of every thug in the school. Nick still bore a scar from the beating he'd received on the first day.

He ate a bowl of cereal, gulped down some coffee and rang Sarah's mobile. He had spent half the night composing the message, but when the moment came every word vanished.

"Sarah, uh, Sarah, look. We have to talk about this, er, please? I know, I know I'm in the wrong, and if I could turn back the clock, I'd never... well, you're not going to believe that, and I wouldn't really blame you. But, anyway, I don't think we should just throw it all away without at least... you know, exploring the possibilities. So, um, well, if you can find it in your heart to... ring me, at least. Not forgive me, not yet. But ring me. Let's talk, please."

He cut the connection and yelled "Fuck!" so loudly the sound reverberated around the house. He imagined her listening with utter contempt.

"You're a mess, Nick Randall," he declared. "A total bloody mess."

Sarah had fared little better. The businessmen she'd been so keen to avoid had spent most of the night tramping on the stairs, slamming doors and flushing toilets. When morning finally came it was only the sad jumbled images of her dreams that convinced her she had slept at all.

She lay in the centre of the spongy double bed and checked her phone. A couple of texts from friends, and then Nick's garbled plea for her to get in touch. She listened to it twice and felt the tears welling up.

She nearly rang him right then. Got as far as resting her finger lightly on the 'call' button. But then the old fears came creeping back. He'd cheated on her. Could he honestly guarantee that he'd never do it again? More to the point, could she believe him?

She switched off her phone.

Hurtling down the M23 in her two-litre Ford Focus, Alex felt that life couldn't get any better. Last night had been a real breakthrough, and today she would consolidate her position.

It was seven-thirty, and the southbound traffic was relatively light. Alex was approaching Handcross Hill, a steep descent into a wooded valley where the road twists to the right and rises just as sharply into the Sussex Weald. Cruising at eighty, she had the outside lane to herself. Not much in the inside lane: nothing bunched up. It should have been a clear run.

The van thought differently. A white Transit, six years old, *Clean me* daubed in the grime on the rear panel. It let her get within a hundred feet and then whipped into her path, doing fifty at best and making no effort to accelerate.

"Cocksucking bastard!" Alex hit the brake and felt the pedal pulsate as the ABS did its work. She couldn't move to the left until she'd passed an old Astra, and the van seemed to be deliberately slowing. She was almost touching its bumper when she cut across to the inside, where a Skoda was ambling along just a few hundred feet in front. She put her foot down to take the van on the inside but the driver had anticipated that and accelerated alongside her.

She risked a quick look and saw the driver's mate leering from the passenger window: shaved head, tattoo on his forehead – or maybe that was the lobotomy scar. He was shocked, though. He'd assumed it was a man behind the wheel.

There was still time to slow down, let them have their tiny victory, but that wasn't in her nature. It never had been.

She stamped on the accelerator, watching the Skoda loom larger through the windscreen. A glance at the van. The driver was leaning forward, perhaps not believing that some bloody woman was taking them on. Both of them snarled, giving her the finger.

She flashed her lights, saw the Skoda driver check the mirror and do a startled doubletake. Alex raised her left hand and jabbed her fingers towards the outside lane: *move over.* Doing seventy-five now and rising, maybe four seconds from a collision.

Three. Two…

The Skoda obediently swerved across lanes, fishtailing as the driver struggled for control. Alex heard a squeal of brakes as the van tried to match the Skoda's speed, but by then she was past them both, moving back out around a juggernaut, not knowing if the Skoda had been rear-ended by the van and not caring. All she could think about was the manic pumping of her heart and the knowledge of her own superiority.

She thought about Sarah, waiting for her. Thought about fucking her.

Thought about fucking *with* her.

By eight-thirty Nick had set up his laptop in the living room, but his mind was still on the message he'd left for Sarah. He'd rung twice more without success. Now he could only hope she was willing to resume contact.

In the meantime, he had work to do. Yesterday's interview with Lauren Doyle was part of an investigation given to him by CBA Insurance, his former employers. Since going freelance two years ago, he'd been careful to stay on good terms with the claims manager, Morag Strutton, and instructions from CBA comprised nearly half of his workload. Today he had to persuade her to let him go on digging.

Leaving the house, he realised he'd done nothing about Howard Franks. The biographer had been pestering them for several months, and no doubt intended to resuscitate all the lurid stories which had so excited the media at the time of Eddie Randall's death.

Nick still believed that the combination of the scandals and Eddie's sudden death had caused his mother's decline. Although Mary Randall had been twenty years younger than her husband, she had developed a drink problem which left Nick and his sister virtually bringing themselves up on their own. A series of strokes in her early fifties left her incapacitated, and she had died three years ago, aged just sixty-two.

At least his mother wouldn't have to suffer all over again. Nick had a sudden irrational conviction that if only Franks had chosen another hapless celebrity victim to drag through the mud, his life would still be properly on track.

He certainly didn't think things could get any worse.

5

Breakfast had been a mistake, Sarah decided. Some foolish impulse had made her order the full English when tea and toast would have sufficed. Now she stood outside the hotel, gulping down the cool morning air and vowing that tomorrow she'd make other arrangements.

Alex arrived promptly at eight-fifteen, speeding into the car park and executing a skilful but noisy turn that aligned the passenger door precisely in Sarah's path. A couple of the hotel staff came to the window to see what had caused the commotion.

"Do you always drive like this?" Sarah said. "I hope I'm going to be safe."

"Safe is boring," Alex retorted.

She spun the wheels and Sarah squealed, grabbing her seatbelt for support.

"You didn't have to wait outside," Alex said.

"I needed the fresh air. Breakfast was a bit greasy."

"You're welcome to stay with me, you know."

"Thanks. I'm not sure what to do about work."

"Why not chuck the job as well? Make a new start."

Sarah felt herself squirming. This was her father's favourite tactic, unleashing a tidal wave of advice that she was powerless to stem.

"I'll think about it," she said.

Alex smiled, her gaze a little too intense for Sarah's liking. For a second her hand rested on Sarah's thigh. "Bad night?"

"Not great."

They drove in silence for a few minutes. Sarah thought

about the message from Nick. It had been totally inept, but also rather touching. She opened her mouth to tell Alex about it, then stopped without quite knowing why.

"You don't owe him anything, Sarah. He's the one that went screwing around."

Sarah stared at her. The woman was uncanny.

"The hardest thing now is fighting the impulse to return," Alex went on. "I've been there myself. A couple of nights trying to sleep alone in an unfamiliar bed, and it's so tempting to give in, go crawling back and let him win. It's an easy mistake to make, but it's a mistake all the same."

Sarah said nothing. Suddenly she knew this wasn't the kind of day she needed. Given the choice, she'd buy a book and walk on the seafront. Alone. But Alex had driven down from Surrey to be with her. Sarah could hardly change her mind now, could she?

Roger Knight lived in a large detached house with four acres of land between the villages of Clayton and Westmeston, at the very foot of the South Downs. Dominating the top floor, the master bedroom had windows to three sides of the property. To the north and west were magnificent views across the Sussex Weald, but it was the south window that inevitably drew Caitlin. On her free days, if Roger was at work, she liked to bring a mug of tea up to the bedroom and sit in the window seat, the imposing mass of Ditchling Beacon looming over her.

She was there when Kevin Doyle arrived. The previous night's argument had been the fiercest yet, and Caitlin decided she'd stay in the bedroom until Roger went out. Now she watched Kevin climb from his flashy red BMW and glance at the house before tossing his cigarette butt over his shoulder. She could have sworn he'd seen her, and the single word he mouthed seemed to confirm it: *bitch*.

"Prick," Caitlin spat in response, and turned away.

If Roger's slavish capitulation to the demands of his ex-wife weren't bad enough, last night he'd spoken to Lynn again and accepted an invitation to his daughter's birthday party. An invitation for one, it turned out.

"I thought you wouldn't want to come," Roger had claimed. "They'll all be there: her parents, her brothers…"

"OK. Supposing I'm not afraid to face them?"

"Oh, Caitlin. It's not like that. It's… it's a question of diplomacy."

"Bollocks."

They were treading familiar ground: Roger couldn't break free from Lynn's influence; Caitlin couldn't understand how much Roger had to sacrifice for the sake of his children. And every time it ended with his simple declaration: "You haven't got kids. You don't know what it's like."

Which always worked. Funny really that he had never questioned its effectiveness. She had vowed one day to tell him about the miscarriage she'd had a month before her thirtieth birthday, but not until she felt sure this was the real thing. Lately she was beginning to doubt it.

From below she heard raised voices. Roger's business was another area about which Caitlin felt increasingly unsure. She knew he had interests in a vehicle repairer and a salvage company, which he assured her were all above board, nicely profitable and extremely dull. Now she was beginning to wonder just what kind of legitimate enterprise cared to employ a man like Doyle?

"I could've kicked his fucking head in. Smartarse wanker."

"Will he go to the police?"

"I barely touched him. He can't prove nothing."

Roger sighed. "I don't mean for assault. The sort of questions he was asking, you have to assume he was suspicious of the claim in the first place."

"I been thinking about that. All these companies jumping up and down about fraud. Just another reason to put the fucking premiums up. Nearly a grand to insure the beamer."

Despite the situation, Roger couldn't help a snort of laughter. "Kevin, you pay your premium with money you've stolen from insurance companies."

"Proves my point then," said Kevin indignantly. "They get their fucking money back in the end." He folded his meaty arms and flung Roger a look that said, *Not so stupid after all, am I?*

"The point is, we have to be careful. We have to make sure they don't make the connections, particularly to me."

"Don't worry, you're in the clear. As always."

Roger narrowed his eyes. "What does that mean?"

Kevin shrugged. His contempt for Roger was never far from the surface, but he wasn't quite ready for direct confrontation with the man who paid his wages.

"What I mean, Kevin, is that our legitimate business is conducted primarily *with* insurance companies. If one whisper of this profitable little sideline gets out, we'll be finished."

Kevin made an incomprehensible noise of disgust and turned away.

"Why don't you sit down?"

"Nah, I gotta go to Portsmouth to look at a couple of reconditioned engines."

"All right. I'll review all the claims paperwork and make sure it's watertight." He heard a thump from upstairs and moved across the room, prompting Kevin to head for the door. "And tell Lauren not to worry."

"I ain't telling her that." He snickered. "Anyway, she's still making up for it."

To you, maybe, Roger thought. "Obviously, if this Randall contacts her again…"

"Keep her fucking mouth shut. She knows."

Roger reached for the handle just as the door opened. Caitlin stood in the doorway, blonde hair awry, holding a robe tightly at her chin.

"Would you like some coffee?"

"Gotta be going."

Caitlin smiled politely. She had been addressing Roger, and Kevin knew it.

"Love some," said Roger. Caitlin started to go but he put his arm around her. She succumbed to the embrace, smiling to hide her reluctance.

"I need to borrow the Range Rover," Kevin said.

"Why?" asked Caitlin.

Kevin kept his eyes on Roger and spoke as if he hadn't heard her. "If the recons are all right I'll bring one of 'em back with me."

Roger dug out his keys and threw them to Kevin. Caitlin used the opportunity to break away and strode towards the kitchen without a word to either of them.

Kevin was amused. "Having a domestic?"

"Not really."

"Thought you got enough earache last time round. Heh heh heh."

Roger ignored him. He couldn't imagine a day when he would need to discuss relationships with Doyle.

"What we gonna do about this Randall, then?" Kevin said when he reached the front door.

"Nothing. For the time being."

"I could scare him off."

"Nothing," Roger repeated. "I'll take care of it."

Kevin shrugged. "You take care of it," he said, "and then I'll scare him off."

He sauntered across the wide gravel drive to where Roger's new Range Rover was parked, tossing the keys high in the air and catching them with a swipe of his meaty fist. For a moment Roger imagined the keys were a bird, plucked from the air and crushed to death. Knowing Kevin as he did, it wasn't an unlikely metaphor.

A hand brushed against his neck and he jumped. It was Caitlin. They watched Kevin start the Range Rover and gun the engine for their benefit.

"He's a nasty piece of work," she said.

"He is."

"You shouldn't have given him the Range Rover."

"It's a company vehicle. He needs it for business."

"Business," she repeated as though it were a dirty word. Closing the door, Roger wondered if perhaps, in his case, it was.

6

Morag Strutton had an infectious laugh, which she failed to suppress as Nick recounted how he'd been forcibly ejected from the Doyle house.

"You think it's funny?" He tried to sound indignant, but found himself grinning.

"The way you're telling it, I do." She shook her head. "In my book it's front page news: Nick Randall's charm fails to win the day!"

"I could have been badly hurt."

"Aww. Don't look so forlorn. What do you want, a wee hug and a kiss?"

Her Highlands accent, softened by more than a decade in Sussex, still pronounced it as "kuss", and the sound gave Nick a shiver of guilty pleasure. He looked away, remembering their night together during a training course in Birmingham, three years ago. It was in the aftermath of his mother's death, but with hindsight that seemed like a feeble justification. Either way, they had agreed afterwards that it must never happen again.

Morag lifted the file on her desk and dropped it with an emphatic thud. "So I'm guessing you'll want to go to work on Mrs Doyle and her delightful husband?"

"Aha. I'd recommend thorough checks on all the participants."

"Should have been done already, but I'll make sure."

"I'd also put a note on the file, warning anyone who might take a call on it."

She regarded him sternly. "Eggs, grandmothers and all that."

"Sorry. Old habits."

"Most of your old habits are best disregarded."

"I was a damn good claims handler in my time."

"I didn't mean professionally." She paused, then asked softly, "How's Sarah these days?"

"She's, er… we're not actually together right now."

Morag nodded. "Thought so. You look bloody awful."

"It only happened yesterday."

"I'm sorry to hear that. Maybe you should take a few days off?"

"I probably will, when she agrees to see me."

"It's like that, is it?"

He nodded. "In the meantime I'd prefer to keep busy."

"At our expense."

"If I'm right, I'm going to save you about thirty grand."

"If you can prove it," Morag reminded him. "I'm under a lot of pressure from Head Office to cut my budget. The cost of assessors is high on the hit list."

Nick snorted. More good news.

"I can authorise another five hundred pounds, maximum."

"Morag, this could be a major fraud I've uncovered here."

"Then you'll have no trouble bringing me some evidence. Whereupon I'll be happy to consider releasing more funds."

He pretended to be disgusted. "I never had you down as a stingy Scot."

"It's not my heritage you should worry about, darling. I've worked in claims all my career and I don't pay out good money unless it's justified." She closed the file and tossed it into a tray, effectively marking the end of negotiations.

He stood and brushed non-existent lint from his tie.

Without looking up, she said, "Oh, and if you've any

other calls today, you'll want to know there's blood on your collar."

He twisted his neck to see. "Is there? Bugger." He'd shaved in a daze, replaying the clumsy phone message over and over in his head.

She walked him to the lobby and gave his arm a quick squeeze just before he stepped into the lift, allowing him no time to respond. "Take care of yourself," she said.

As the doors closed he felt a sudden rush of hopelessness. Was this the future, slowly becoming an object of pity?

The CBA building was a characterless concrete pile in the heart of what had once been Brighton's financial district, before the banks turned into wine bars and offices into apartments. Parking was almost impossible, but Nick had squeezed into a gap between Morag's car and the Renault Laguna next to it.

The Laguna's owner, a tall bearded motor engineer called John Folsom, was sitting on the bonnet of Nick's car, smoking with evident pleasure.

"Sorry, John. Are you off somewhere?"

"Inspection in Bexhill. No hurry." He fished out the packet and offered it to Nick, who shook his head.

"Gave up years ago. Bad for your health."

"Hmm. Don't believe it myself."

They exchanged small talk for a minute or two, and then something occurred to Nick. "I don't suppose you inspected an L-reg Escort, written off a couple of weeks ago? Name of Doyle."

Folsom took a long drag on his cigarette. "Whereabouts?"

"The accident happened near Crawley. Supposedly."

"Hmm." He pulled a face. "Yes. In a breakers' yard. A heap of shit, if memory serves."

"The car or the yard?"

Folsom snorted. "Both."

"What was this place called, can you remember?"

"Yeah. Griffin Farm Breakers. No more than a glorified scrapyard." He dropped his cigarette butt on to the ground and trod it down. "On to something, are you?"

"Maybe. How do I find this place?"

"It's not easy. Little country lane near Rusper." He rattled off directions and added, "You'll need your welly boots. Place is a mudbath."

As Nick opened his car door, Folsom added, "In fact, the Escort was filthy. Looked like it had been in the yard for weeks."

Howard Franks's study was his pride and joy: the fulfilment of the dream that had sustained him through six years as a put-upon reporter for a ghastly local rag covering the Lincolnshire coast, then more than fifteen as a hack on a national tabloid.

He'd knocked through two bedrooms to create a room that ran the length of the house and combined an office with a den, entertainment suite and media centre. There were two desks, one of contemporary design with a £2000 ergonomic chair, the other a reproduction mahogany pedestal desk with a captain's chair in green leather. He had a top of the range Dell PC on the former, and on the latter a 1920s Underwood Number 5 typewriter that he never used but which looked splendid.

There was a huge plasma TV mounted on the wall, linked to a digital camcorder trained on a couple of easy chairs. It was here he liked to practise his interviewing technique, fending off imaginary questions with an aplomb he could rarely muster in real life. In his loftier moments he liked to imagine himself a guest on Leno or Letterman. Usually he had to make do with the lesser shows, the breakfast slots, the pre-filmed segments, but he was determined to change all that one day.

Not with his present subject, if he was realistic. Eddie Randall's story might just swing him a slot on Parky or Jonathan Ross, but he wasn't counting on much foreign interest. What he needed from this book was enough attention in the UK to justify an A-list commission: a movie actor or an international sports star.

For now, though, he had to make do with dear old Eddie. After months of research, Howard had a sneaking admiration for his subject. On the surface Randall had maintained a fairly clean image, certainly by the standards of his day, when actors could openly visit disreputable nightclubs and mingle with underworld figures. But dig a little deeper and you found, as with many of his peers, Eddie ran the gamut of vices: alcohol, drugs, gambling and sex. And it was the sex Howard needed to focus on. It was sex that would get his book off the shelves.

And while on the subject, it was sex he was in need of himself. Unfortunately Lindsay had risen horrendously early and seemed eager to get to work. While she showered he spent some time nurturing an erection, and when she returned he threw back the duvet to display the result.

"Very impressive," she said. "What do you want me to do with it?"

"You mean you have to ask?"

"Sorry. Duty calls."

"Forget the office for a while. Go in late."

"Unlike some of us, I can't choose how many hours I work."

Indignantly he flipped the duvet back over his body. "You know mornings are the best time."

"They're the best time for lots of things, not just throttling that little worm." She saw how offended he was, and chuckled. "Maybe tonight, OK? Now go back to sleep."

He'd taken her advice and woke at nine feeling thick-headed and lethargic. Now another hour had passed and he'd done nothing except sit at his computer and day-dream, a Jamie Cullen CD on the hi-fi and an Eddie Randall comedy running silently on the TV.

He needed action today, he realised. Best to get out and do something, however minor, that progressed the book in some way.

Pay the darling Randall children a visit, he thought suddenly. Keep the pressure on. They'd send him packing, but so what? Working on a tabloid had given him a skin like armour-plating.

And tonight, if Lindsay wasn't able or willing to satisfy him, he'd find someone else who was.

In Alex's car, heading out of Eastbourne, Sarah realised she was beginning to count down the minutes until she could be alone again. She vowed that if Alex suggested any more excursions, she'd have an excuse ready.

At her first sight of the Arndale Center, Alex had said, "So where are the designer shops?"

"I don't think there are any. Eastbourne's more of a retirement resort."

"The last resort, more like. You'd have to drag me kicking and screaming to live somewhere like this."

"I think it's quite charming. Not so raucous and in-your-face as Brighton."

"At least Brighton has some decent boutiques."

"I'm not interested in a flashy outfit."

"Something practical, then. Just make the bastard pay."

Sarah stopped abruptly. "Don't talk about Nick like that. You don't know him."

Alex seemed slightly amused, and Sarah felt patronised. That's right, she thought. The little woman's not afraid to defend her philandering husband. Well, fuck you, Alex.

But she didn't say any of that. She stared at the ground and muttered, "Sorry. Didn't mean to snap."

In Next, Alex accompanied her into the cubicle, ostensibly to try on a dress she'd noticed, although Sarah couldn't rid herself of the impression that Alex didn't want to let her out of her sight. As she undressed she could feel Alex's gaze on her, as hot and heavy as a spotlight. It reminded her of the supermarket job she'd had at college, the manager notorious for his wandering hands.

She had met Alex a couple of months ago at her local gym, which Alex used when her job as a pharmaceutical rep brought her to Brighton. Sarah hadn't felt anything untoward at the time, but then she probably hadn't been looking out for such things. Or was it that Alex had kept her inclinations to herself until now, when Sarah was in a vulnerable position?

Alex stripped to her underwear without any inhibitions, chatting merrily the whole time. Once down to a black bra and matching high-cut knickers, she seemed in no hurry to put on the dress. Instead she held it to her body and said, "What do you think?"

"Very nice," said Sarah, risking the briefest of glances.

"Sure?"

Sarah shrugged. "I hadn't pictured you as someone who'd wear skimpy dresses."

"Part of my secret personality," Alex said slyly. "For special occasions."

In the end she didn't buy it, but she did encourage Sarah

to get some trousers and a couple of tops. Afterwards they decided to have lunch at a pizza place, though neither of them was very hungry. Both ordered salads and consumed them with little enthusiasm.

"You look deep in thought," Alex murmured as they waited for the bill.

"Sorry. Tired, I think."

"We could go back to the hotel if you like?"

A vision of Alex slipping into bed beside her, the lacy underwear discarded, made Sarah gulp. Last night, Alex's kiss had thrilled her, but today she was another person: brittle and immune to affection.

"No," she said. "Let's have a walk."

They drove out along the clifftop road and parked at Birling Gap, in the midst of the famous chalk cliffs known as the Seven Sisters. As they joined the well-worn path up the hill, Alex linked arms with Sarah and snuggled against her for a moment. Sarah instinctively tensed, then forced herself to relax, never suspecting she'd just missed the last chance to save herself.

7

After speaking to CBA's motor engineer, Nick was keen to find out more about the salvage company that had collected Lauren Doyle's car. Unfortunately he had two other calls to make that morning, so a drive out to West Sussex would have to wait.

The first task was a locus report: preparing a detailed plan of an accident location to help determine liability. Then he took a statement on a car theft from an elderly Latvian refugee who allegedly spoke no English. Translations were provided by his son, a shady-looking character who had almost certainly owned the car in question. All Nick could do was make his observations. The insurers would have to decide whether to pay out.

By the time he'd finished his stomach was rumbling. He parked in the High Street and was buying a chicken salad sandwich when his mobile rang. His first thought was Sarah, but it was his sister.

"Nick! Thank God your phone's on."

His heart started thumping. "What is it?"

"Howard Franks," she said, her voice shaky. "He's outside."

They climbed the hill into a blustery wind, swirling and howling around them. Sarah had to keep pushing her hair back from her face. Alex, whose long hair was tucked inside her coat, produced a beanie hat from her pocket.

"Have this."

Sarah laughed. "I'll look an idiot in that."

"No you won't. Keeps your ears warm as well." Alex put the hat on and pulled it tight around her scalp. "See?"

"I'm not convinced."

"Fair enough. I'll wear it then."

They walked mostly in silence, saving their breath for the steep incline. At the top of the hill they paused by the Belle Tout lighthouse, which Sarah explained had been the subject of a groundbreaking engineering feat five years before, when the entire property had been moved seventy feet back from the cliff edge.

Alex was mystified. "Why did they do that?"

"To stop it falling into the sea. The cliffs are constantly eroding."

"But all they've done is postpone the end. What's the point?"

"That's a very fatalistic view."

"I don't believe in delaying the inevitable," Alex declared. There was a distant look in her eyes. "Better to confront it."

Sarah waited for her to elaborate, but Alex was staring out to sea. *I don't know her*, Sarah thought suddenly. She shivered.

Alex noticed the movement and put her arm around Sarah's shoulders, then suddenly kissed her hard on the lips, her tongue pushing at Sarah's mouth but finding resistance.

Sarah's stomach clenched with nausea. She pushed Alex away and wiped her mouth. "Don't do that."

"You like it."

"No I don't. I'm not interested in… whatever it is you want."

Alex seemed amused. "And what's that?"

"To destroy my marriage."

"Nick's done that for you. It's over."

"No," Sarah shouted, all her anger bursting free. "I'll decide when it's over. *I'll decide.*"

She strode away, deciding in that moment to walk on to Beachy Head and catch a bus into Eastbourne. A second later she felt Alex's footfalls behind her, a hand brushing against her arm.

"What's got you so upset? It was only a kiss."

"I don't want to be kissed by you. Or told what to do, or how to feel."

She kept on walking, aware of Alex a step behind but making no move to stop her. Bitterly she remembered occasions when she and Nick had argued like this, Nick hanging back, waiting for her temper to cool.

"Why should I throw away everything we had together?" she exclaimed. Alex didn't reply. "You didn't hear the message he left me this morning. It was so sweet. I know he's been unfaithful, but Christ, there are millions of men like that. Some women walk out, and some decide to stay. You have to do what's best for you. And if I choose to give him another chance, that's my business and nobody else's. Do you understand?"

Sarah turned. Alex had dropped back a few paces and was studying her with a clinical efficiency.

"Something's happened to you," she said. "What's changed?"

"What do you mean?"

"Something you're not telling me. What is it?"

Sarah shook her head and began walking again.

"Tell me," Alex shouted. "Tell me, you bitch!"

Sarah should have ignored the insult, but she couldn't. She spun on her heels and spoke through gritted teeth. "It's none of your bloody business, but I think I'm pregnant."

It took Nick half an hour to reach his sister's house, and as he drew up behind a silver Lexus the driver's door opened and Howard Franks emerged. It was the first time Nick had seen Franks in the flesh, and his first reaction was surprise that the writer was so diminutive. Franks was no more than about five feet five, slightly built, with immaculate silver hair and the kind of artificial tan that looked about as convincing as a coat of creosote.

"What are you playing at?" Nick demanded.

Franks swept his hand in the direction of Diana's house. "Your sister declined to speak to me. I felt it best to give her some time to reconsider."

"Haven't we made it clear that we're not going to help you?"

"You've made it abundantly clear. The fact is, I have absolutely no intention of abandoning this project. I can write it without your contribution if I have to, but I'm trying to do you and your family a favour. Your involvement would help to provide a balanced view."

"And it also legitimises whatever scurrilous lies you choose to include without our knowledge."

Franks chuckled. "If that's the stumbling block," he said, "let me give you a flavour of my discoveries so far. Does the name Ted Wheeler mean anything?"

Nick instinctively shook his head, but at the same time he felt a flicker of recognition: had his mother perhaps mentioned that name, many years ago?

Franks continued, "What about Leslie Jones?"

"Just get to the point. Who are they?"

"Jones was a small time criminal, working for Wheeler, amongst others. I've reason to believe he tried to blackmail your father, possibly in relation to some of Eddie's… shall we say, extracurricular activities."

"Got any proof?"

Franks laughed, as though the very idea of needing proof

was a quaint anachronism. "I'll have enough to keep your lawyers in their traps, if it comes to that."

Nick looked away, not wanting Franks to sense the dread unfurling in his stomach. Trying to maintain a defiant tone, he said, "So what about this Leslie Jones?"

And although he braced himself for something unpleasant, he was completely unprepared for the answer Franks gave him.

"Your father had him killed."

"You think?" said Alex. She took a wary step forward, unsure how to deal with this new, assertive Sarah.

"I came off the pill when I found out about Nick. I didn't go near him for ages, but then…" She shrugged. "I needed him."

Alex snorted contemptuously. "How long have you known?"

"A week or two. I haven't done a test yet, but normally I'm pretty regular."

"Then why walk out on him?"

"Because I was so scared, knowing I'd be getting fat and unattractive. If he can't keep it in his pants at the best of times, what will he be like when I'm waddling round with a screaming brat clamped to my boob? I left because I needed time to think, but all I've had is you nagging, undermining, manipulating me."

"Because you're so spineless."

"Maybe. Maybe I am. But I'm willing to try again, and I want you to piss off out of my life."

A seagull rose suddenly on the updraft, unleashing a screech of displeasure at the presence of humans so close to its habitat. Sarah flinched, turning towards the sound, and Alex rushed at her, pushing her closer to the cliff edge.

"Only too happy to oblige," Alex snarled. "You've served

your purpose."

Holding Sarah by the shoulders, she wrestled her to the brink. Sarah opened her mouth to scream, but the feeble sound that emerged was snatched away by the wind. She tried to clasp Alex but could only clutch at the shiny fabric of her coat. Even in desperation her strength was no match for the other woman. Her body twisted into the void, feet kicking uselessly at the loose chalk of the cliff face, fingers grasping, horror and pitiful confusion on her face as Alex broke free and lurched away from the edge. Then she was gone.

Alex fell to the ground and was still for a moment, breathing fast. Despite the noise of the wind and the waves, she was sure she heard the body hit the rocks. It sounded like the end of something and the beginning of something.

Rising to her feet, she looked around for anyone who might have seen what happened. A couple of people were walking towards Beachy Head, but they had their backs to her. There seemed to be no one else in sight.

She had been lucky. Not for the first time.

She started jogging, taking a circular route halfway down the hill that would avoid going too close either to the lighthouse or to the road. She watched a couple of cars negotiate the bend near the cliff edge and continue towards Birling Gap. The drivers were too far away to make her out, but still she pulled the hat tight over her head and hunched her shoulders.

If the murder had been witnessed, the police would pick her up before she made it back to the car. The knowledge gave her an incredible thrill, lending a heightened aware-ness to every sensation: the springiness of the wild grass, the delicious salt taste of the wind, the mournful cry of gulls.

This was a deviation from her original plan, but an

enormously satisfying one. She was glad to be rid of the miserable whining bitch. And she hadn't had to go through with the sex, which was a bonus.

She reviewed the day's events, trying to pinpoint where she might have left incriminating evidence. Her foolish manoeuvre in the hotel car park had brought people to the window. Had anyone taken the number? She didn't recall seeing security cameras outside the hotel, but that didn't mean they weren't there.

No doubt plenty of the shops in Eastbourne had captured them on CCTV, but there was little she could do about that. Just had to hope the images were poor quality.

The other question was DNA. There was a possibility she'd left hairs or traces of skin on Sarah, but to find them the police would have to be quick: one high tide and any evidence would be erased.

It took her ten minutes to reach the car park, and the handful of people in sight paid her no attention. She drove away cautiously, half-expecting to hear sirens approaching, but once she reached the main road towards Brighton the excitement returned, and with it the understanding that once again she had got away with murder.

She saw now how this development could bring her a step closer to her goal, while also allowing her a breathing space: no more time wasted on the sham of inane friendship and pathetic female bonding.

Coming out of Brighton on to the A23, she picked up speed and switched on the CD player, turning it up loud. She needed to get home; she needed food and a bath and nourishing sleep.

And she knew Sarah wouldn't linger long in her dreams. Instead it would be her brother's face she saw below the water, his eyes wide with confusion and pleading to be spared.

8

"That's ridiculous. And you'd better warn your publishers that we'll instruct lawyers to scrutinise every word of your crummy little book. One unsubstantiated allegation and we'll have you in court. Do you understand?"

Nick jabbed a finger angrily at Franks's face, and saw a tiny flash of unease in the older man. It was an unwelcome reminder of how he must have appeared when Kevin Doyle sprang at him the day before.

"I'm prepared for that," said Franks, quickly regaining his composure. "And I haven't come here to exchange schoolboy threats. I want you to understand the gravity of the crimes your father committed. When you've had time to consider it, I'm sure you'll see the benefits of collaboration."

He turned away and opened his car door. For a moment Nick was nonplussed, almost disappointed that the confrontation had ended so abruptly. Franks started the engine and then lowered the window. "Think about it," he called cheerily.

Nick waited until the Lexus was out of sight and then walked up the drive. Diana must have been watching, for the front door opened as he approached.

"I feel like a terrible coward," she said. "I just couldn't face him. I didn't want to get upset in front of the kids."

"You did the right thing. He should never have come here."

They went into the kitchen, and Nick spent some time with the children while Diana made Ryan some toast and put on a DVD.

"*Finding Nemo* as babysitter," she sighed. "What a terrible mother I am."

"We were always glued to the TV," Nick reminded her. "Didn't do us any harm." He made himself go cross-eyed and she laughed, then sniffed and rubbed away sudden tears. He was aware of her steeling herself, taking a deep breath.

"I assume it's bad news?"

"It's ludicrous. Insane. He says Dad had someone killed."

There was a moment while Diana processed the words and attempted to make sense of them. She gave a snorting, spluttering laugh of disbelief.

"But why? Why would he…?"

"He claims the guy was a lowlife villain who was black-mailing Dad."

"Blackmailing him for what?"

Nick saw that Diana's hands were shaking. He stepped closer and put his arm round her.

"He didn't say."

"Or doesn't know?"

Nick shrugged. "Maybe."

"So it could be just a lot of… baloney."

He said nothing. Diana was four years younger than him, and had been only five when their father died. Unlike Nick, she had been shielded from the discovery that big-hearted comic Eddie had left his family almost penniless, not to mention the trail of lovers crawling out of the woodwork for their double-page spreads in the *News of the World* and *Titbits*.

Diana produced a tissue from the sleeve of her sweater and blew her nose. "Do you think we should co-operate with him?"

"I don't know. He could take whatever charming anecdotes we give him and ignore them altogether, or even twist them into something nasty. We can't trust him."

"But maybe if we're on the inside we might be able to influence him in some way."

"Appeal to his better nature?" Nick asked sarcastically.

"All right. Forget that idea." She blew her nose again. "Do you want a drink?"

"I'm fine."

"Sure? I'm going to have a glass of wine."

Nick glanced at his watch, pretending to be shocked. "Really?"

"Sod it. Medicinal purposes. Sure you won't join me?"

He shook his head. Pouring the wine, she finally asked the question he'd been dreading.

"Has Sarah been in touch?"

"Nope."

"Have you spoken to her friends?"

"She told me she was in a hotel, and there are a hell of a lot to choose from." He didn't add that, to his shame, he barely knew the three or four friends that were exclusive to Sarah. It was as if she'd deliberately kept them away from him, perhaps fearing he'd jump into bed with them at the first opportunity.

"What you did was so stupid," Diana said, more weary than angry. "Why on earth would you risk everything for a bloody one-night stand?"

Nick struggled to find a reply. He suspected the question had been phrased to illustrate that the son was going the way of the father.

"If Sarah gives you another chance, tell me you won't do anything like that ever again." She took his hands in hers and squeezed them. "Promise me."

"Of course I won't," he said, flinching at the intensity of her gaze. "I've learnt my lesson."

"Are you sure?"

"*Yes.*"

"Don't snap. I just want to know that you mean it."

The back door opened and Patrick walked in. "Hey, you're becoming a fixture," he said. "Shall I sort out the spare room?"

He was joking, but Diana nodded. "Good idea. You could eat with us and stay over."

Nick was tempted, but shook his head. "I wouldn't say no to dinner, but I have to get back. The work's piling up."

"I'm surprised you can think about work with all this going on."

"So am I. But I still have the bills to pay. Life goes on."

Diana raised her glass as if making a toast. "Life goes on," she echoed.

Howard Franks returned to London feeling more than satisfied. Nick Randall's intransigence was a trivial setback compared to some of the situations he'd experienced in his tabloid days. The expression on his face when he heard about Leslie Jones's death had been worth the journey on its own.

From now on, Nick and Diana knew exactly what they were facing. Franks felt it was only a matter of time before they agreed to talk to him.

Nick had been sharp, though, understanding why he was so eager for their collaboration. Armed with quotes from Eddie's family, Franks could claim far greater legitimacy for the other, more salacious aspects of the book. And having agreed to contribute, they could hardly claim the finished result was an unauthorised account.

On the way back he tried calling Lindsay but got no answer. Taking the chance that she'd be keen to hear about his latest masterstroke, he stopped off at the delicatessen in Archway Road and bought borlotti beans, pancetta and double cream. He was a keen amateur chef, and had spent thousands on a gleaming Poggenhall kitchen. Tonight he had in mind a Jamie Oliver risotto followed by Nigella's bitter orange ice cream.

And then sex. Definitely sex, after last night's disappointment.

But when he reached home there was a message from Lindsay. She was drowning in paperwork and wouldn't be able to see him for a couple of days. To make up for it, she suggested he book a table at the best restaurant he could find on Saturday night and afterwards she'd give him, in her words, a blow job to die for.

The message gave him an erection. He listened to it twice more and knew he couldn't possibly wait until Saturday. Four days, for Christ's sake.

Checking his other messages, he learnt that he'd been invited to appear on a Channel 4 reminiscence show about footballers and their indiscretions. His transition from journalist to biographer had encompassed a stint as ghost-writer of a couple of tedious sporting autobiographies, one of them by a former Premiership player. Franks rang his agent and said he'd be delighted to appear.

After taking a shower he put on a Norah Jones CD, poured a large gin and tonic and consulted his little black book.

His first choice, Geraldine, was in the Maldives. Lucky bitch. Fiona couldn't talk because hubby was close at hand but not in sight, raising the possibility that he was listening on another extension. Franks threw in some nonsense about the TV invitation and hastily terminated the call. Hubby in this case was built like a brick shithouse and had never seemed overly fond of Franks.

Penelope was the ex-wife of a Labour peer; her maid delivered a long unintelligible message that he cut off halfway through. Those options exhausted, he rang a favoured escort agency based in Kensington and was overjoyed to learn that Teri was available for £350 per hour, or £2000 for the night. He booked the whole night to show he was both virile and generous, but knew he'd be exhausted by midnight.

He put the phone down, his good mood restored by the promise of physical gratification. The added benefit of an escort was that he needn't make much effort. For two grand it was only his pleasure that mattered.

Of course there was always a chance that Lindsay would turn up unannounced, as she had a couple of times after declining a date. Tough. The fact was, Lindsay's independence was becoming a bit tiresome. And now she was no longer needed for the book, it was time to think about ditching her.

Just as soon as he'd lined up the next one, of course.

9

Nick woke the next morning feeling full of vigour. It didn't matter that Sarah was still gone, or that Franks had accused Eddie of murder, or that he had reports to write and visits to make: some inadvertent chemical imbalance in his brain had made the air coming in his bedroom window smell fresh and inviting, the cry of the seagulls romantic and tender. He felt so infused with energy that he left the house at seven-thirty in shorts and a t-shirt, shuddering at the cold but determined to warm himself up with a quick run along the seafront.

His route took him west to the end of the promenade and then along the access road by the side of Shoreham harbour. Then he headed inland to Boundary Road, where he knew there would be a bakery open. Laden with fresh rolls and a couple of jam doughnuts still warm from the oven, he returned home and had an unhealthy but delicious breakfast.

Afterwards he wrote up yesterday's reports, then he rang the insurers of the other vehicle involved in the Lauren Doyle claim. While on hold, enduring a sugary ballad by the Carpenters that would torment him for the rest of the day, he leafed through his file of papers. The Renault Espace had allegedly sustained heavy rear damage, and he learnt that repairs had been authorised to a garage called Knight's Accident Repair Centre.

"Do you have the invoice there yet?" he asked.

"No. We only authorised... what is it, three weeks ago."

"That's great. Thanks." He called up Yell.com and quickly located the bodyshop in an industrial park on the edge of

East Grinstead, about six miles from the M23. With a major repair, three weeks wasn't a long time. If this was a genuine accident there was a good chance the vehicle would still be at the garage.

His next call was considerably more difficult. It was to the converted barn near Bergerac where Sarah's parents lived. The property had been magnificently refurbished by Gerry and his wife Lisa, an interior designer, and their two-year labour of love had been the subject of a makeover show on one of the satellite channels.

Nick was hoping that Lisa would answer. Instead he heard a gruff, "*Bonjour*?" and felt his good cheer begin to deflate.

"Gerry, it's Nick. Nick Randall."

"Hmph. To what do we owe the pleasure?"

Gerry had never been one for chit-chat, and Nick was frankly eager to get it over with. "Sarah and I have separated," he said. "I thought I should let you know, because she walked out two days ago and I've heard nothing from her."

In the silence that followed, Nick had a vivid image of Gerry squeezing the receiver and wishing it was Nick's throat. "Has she been in touch with you?" he added.

"Wait," Gerry ordered. Urgent voices in the background, and then Lisa took the phone.

"Nick, what's happened?" Distressed but sensible: not out for his blood just yet.

"I'd rather not go into that right now," he said. "I'm just concerned to know she's all right."

"We haven't spoken to her for a week or more. Is there any reason to fear for her safety?"

"Oh no. She told me she'd booked into a hotel, but she's not answering her mobile."

"I'll ring her straight away."

"Thanks. Can you let me know how she is?"

A pause while Lisa wrestled with her conscience. "I'll see what I can do," she agreed.

He put the phone down, glad of the distance between them. If Gerry had still lived in Sussex he would have turned up on the doorstep within half an hour, ranting about his feckless, waste-of-space son-in-law and probably challenging him to a fistfight. Thank God for the appeal of the Dordogne.

Roger Knight arrived for work at just after ten, parking in the space reserved for him as managing director. Knight's Accident Repair Centre was the flagship of his business empire, a state-of-the-art bodyshop occupying twenty thousand square feet. It had been launched just over six years ago, with an opening ceremony performed by an ex-Formula One commentator and a C-list glamour model. It had contracts with half a dozen insurers, including a couple of the biggest players, and a turnover approaching a million pounds a year.

And it was barely breaking even.

The business had evolved from a used car dealer-ship owned by his uncle, Ray McPherson, a dynamic entrepreneur and villain of the old school. Together with a couple of even more unsavoury characters, Ted Wheeler and Mickey Leach, he'd had interests in various businesses, both legitimate and bent: pubs and loan sharking in South London, Kent and Surrey, a club and a massage parlour in Soho, a garage in East Grinstead and a scrapyard run from a farm in West Sussex. Ray had died childless ten years ago, leaving Roger the car dealers and the farm.

The scrapyard was still in the process of evolving into a fully-fledged salvage company. Against his better judgement, Roger had given responsibility for that to Kevin Doyle, while he concentrated on the bodyshop.

The idea for the fraudulent claims had come from Barry Harper, a partner in a firm of solicitors with historic links to McPherson, Wheeler and Leach. He'd pointed out that Roger had a perfect opportunity: the dealership and salvage yard gave him access to cars, the bodyshop offered control of the repair process, and Barry his friendly solicitor took care of the spurious medical reports.

The scam, essentially, was a simple one. Two vehicles, one low-value and one high, were acquired and insured with different companies. The driver of the low-value vehicle reported a straightforward accident: rear-ending the expensive car filled with people. A claim was made for the vehicle damage, hire charges and injuries to the occupants. If they kept the claims straightforward, the evidence was rarely disputed. Even if an insurer insisted on their own medical examination, the symptoms of whiplash were easy to fake.

This was their nineteenth claim. So far they'd collected nearly £300,000, with at least another £400,000 in the pipeline. Barry had urged them to take their time. "Wanting a quick settlement makes them suspicious. And besides, the longer the claim's outstanding, the more they expect to pay out."

Most of the injury compensation was being laundered through the car dealers and salvage yard – if Kevin sold a reconditioned engine for £700, the books would show £1500. Roger suspected that Kevin was also creaming off some cash for himself, but for the time being he was fairly relaxed about that. It gave him some leverage, should he ever need it.

At heart, though, Roger remained uneasy about the

fraud. He told himself it was providing a much-needed cash injection, and that he'd close it down once the legitimate businesses were trading profitably. But when it came to making that decision, he knew Barry Harper and Kevin Doyle might have something to say. What he would do if his partners disagreed was something that regularly kept him awake in the early hours.

He was staring at the framed photos of his children without really seeing them when the receptionist, Angela, leaned into the room.

"There's an insurance assessor here," she said. "Wants the bodyshop manager."

Roger frowned. "Can't George see him?"

"It's about the Renault Espace," she hissed. Unlike the bodyshop manager and most of the other staff, Angela knew about the profitable sideline, and indeed received a little cash bonus in her pay packet every month.

"Well done," said Roger. He'd taken her into his confidence for just such eventualities. "Do you have his name?"

"Nick Randall," she said. "It's funny. I'm sure I know him from somewhere."

Nick sat on a plastic seat in the reception area, which was exactly like every other bodyshop reception he'd ever seen: bland décor, piped music and a selection of stunningly dull leaflets about legal expenses and car breakdown cover. He considered sampling the coffee from the drinks machine in the corner, but experience told him not to bother. Instead he checked his phone for messages, then tried Sarah's number again, but her mobile was still switched off.

The receptionist reappeared, followed by a tall, well-built man in an expensive suit. He beamed and extended his hand.

"Roger Knight. I'm MD here."

"Ah. I was hoping to see…"

"Our bodyshop manager's tied up, but I'm sure I can help. Come this way."

He led Nick through a narrow corridor and into a nondescript office, modest by executive standards. Apart from a couple of plants, the only human touch was half a dozen framed photographs of children.

Nick sat down, declining an offer of refreshments. He realised Knight was studying him curiously.

"You look familiar. Have we met before?"

"I don't think so."

"Would I have seen you on television?"

"That was my father," said Nick. "Eddie Randall. He was in a lot of British films in the fifties and sixties."

"Of course." Knight was nodding enthusiastically. "Funnily enough, I think my uncle used to know him. There was a picture of them both in his hall for years."

Nick opened his briefcase and pretended to sort the contents rather than betray his interest in this news. "Was your uncle good friends with him?"

"That I can't say. He died ten years ago. But I know he had interests in a club in Soho for a time, back in the sixties." Knight rested his hand on his PC mouse as though it were a comforting pet. "Now, how can I help you?"

Nick produced a business card and placed it on the desk. "I'm investigating a claim for CBA Insurance. I believe you're repairing the other vehicle, a Renault Espace." He handed Knight a copy of the claim form. "Heavy rear-end collision. Quite a large job, I should think."

Knight examined the papers, but his expression gave nothing away. "What exactly is CBA concerned about?"

"To put it simply, we don't think there was any such

accident."

Knight frowned as though he had misheard. He peered a little closer at the computer screen.

Nick added, "As you probably know, not all staged accidents actually happen. In some cases it's a completely paper-based event, putting forward previously damaged cars as evidence of the loss."

"And you think this vehicle…?" Knight looked concerned. "Well, I'd better see what I can find."

He started tapping at the keyboard, which gave Nick an opportunity to observe him. He put Knight in his mid-forties, but looking pretty good: only a few lines on his face, a hint of grey in his slightly bouffant brown hair. He had the plump friendly face of a young Bill Clinton, and brown eyes that shone with intelligence. His immaculate appearance only served to remind Nick that his own hair was due for a trim, and he had blood on his collar.

"Nearly there," Knight murmured, glancing at Nick, who turned his attention to the photographs. His eyes were drawn to a group picture, where a woman with short blonde hair and sparkling eyes was embracing two of the children. Despite her smile, Nick had the impression that she didn't feel entirely comfortable.

"Do you have kids?" Knight asked.

Nick thought of Sarah, and the conversation they'd never quite managed to have. "Not yet," he said.

Knight gestured at the photographs. "They live with their mum. In Aberdeen."

"Must make it difficult to see them."

"Oh, I'd happily fly up there every couple of weeks. No, it's Lynn who makes it difficult."

"Your ex-wife?"

"Mm. Let me give you some advice. If you're lucky enough

to have children, stay with their mother." He sighed, clicked heavily on his mouse and a printer whirred into life. "We certainly have this job on our records. I assume you'd like to see the repair documents?"

Nick leant forward. "It's already been repaired?"

Knight greeted the question as a compliment. "We pride ourselves on a quick turnaround."

"Did the insurers inspect the vehicle?" Nick tried not to sound uncertain, but his theories about the claim were starting to look doubtful.

"Via our imaging system. The job was approved by their engineer." He handed the papers to Nick. "Are you sure you won't have a coffee?"

"No, thanks." Nick saw that the job had been costed on a computerised estimating system, which detailed precise repair times for each stage of the process. Together with half a dozen digital images of the damage, it was more than enough to justify authorising repairs.

"Do you mind if I keep these?" he asked. "They might come in handy at some stage."

"Of course." Knight sounded amused, as though he was aware that Nick had been wrong-footed.

Nick put the papers into his briefcase. "When you have a moment, can you check your records to see if this policy-holder has had other repairs carried out here?"

"I'd be happy to."

Nick made for the door, then paused: the old Columbo method. "While you're at it, have a look for the name Lauren Doyle as well."

Knight seemed to flinch. "Lauren...?"

"The other driver involved."

"Oh, I see. Yes, yes, I'll do that."

"Thanks." Nick grinned. Suddenly he was feeling better

again.

Leading him back to the reception area, Knight said, "We sometimes encounter problems collecting on our non-contract work. Do you offer any debt recovery services?"

"I've done a bit of that for insurers."

"Excellent. I might be able to put some work your way, then."

He saw Nick to the exit, where they shook hands. Knight's grip was too firm, and a little damper than it had been the first time.

"Pleased to meet you," he added. "Let me know if you need any more help."

"I'll do that," said Nick, wishing he had a more pithy response to hand, but satisfied that the other man understood what had just happened. Knight's reaction to Lauren Doyle's name had given him away: he *knew* something wasn't right about the claim.

10

As soon as Nick's Audi had pulled out on to Copthorne Road, Roger went back to his office and grabbed up his phone. Kevin Doyle answered on the third ring.

"I've just had Nick Randall here."

"That fucking investigator?"

"He wanted to know about the Renault. He was surprised we'd repaired it so quickly."

"Did you show him the invoice?"

"Of course," Roger replied coldly.

"You reckon he'll be happy with that?"

"There's no reason why he shouldn't be," Roger said, but he felt less sure than he sounded. He didn't know if his reaction to Lauren Doyle had been noticed: only the merest flash of recognition in his eyes, something he'd been helpless to prevent. Surely you'd have to look very closely to notice a thing like that?

But Nick *was* looking closely, he reminded himself. He's trying to prove a fraud.

"Fuck!" The usual eloquent outburst from Doyle broke the silence. "D'you want me to come over?"

"No. We shouldn't be seen together here. I'll meet you at the farm in about an hour." He took a breath and added, "We might have to hold fire on the new claims."

He thought Kevin would protest, but there was only a disaffected grunt that could have meant anything. He concluded the call, then opened an internet connection on his PC and typed *Eddie Randall* into Google.

Know your enemy, isn't that what they said?

*

Meanwhile, the enemy was buying a sausage sandwich from a greasy spoon close to the M23. Then he drove west, skirting Crawley to avoid traffic, and parked in a country lane a couple of miles from Gatwick. Taking care not to spill HP sauce on his suit, Nick studied Lauren Doyle's description of the accident.

According to the initial telephone notification, the collision occurred in the vicinity of Ifield golf club, close to where he was now parked. However, on the claim form Lauren had put the location down as Slaugham, which was about eight miles further south. Was that simply carelessness, or did it mean something more?

He was mulling it over when his phone rang. Diana.

"I've been trying Sarah's number all morning and getting nothing."

"And?"

"And… I don't know. How long should we leave it before we report her missing?"

Nick had been wondering the same thing himself. "I thought tonight, if there's still no message from her."

After the call he tidied up, wiped the inevitable blob of sauce from his trousers and wandered along the lane. Reaching a gate, he picked his way carefully around the puddles and stood watching a tractor ploughing the far side of the field, seagulls drifting like litter in its wake. He thought how satisfying such a task must be, no uncertainty about either the objective or the result, the evidence of your progress displayed in each strip of glistening earth. Life on the farm.

And then he thought: *farm*. Remembering what CBA's engineer had told him about Lauren Doyle's Escort. The vehicle had been inspected at a run-down salvage yard near Rusper, which was only a couple of miles from the location she'd first given to the insurer.

"They realised it was too close," he muttered to himself. And recalled Folsom saying the Escort looked filthy. It hadn't been towed there after the accident: it had never left the yard in the first place.

There was a road atlas in the car, but it wasn't much help in locating the yard. He rang Morag Strutton and asked her to check the file. Griffin Farm had charged CBA for recovery and storage, the invoice no more than a page from a spiral notebook with a rubber-stamped heading.

After relaying the directions to him, she said, "Why do I sense you're really enjoying this one?"

"Because I know I'm right," he said.

"Cocky bastard," she laughed, and put the phone down.

With the benefit of directions, the farm was easy to find. Without them, it would have been virtually impossible. The private road which led to it was screened by trees, and for the first fifty yards it was no more than a muddy track. Brambles and nettles grew high on each side, obscuring his view of the farm.

After quarter of a mile the road twisted to the right and Nick found himself passing through high metal gates into an open yard full of rusting wrecks. A large German Shepherd appeared from some sort of workshop, followed closely by two Rottweilers.

Nick pulled up in the yard, and against his better judgement started to open his door. The German Shepherd let out a long deliberate growl, and Nick shut the door.

Hearing a shout from behind him, he looked in his wing mirror and saw a man in overalls climbing down from a JCB excavator. Another shout and the dogs dispersed, but Nick still thought twice about getting out. He opened the window instead.

"Who're you?" the man asked, thumping a grimy hand on the roof of the car and peering inside. His breath made Nick want to recoil.

"My name's Randall. I work for an insurance company."

"Nobody here now. Need an appointment." The man's gaze was unrelenting and hostile: the dogs seemed almost tame by comparison.

"You're not open to the public, then?"

"Auction days only. You come to buy?" The man was chewing something as he talked. He spat into the dirt below Nick's car.

"I'm interested in a car you recovered. A 1994 Ford Escort."

"Can't help you."

"Well, is there someone —"

"Best get off if I were you."

The man turned and walked back to the JCB, climbing into the cab. Nick remained where he was, hating himself for feeling intimidated but aware that he'd gain nothing by ignoring the advice. There was a rumble as the excavator lurched forward, and Nick realised it was heading straight for him.

Scrambling with the gearstick, he yanked on the wheel with his other hand, trying to turn the car on a full lock. The JCB accelerated, its hydraulic metal claw missing the rear bumper by inches. The Audi slithered on the mud and he lost control trying to straighten up, clipping the passenger mirror on the gate post. Once in the lane he checked his mirror and saw the JCB had come to a halt, the driver doubled over with laughter.

Roger was less than a mile from the farm when he saw a familiar blue Audi heading towards him. He spotted an opening on the right and threw his Saab into what turned out to be a long gravel driveway leading to a thatched cottage. He waited until Randall had passed, then reversed and drove out.

At the farm Kevin Doyle was standing by the JCB, talking to Jim Harvey. Jim was a thirty-year-old car thief who worked for them on a casual basis, between spells in prison. Jim's idea of a recreational Saturday night was to down eight pints of lager and kick someone's head in.

"He was here," Kevin said.

"I know. I just passed him."

"Did he see you?"

Roger shook his head. "More to the point, did he see *you*?"

"Jim got rid of him." Kevin and Jim exchanged a malicious smile.

"Politely, I hope? We don't want to make him any more suspicious, do we?"

One of the dogs barked at Roger, who gestured carefully at it. "Get rid of them," he said to Jim. He noticed Jim glance at Doyle before jumping down from the cab and whistling to the dogs.

Roger followed Kevin into the cramped office in the main building and shivered. The paraffin heater in the corner was throwing out a noxious smell but precious little warmth. Kevin's desk was cluttered with invoices and letters and even a few car parts. And a tiny bag of cocaine, sitting on a Parkers valuation guide.

"Can't you keep that rubbish out of sight?" Knight complained. "What if he'd come in?"

"You think he was gonna get past the dogs?"

Roger grunted. He was still considering how narrowly he'd avoided being seen. If he hadn't recognised Randall's car in time it would be as good as over by now. It was bad enough that the salvage yard was in Doyle's name, but anyone digging deeper would soon find the link to Roger.

"We've put ourselves in a stupid position," he said. "Too many coincidences."

The irony was, they'd never intended to use Lauren Doyle, but one of Barry Harper's contacts cried off at the last minute and Kevin put her name forward, expecting any investigation to be no more than a formality.

"So what's he got?" Roger said. "The Espace is linked to the bodyshop, which is clean as far as he knows. He's got Lauren and the Escort. If he does a DVLA trace and gets the previous owners, he'll find it was brought in here three months ago."

"He won't go back that far," Kevin said. The cocaine had disappeared and he was lighting a cigarette.

"Do you want to take a chance?" Roger asked. "The previous owner can confirm it was towed here with heavy front damage, a perfect match with the damage reported by Lauren. Then he finds the claimant's husband runs the salvage yard."

"So let's do what I said in the first place."

"Kevin, if you beat him up, what's going to happen? He'll go straight to the police, and then maybe they'll take a closer look at us."

"They don't give a toss about insurance fraud. Anyway, I'm not saying just a beating. Let's make it more permanent." Kevin drew on his cigarette, then coughed and gurgled the phlegm.

"Kill him? You'd kill him for this?"

"We're making thirty grand a month. You want to give that up? 'Cause I fucking don't."

Roger said nothing. This was precisely the reaction he'd expected, but it gave him no satisfaction to be proved right.

He waited for Doyle to continue.

"As far as we know, it's just him that's interested in us, yeah? We make it look like an accident. Get him off the scene now and it's problem solved."

"And what if the insurer instructs someone else?"

"I've been working on Lauren," he said, and his tone made Roger shudder. "She ain't gonna slip up again."

"I don't like it."

"What fucking choice do we have? Walk away from all that cash."

"If we have to, yes."

"No fucking way." Kevin jumped to his feet, sweeping a stack of papers to the floor. "You can bale out if you want, but not me."

It was the most emphatic show of defiance in the five years they'd been working together. *I've given him too much independence*, Roger realised. *Now he thinks he can go it alone.*

"That's not what I mean," he said.

"Don't talk to me like I'm fucking stupid."

"Then don't act like it," Roger responded, meeting Doyle's gaze and holding it until he saw the other man's shoulders drop. "I'll think of something, don't worry."

"Yeah? Well it had better fucking work," Kevin snarled, "or I'll do it myself. My own way."

After his brush with danger at the salvage yard, Nick was bristling with anger and even more determined to prove the claim was fraudulent. En route to his next call he stopped at Ardingly reservoir and made detailed notes of his meeting with Roger Knight and the visit to Griffin Farm. Then he took a half-hour walk along the nature trail that circled the reservoir, envying the few fishermen their untroubled pastime. He also tried Sarah's mobile, but to no avail.

The next appointment was at a smart executive home in Haywards Heath, where the lady of the house immediately began to berate him for the shortcomings of her insurance company.

He wasn't in the mood to hear it, and wasted no time in voicing his misgivings about her claim. "No one buys a plasma screen television and throws away the receipt," he said bluntly. Her grand manner fell away, replaced by open-mouthed astonishment. "And no one forgets to include it on the police inventory."

She let out a sob and blamed her husband, who was a chartered accountant and ought to have known better. Nick might have told her that in his experience, white-collar professionals were the worst.

After two more calls he drove home on autopilot, nearly missing a red light on the Old Shoreham Road. When he got in he made straight for the fridge and opened a beer. Barely six o'clock, but what the hell? He was his father's son, wasn't he?

He laughed in the silence and wondered if he was already cracking up. There was a message from his sister, reminding him to ring the police about Sarah.

Quite right too. But beer first, and perhaps a sandwich. And there were reports to write.

He recharged his mobile phone and powered up the laptop. Deciding he didn't have the energy to make a sandwich, he opened a large bag of Doritos and washed them down with another beer while writing up the day's visits. At some point he moved on to the couch, where he shut his eyes in order to think more clearly.

When he woke it was dark outside and strangely there

were three empty beer cans on the table. He could have sworn he'd stopped at two. The laptop had gone on to standby and there was a strange ringing noise he couldn't quite identify.

The door. Someone at the door.

He struggled to his feet, wincing at pins and needles in one arm. His bladder was painfully full and he had the beginnings of a headache. He saw with a shock that it was gone eight o'clock: he'd been asleep for at least an hour.

He opened the door and found himself facing a thin man in a police constable's uniform and a motherly middle-aged woman in a dark suit. She identified herself as Detective Chief Inspector Melanie Pearce, her companion as Constable Wilcox, and asked if they could come in.

He nodded and stepped back, only now thinking to ask why they were here.

"It's about your wife," DCI Pearce said.

He felt a wave of relief, quickly replaced by confusion. How could they have found her so quickly? He wasn't even sure he'd reported her missing yet.

He led them into the living room, desperately trying to clear his fogged mind. Had he rung them before he fell asleep? And if he hadn't, why were they here?

The answer was on the detective's face, her sorrowful averted gaze while waiting for him to be seated. Just like a child at storytime, he thought, and had to suppress a mad laugh. *Are you sitting comfortably? Then I'll begin.*

In his lap, his hands began to shake like landed fish. The constable, whose name he had already forgotten, watched him curiously for a moment and then cleared his throat as if about to speak. Nick looked at him, waiting for the words to emerge, but in fact it was DCI Pearce who brought his world crashing down.

Part Two

June 1968

A perfect day at the races: the sun shining, stunning views in every direction. Sea, town and rolling downland.

Surveying his new friends, Eddie thought it appropriate that they should meet up in Brighton, the setting for Graham Greene's famous book. Also known as London-by-the-sea, and famous for its tawdry image, the location of choice for a dirty weekend, a bit of slap and tickle with the mistress. Not in Eddie's case, though: too close to home for all that. Mary was only a few miles away in the house in Alfriston, stuck with a bawling baby and about as much fun these days as an enema.

No, the real treat was planned for tonight, back up in town.

After a few drinks Eddie and his friends went for a stroll around the course, exchanging wisecracks with the bookies and the great unwashed. He loved the reaction of the crowd, the whispers, the double-takes. He was no Peter Sellers or Sean Connery, but most of them knew his face, and what's more they liked it.

Of his companions, Mickey Leach was also familiar, but you got a very different reaction from anyone who recognised him: the smiles wiped away like blood off formica, people jostling to get out of his path. Even some hissing from a couple of unwise punters, although today Mickey was happy to let it pass. Down here he was primarily known as a slum landlord, notorious for his Rachman-like methods.

Mickey's interests went way beyond that. He was part of a loose affiliation of self-styled entrepreneurs making hay while the sun shone on swinging London. Eddie had been taken into the fold following a little misunderstanding about some money he'd lost on the horses. That all changed when they realised who he was. No question of wiping the slate clean, of course, but he was invited to renegotiate the debts, and new lines of credit were immediately made available.

With the help of some informed tips, his luck had turned and seen him clear the money he owed, and then some. Today they were out to celebrate. There was even talk of Eddie taking a share in their club, Lewds, maybe becoming a kind of resident entertainer – as he said, he had a pretty good set of pipes. "Used to knock 'em dead at the troop shows in Burma."

After four races he was up a hundred, Mickey had won about half that and Ted Wheeler was thirty quid down. Ray McPherson hadn't bet more than about thirty shillings; said it was a mug's game. They ribbed him about it all the way back, Ted's big old Daimler weaving a little on the London road. They were all pissed: Ray was nominated to drive because he held his drink better than the rest of them.

In the car they drained another bottle of Hennessy and aimed the empty at a bus stop in Purley Way. Mickey produced some uppers and they snatched them from his hand like kids taking sweets.

When Eddie was high he started telling them about a small role he'd had in a Dennis Wheatley adaptation made by Hammer out at Elstree the year before. That's where the idea for the ceremony came from. By the time they got to Soho they had it all planned. Mickey even sent one of his lackeys to the butchers in Brewer Street to see if he could blag some pig's blood, but the butcher wasn't having any of it.

"Fuck it," Mickey said. "We'll do without."

"Or make our own?" Ted suggested. No one quite knew what he meant, but he seemed to think it was funny, so they all laughed.

They'd arranged it so that the main bar would stay open till one in the morning. The real party would kick off upstairs at about midnight and go on for the rest of the night. When they got there, one of the staff was carrying up crates of light ale. He gave them a sour look, his gaze lingering on Eddie.

"Who's that miserable sod?" Eddie asked.

"Les Jones," said Ted. He put on a strong Welsh accent: "Or Jones the Twat, as I now rename him."

"Still goes to church, does our Leslie," said Ray. "Strict Presbyterian upbringing, you know."

"So what's he doing in this place?"

Mickey chuckled. "He was here when I was choosing the girls. 'Sordid!' he kept saying. 'Sordid behaviour.'"

"You know what his problem is?" said Ray. "He ain't getting enough himself."

"If you saw his missus you'd say that was a blessing," Ted retorted.

"Yeah, and he ain't having any of tonight's lot even if he wanted it. Cream of the crop, I'm telling you." Mickey shot a conspiratorial glance around the club, even though it was now empty apart from the four of them.

"Eight girls in all, most of 'em dancers or strippers, bloody good ones an' all. And then a couple that are really something special. Never been touched."

There were some sceptical noises, but Mickey shook his head vehemently. "Straight up. My boys searched high and low for these virtuous little darlings."

"Bet they never found none in Leytonstone," said Ray. Mickey was from Leytonstone.

"Yeah, and you wanna know the age range?" Mickey lowered his voice. "From nineteen..." A dramatic pause, and Eddie thought he'd go up from there, probably they all thought that, but instead Mickey said, "Down to fifteen." His eyes shining with something gleeful and hungry that, had they admitted it, was present in them all.

Ray whistled. "Fucking hell."

"Too right, fucking hell," Ted said. "It's what we're gonna do and it's where we're gonna go."

And they laughed again, and slapped Mickey on the back, and then Eddie remembered a joke he'd heard about the Bobby Kennedy assassination, and nobody noticed the disapproving lackey passing by to fetch another crate of beer. After all, the Joneses of this world were here to fetch and carry and keep their mouths shut.

11

Saturday morning, with a day to herself, Alex decided on a walk. Her current home was a cramped one-bedroom flat above a furniture shop in Old London Road, a couple of minutes from the centre of Kingston on Thames.

For most of her adult life she had travelled frequently, rarely staying in one place or one job for longer than a year. Despite the privations of her childhood she'd managed to go to university and scraped a 2:1 in biology. Her chequered career included time as a lab assistant in various hospitals and clinics, as well as a position with a pharmaceutical company in Canada that might have offered a real opportunity for advancement. An incident over some missing drugs had put paid to that – not to mention the suspicious death of her immediate supervisor, a well-known bully and misogynist.

Leaving the flat at just after nine, the blustery wind took her by surprise: one of those days that looked nicer than it was. After collecting coffee and a Danish from her local café she negotiated a path around the Bentall centre, avoiding clusters of sulky teenagers sucking on cigarettes, thumbs prodding moronically at their mobile phones. In her world these people would be exterminated like rats.

She crossed Kingston Bridge, heading for the river walk towards Hampton Court. To her right was a new development of luxury riverside apartments, priced at about half a million each and utterly beyond her means. She'd resolved that one day she'd do whatever it took to acquire those means, but that was for the future, when her current project was complete.

Project Randall.

It was eleven days since she'd thrown Sarah Randall to her death. In that time she had rid herself of any potentially incriminating evidence, including the Focus, which had been registered under a false name. From now on she would use hire cars, paying cash and supplying a fake driving licence.

The first report of Sarah's death appeared in the Brighton *Argus* two days after the murder. It merited no more than a paragraph: the body of a woman had been recovered near Birling Gap, identified as Sarah Joanne Randall, thirty-three, of Wish Road, Hove. The body was taken for a post mortem at Eastbourne District General Hospital, and police enquiries were continuing.

Three days later the same paper ran a full-page article. It reported that a post mortem had been carried out, and the inquest opened for identification purposes and then adjourned. There was a passing reference to Eddie Randall, and Nick was described as devastated. Most importantly, it confirmed that police were not treating the death as suspicious.

The following day the national papers pounced on the news. Most of the tabloids ran stories along the lines of *Late Star's Daughter-in-Law in Mystery Death Plunge.* Some featured photographs of Nick as a child, and much larger ones of Eddie Randall in his heyday. Only one thought to include a picture of the victim herself: a cropped portrait from her wedding.

Virtually every article mentioned Howard Franks. One paper reminded readers that it had serialised Franks's last book, and devoted more attention to the forthcoming biography of Randall than it did to Sarah's death. It riled Alex that someone else should be profiting from what she'd worked so hard to achieve.

Not treated as suspicious. That was all that mattered.

Ironic, really, when she considered the reaction to her own father's death. He'd been tossed into the path of a train. The driver had witnessed two figures on the bridge, had seen the body fall but couldn't stop in time. Nobody had stood trial or been charged. There hadn't even been any confirmed suspects. The police carried out barely a dozen interviews, none of which produced any other lines of enquiry.

"They didn't want to know," Alex's mother had raged, night after night. "Bastard police don't give a monkeys for my Leslie."

My Leslie. Alex always remembered that, the bitterness in her mother's voice. The truth was that Hilda had hated Leslie, and he had despised her. He stayed with her for one reason and one alone: Alex. He couldn't deal with Billy, the crybaby, the mummy's boy who was wrong in the head. Leslie cared only for his daughter.

"You're my future, lady, you know that?" he used to say, stroking her hair as she lay in bed. When he returned from the club in the early hours he'd always come in her room and kiss her forehead. Sometimes she'd pretend to be asleep and she could feel him watching her, adoration pouring out of him like heat.

And then one night he didn't come home. Childhood was over. Cancelled. Stolen.

By Eddie Randall, according to Hilda.

Alex couldn't remember when she'd first heard the name, but for the whole of her childhood it became a familiar litany. Whenever she was denied something, whenever she had to go without, the response was always the same: "Blame Eddie Randall."

She turned on to the river path, noticing a couple of

horses in the field to her right. She'd gone through a few years of equine infatuation in her childhood. Not that she'd ever stood a chance of riding one. *Black Beauty* on TV was the closest she got.

It wasn't until she was thirteen, in early 1972, that Alex finally confronted her mother. "If Eddie Randall killed Dad, why haven't the police done anything about it?"

"You think they listen to the likes of us?" Hilda had said scornfully. "He covered his tracks, didn't he? Folk like him, they get others to do the dirty work. Then it's just my word against his."

For the first time Hilda divulged that Leslie had been involved in a 'financial arrangement' with Randall, which Alex had correctly guessed meant blackmail. After Leslie's death Hilda had even managed to contact Randall by phone, but the actor flatly denied any involvement in his murder and refused to meet her.

"What good would it have done, anyway?" Alex had asked.

"I dunno. I wanted to look him in the eye. Then I'd know if he was telling the truth."

"So what? You just said the police would do nothing."

Her mother had sniffed and looked evasive.

"You'd ask him for money?" Alex guessed.

"And why not?" Hilda responded savagely. "You think he doesn't owe us? Think I enjoy working my fingers to the bone at two bloody jobs, trying to keep you fed and watered and out of mischief? Compensation is what it would be. It's only what I'm due."

But Randall had just laughed off Hilda's clumsy attempt at extortion, and Alex didn't know who she despised more: Randall for the original crime, or her mother for being such an inadequate opponent. Even at thirteen Alex knew she wouldn't have taken no for an answer. She'd have searched for a way to make Randall admit his guilt, no matter what it took.

12

The unreality gripped Nick when the police dropped their bombshell and didn't let go for eight days, when exhaustion finally rewarded him with ten hours of heavy dreamless sleep. He awoke with the savage realisation that Sarah was gone, but his recollection of the preceding days was as hazy as his memories of childhood. He had only fragments, vivid but unreliable, which might just as easily have belonged to someone else.

DCI Pearce gently informed him that a body believed to be that of his wife had been discovered at the foot of the cliffs east of the Belle Tout lighthouse. The circumstances suggested that she had either fallen or jumped to her death.

He'd insisted on identifying the body straight away, although DCI Pearce made it clear he could wait until the following morning. He remembered the journey in the police car, the crackle of routine messages on the radio, familiar landmarks passing unrecognised, but nothing of the identification itself. Except the knowledge that it was Sarah.

He spent the next day at his sister's. Patrick took compassionate leave and disappeared with the kids, while Diana sat with Nick and they talked. And at some point he'd made the phone call to France, and Gerry Clarke had bellowed and thrown the receiver down. Diana was in tears later, fielding hysterical calls from Lisa Clarke and Sarah's sister, Elaine.

The police returned, asking him about his movements on Tuesday March 23rd, all perfectly routine. Later they confirmed they were not treating the death as suspicious. An inquest was opened and adjourned, the body released for burial. Then DCI Pearce gave him the shattering news that Sarah had been in the early stages of pregnancy.

The funeral took place a week later, at a cemetery in Hove. For days the weather had been overcast with frequent squally showers. Now the sky was washed clean and offered the bitter promise of spring, tiny pink and purple shoots bursting through the grass around the grave.

The service was low key and stilted, nothing like the big showbusiness celebration his mother had masterminded for Eddie Randall. Everyone seemed too shocked to grieve, and from Sarah's family came the first indication of what promised to be a fierce animosity. Gerry lunged at Nick as they filed back to the cars and had to be dragged away by Pat and one of Nick's cousins. The wake was hastily rearranged; Sarah's family withdrew to their Brighton hotel while the Randalls convened at Nick's home.

The day after the funeral Diana rang to say there were reporters outside. Her phone rang each time she renewed the connection. Later she had to confess that she'd told Howard Franks about the tragedy and asked him to leave Nick alone, never imagining he would tip off the papers in order to generate interest in his book.

It was around the same time that Nick heard himself described as a widower. Surely that word belonged to a frail old man in a cardigan, struggling to cope after forty or fifty years of marriage?

After the funeral he received a letter from Sarah's sister, Elaine. She refused to believe that Sarah would have taken her own life, no matter what the provocation. The police would be asked to carry out a thorough investigation, paying particular attention to Nick's conduct in recent months.

Waking clear-headed for the first time, Nick re-read the letter and knew that the coming weeks would be more turbulent than his sister had maintained. But at least Elaine's prescience had one benefit: when the police returned to see him, they weren't entirely unexpected.

On Friday April 2nd a sixty-two-year-old man from Polegate walked into Eastbourne police station and announced that he had seen Sarah Randall before her death. He'd missed the original report in the local papers, and only realised he might possess significant information when he read an article about Eddie Randall's daughter-in-law in the *Sun*.

"It was from a distance, like, but I'm positive that's who I saw. I was on my way back to the car when I turned round to call the dog. I saw this woman up near the lighthouse, dark hair, wearing a red jacket. Just like it said in the papers. Only she wasn't on her own. There was this feller with her, he had his arm round her shoulders and they were kissing. Lucky sod, I thought. I turned away, didn't want to be gawping at 'em, like. But I thought I better report it. I mean, why'd she wanna go jumping off a cliff when she's with her bloke?"

Nick was interviewed under caution at Eastbourne police station, and invited to have a solicitor present if he wished. He declined.

This time there was no sign of matronly, sympathetic DCI Pearce; in her place a burly middle-aged detective inspector called Flynn and a young female DC, Kaur, both of whom were distinctly cool towards him. They went through his movements in meticulous detail, and he thanked God it hadn't been a quiet day when he might have parked in a lay-by and read the paper.

With the possible sighting of Sarah they were able to estimate the time of death at between two and five pm on the Tuesday afternoon. At that time Nick had finished taking a statement in Hailsham and then driven frantically to his sister's house to confront Howard Franks. This could be confirmed both by Diana and by Franks himself, whose tip-off to the media had brought the witness forward in the first place.

DS Flynn floated the suggestion that Sarah had been having an affair, and Nick was asked if he could name any possible candidates amongst her colleagues or friends. Nick was aghast at the suggestion that his wife might have slept with someone else, and then saw the terrible irony in that.

"I really don't know. Maybe someone at her office."

"What about her female friends?" asked DC Kaur.

Nick frowned. "What do you mean?"

"Well, is there anyone she's likely to have confided in?"

"There was someone she met at the gym a little while back. I think they got quite friendly."

"Name?" Flynn barked.

He shifted in his seat. "Alice, possibly."

"You did live together, I take it?" asked Kaur sardonically.

"We were having problems, as you know," Nick said. "In that situation you don't communicate very well."

"We'll need her address book," said Flynn. "We'll also be following up any calls made on her mobile phone over the past few weeks."

"What I can't understand is why, if she was having an affair, she would have died the way she did?"

"We're still trying to determine exactly how she died," Kaur reminded him.

"Could have been a lovers' tiff," Flynn added. "Just in

the wrong place and time. Very passionate, these illicit relationships." He was clearly relishing Nick's predicament, and Nick felt a wave of hatred towards him.

"Then why not come forward, if it was an accident? I can't believe anyone I know would be capable of just… leaving her there."

"You'd be surprised the things people are capable of," said Flynn darkly.

After three hours he was allowed to go, and he sloped out of the police station feeling as guilty as if he'd killed Sarah with his bare hands. No doubt that was exactly what the interview had been intended to achieve. That night, for the first time since learning of her death, he drank himself into a stupor.

After lying unconscious on the sofa for hours, he woke at four in the morning and threw up on the living room carpet. He cleaned up then stumbled into the shower, by which time the first traces of light were showing through the curtains. He felt tired and wretched, but rather than go back to sleep he forced himself outside.

There was a sharp westerly wind, but the sky was blue with only a light scattering of cloud. Jogging across the road in front of a milk float, he spotted a police car cruising slowly along the promenade, flashing strobe-like in the gaps between the beach huts. Nick faltered, wondering for an awful moment if they were sneaking up on him. And then he dismissed the idea and ordered his reluctant legs to advance. The car drew level with him as he approached, and the driver sent him a quick once-over before moving on.

Nick sighed, relieved but also despondent. Was this how it felt when you had committed a crime? And if someone out there had killed Sarah, was he feeling like this right now, waiting for the knock on the door?

And the worst question of all: did Nick know him?

The further he walked, the better he felt, so he ended up going as far as the dilapidated West Pier, where he stopped briefly and watched the early joggers, rollerbladers and dog walkers competing for space on the prom. By the time he got home it was nearly eight o'clock. His head felt clearer, but no less confused.

He was finishing breakfast when the doorbell rang. He checked the window and saw the familiar form of DCI Pearce. He had another horrible premonition: somehow he'd been framed for Sarah's death, and she was about to arrest him. Had another officer gone round the back to prevent his escape?

He opened the door, picturing his father-in-law's immense satisfaction as a life sentence was passed, and then Pearce said brightly, "Good news. You're in the clear."

Nick noticed that instead of the usual tailored suit, Pearce was wearing a woollen jumper and denim skirt. "Is this an official visit, Chief Inspector?" he asked.

"Melanie, please." She grinned. "I happened to be in the area, and I thought you'd want to know as soon as possible."

"I appreciate it." He made some more coffee and led her into the living room. Pearce wrinkled her nose.

"Sorry about the smell," Nick said. "I was, er, taken ill."

"You might want to use some carpet cleaner. I don't think that's quite enough." She indicated the kitchen roll on the floor.

"I can see why you're a detective."

"Luckily for you I'm a keen one. I've spoken to various people about your alibi." A smile crept on to her face. "Mr Franks seemed positively disappointed to be verifying your whereabouts."

"It's a better story if I'm under suspicion."

"I daresay. Because of the media interest, I've authorised a statement confirming that we've ruled you out as a suspect."

Nick's relief was so great that Pearce looked slightly embarrassed. She let out a sigh. "The next bit's not so good. We went back to the Parkside and found one of the kitchen staff who recalled Sarah waiting in the car park."

Nick leant forward in his seat. "Did they see…?"

"I'm afraid not. A car pulled in at speed, collected your wife and took off like a maniac, in the words of our witness. They didn't get the registration mark, but they think it was a black Ford Focus."

"Not the rarest of cars, then?"

"I'm afraid not."

Nick gave a sarcastic laugh. Pearce smiled, then regarded him sadly. "You looked the image of your dad then. I remember watching that sitcom when Trevor and I were first courting." She sighed wistfully. "Was that really thirty years ago?"

"I used to get teased at school," Nick said. "Kids wanting to know why he wasn't in something decent, like *Dr Who*."

Pearce laughed, and so did Nick, and for a moment they were simply friends sharing a fond reminiscence. There was a maternal warmth about Pearce that Nick found tremendously comforting, and he suspected that Pearce knew it too.

He said, "What about the witness at Beachy Head?"

"He wasn't close enough to see a face."

"So all we've got is a boy racer in a black Focus?"

DCI Pearce clasped her hands together on her lap and nodded. "We're still checking CCTV cameras in the area, and we'll continue to interview her friends and colleagues, but there's a real possibility that he'll never be identified. And even if we do locate him, we still have no evidence of foul play."

"Apart from the fact that he's not come forward?"

"That's not enough to support a prosecution," she said gently.

"Do you think it was an accident?" His voice thickened. Pearce looked away, gave the question the time it deserved before meeting his eye.

"I can't rule it out," she said. "Perhaps he panicked, and now he's too ashamed to contact us. Perhaps… he's also in a relationship."

Nick didn't want to think about this. He pressed on, unable to keep the emotion from his voice. "But equally, he might have killed her and got away with it?"

Again DCI Pearce took her time to respond, but eventually she nodded. "It makes me sick to say so, but yes. He might have got away with it."

13

Roger Knight saw a brief item about Sarah's death on a local news bulletin, but he didn't make the connection with Nick Randall until he picked up a *Daily Mail* and found a whole page dominated by the story. His initial reaction was shock, then relief as he realised the news might stop Randall snooping around.

This in turn was followed by a thought so horrifying that he must have exclaimed out loud. Caitlin, reading W H Auden alongside him on the sofa, turned to see him drop the paper on the floor.

"What is it?"

"Doyle. The stupid fucking…"

Caitlin frowned. "You're talking like he does. What's he done?"

"I don't even want to think about it." He hurried to his study and logged on to the internet.

According to the *Sussex Express* website Sarah Randall was thought to have died during the afternoon of March 23rd. Roger checked his diary and found that this was the day after Nick Randall interviewed Lauren Doyle. He knew Kevin had reacted violently during Nick's visit, but would he really have taken such drastic measures so soon?

He wanted to say no, but knowing Doyle as he did, anything was possible.

Kevin's mobile was switched off, and he wasn't answering his landline. Roger left messages on both numbers and then had to stew for the rest of the evening, which in turn caused a row with Caitlin. Even a late call from his eldest daughter failed to lift his mood. He was hoping to hear from Doyle, and made the grave error of saying so.

"Great!" Sally had exclaimed. "You'd rather talk to one of your employees than your own daughter!" And the conversation had continued in the same tone, despite Roger's agreeing to fund a new Xbox, the current one having been broken during a party.

In the end he didn't speak to Kevin until they met up the following day. Doyle punched the air with delight at the news.

"So you weren't involved in any way?"

"Course I wasn't. Why would I chuck her off a cliff? There's no fun if you don't get to see 'em suffer." He cackled with laughter, all the more amused by Roger's distaste. "Anyway, there's no way he's gonna care about a few iffy claims now."

Roger shrugged. "I'm not so sure. What if Nick Randall reacts as I just did?"

Kevin considered it for a moment. "I'll make sure I'm covered for the day it happened. You'd better do the same."

"I already have," Roger said.

"Maybe he did it?" Kevin added. "Husband's always the first one they look at."

Roger tapped the paper. "They say the police aren't treating it as suspicious. That means suicide."

"Either way we're in the clear. Fucking brilliant!"

Roger was far from convinced, but he decided against voicing his fears. A couple more claims had recently settled, bringing in nearly thirty thousand pounds. They'd already acquired cars and taken out insurance in preparation for the next batch, but Roger argued strongly that they should put these on hold for a while. Kevin couldn't see why, but eventually he skulked out with an agreement to do nothing until Roger gave the word.

Maybe it's going to be OK, Roger began to tell himself. Maybe we've ridden the storm, and now we're through the other side.

He could say it as often as he liked, but in his heart he didn't believe it. Either Nick would be back, or someone else would take his place.

Howard Franks was in a state of giddy excitement. For days the phone had rung constantly, a stream of journalists clamouring for information on Eddie Randall, and everything was supplied on the strict understanding that they included a plug for the book.

Diana's call had been a welcome surprise. When she tearfully explained that Nick's wife had apparently committed suicide, his initial disappointment quickly turned to elation. It took a considerable performance on his part to maintain a sympathetic demeanour when in reality he wanted to whoop with joy. And his agreement to leave Nick alone in no way precluded him from phoning an old friend on the *Sun*.

To demonstrate that he bore no resentment for the way they had treated him, he sent them a hardback copy of his 1999 biography of a minor celebrity who'd overcome breast cancer, complete with a handwritten dedication: *To Diana and Nick: May it inspire you.*

Then it emerged that a witness had seen someone with Sarah Randall just prior to her death. Howard began to entertain delicious fantasies about publication being timed to coincide with Nick's high-profile murder trial, but those were shattered when a Sussex detective asked him to confirm Nick's account of their confrontation outside Diana's home.

Providing such a crucial alibi was, in Howard's mind, an act of selfless generosity that should not go unrewarded.

And with his publishers now desperate for a finished manuscript, Howard knew it was time to force the issue.

His stroke of genius was prompted by Lindsay, who'd kept her word and met him for a meal at Almeida. She seemed thrilled by the publicity he was generating, and it was clear that he'd risen in her estimation as a result.

The following Saturday they were discussing the events of the past week after a long and exhausting afternoon in bed. She was lying against him, her breasts squashed against his shoulder, her fingers playfully combing his pubic hair. His strategy was launched on a long forlorn sigh.

"Don't be sad, honey," Lindsay said.

"But I *need* their contribution. I don't want to give up on it."

"That's got to be the last thing on their minds right now."

"Maybe. Maybe not." He fixed Lindsay with a meaningful stare. "What about an entirely fresh approach?"

She snorted. "Why do I get the feeling this involves me?"

"Because you're remarkably perceptive woman. Among other things."

She laughed and gave the hair a tug, just the right side of painful. He could feel blood rushing to the area.

"Supposing I employed an attractive research assistant?"

She brushed her hand lightly over his balls. He shivered.

"And just how will you repay this attractive research assistant?"

He thrust his groin towards her hand, which hovered tantalisingly out of reach. "A credit in the book?"

Her hand dipped, squeezed, moved away. "Mm. 'To the indispensable Lindsay, for providing a full range of services.' How does that sound?"

He chuckled, feeling his heart rate increase. He hadn't

achieved a second erection this quickly for months.

"Maybe."

"So what would I have to do?" She shifted on to her knees and moved down the bed.

"Just talk to Nick. Appeal to his better nature."

"Hmm. I'll think about it."

She pursed her lips and moved closer. His penis twitched with excitement.

"You're gonna owe me."

"I know. I know."

"On top of what you already owe me." Grazing the head of his penis with her teeth. "And always you want more." Caressing it with her tongue.

He groaned. "Yes. I'm a…"

"Greedy boy."

"Greedy," he echoed. He saw her eyes flare but wasn't sure if she was amused or offended. That was the trouble with Lindsay. He couldn't read her like he could read most women. Perhaps that was what kept him… what kept him…

But now she had stopped teasing, and rational thought became impossible.

14

Woken in the early hours of Sunday morning, Nick heard a ferocious gale hurling rain at the windows. He shivered and turned towards Sarah for warmth. It was only when he rolled on to the empty mattress that he remembered, and the shock was nearly as great as it had been the first time. He pulled the duvet around him, curled into a foetal position and sobbed loudly enough to obscure the howling wind.

The day dawned fresh and bright, the wind easing as the weather front moved eastwards. Nick slept late, and it was only the simultaneous ringing of his phone and the doorbell that finally roused him.

He trudged downstairs to find Diana peering through the window, her mobile clamped to her ear. Patrick and Ryan were watching anxiously from the car.

"Where have you been?"

"Sleeping."

"It's nearly lunchtime."

"I had a bad night," he snapped, and then regretted it when she gave him one of her reproving looks.

"I've brought some food," she said, as Pat popped the boot and got out of the car.

"Why?"

"I remember the state of your fridge when you were a student. Lager and a lump of cheese, am I right?"

Nick shrugged. "I had to bin the cheese."

"Pat's going to take the kids to the Lagoon while we start on the clear-out."

"But the police might want…"

"DCI Pearce gave me the OK."

Nick frowned. His sister and the detective had been colluding.

"She thought it would do you good," Diana added. "Part of the healing process."

They went inside, and for a brief period the house rang with noise and laughter as Ryan ran manically from room to room, perplexed by the concept of a home without toys. Diana had told him that Auntie Sarah was living in France for a while, sparing Nick some awkward questions. The real explanation could wait until he was older.

Once they'd gone, Nick trudged upstairs behind his sister, who was wielding a roll of heavy-duty plastic sacks. It was a grim task, but one he knew he must confront: a way of disabusing himself of the notion that it was all a terrible mix-up, that one day soon she would return.

After the funeral Sarah's sister had asked to keep anything Nick would otherwise discard. Unsure where to begin, he hung back as Diana opened the large double wardrobe and surveyed the contents.

"A hoarder," she said sadly.

"You haven't seen the shoes yet," he said.

Diana rolled up her sleeves and quickly got to work, chattering brightly about nothing in particular while Nick sat on the bed, contributing a well-timed "umm" or "uhuh" when he felt it was required.

"What about the rest of her things?" she asked, when the first wardrobe contained no more than dust and empty hangers. "Her jewellery?"

"She left it to me," Nick said. "I guess I'll give it to Elaine and her parents."

"You're allowed to keep it, you know."

"But why?" he said, when really he meant, *I don't feel*

entitled, and Diana didn't press him.

On top of the wardrobe there was a large box full of old records and cassettes. Diana fetched a duster and gave each item a wipe before handing it to him. Most of the records had warped with age, and none had been played for years. Nick shook his head sadly as he studied them: Shalamar, Wham, Depeche Mode; it struck him that they were dismantling a life.

"Leave them," he said. "Let's put them back." And he could hear his voice didn't sound right, Diana watching him with a terrible pity, and then her image blurred and he knew he was going to weep for the first time in someone else's presence.

She held him and let him sob, soothing him as she would soothe her children, protecting him as he had once protected her when Dad died and Nick, at nine, became the man of the house.

"I feel so guilty," he said at last. "To think she might have been seeing someone, someone who was responsible for her death, and yet I have *no idea* who it could be."

"None of it makes sense," said Diana. "I think the witness must be confused, perhaps saw someone else. I'm sure Sarah was on her own. It was just a dreadful accident."

Nick gave her a fond smile. She was choosing to ignore the hotel staff who'd seen Sarah climbing into the black Focus. And the calls to her mobile that had been made from an untraceable phone.

Still, DCI Pearce's advice had been to choose whichever explanation offered him the best chance of peace. She hadn't actually used the hideous word *closure*, but that was what she meant. Maybe they were both right, he thought.

Later he helped her load the bags for Elaine into the car. Sarah's family were refusing to have anything to do with him, so Diana had volunteered to deliver the possessions to their hotel.

"For what it's worth, I think they're being pathetic," she said.

He disagreed. "I wasn't a good husband to her. They have every right to blame me."

"No," Diana said. "You've got to stop thinking like that."

That night Nick came across one of his dad's movies on Channel 5: *On The Tide*, a gritty thriller with Eddie, aged thirty-six, playing a police sergeant. It was an unwelcome reminder that Nick had given no further thought to Howard Franks, and the allegation that Dad was responsible for murder.

Another prompt that he couldn't ignore. Life had to get started again.

Sunday evening, Roger Knight was sitting on the sofa, a beer and a bowl of peanuts at his side, watching an old film starring Eddie Randall.

Roger immediately saw why Nick had looked familiar. It wasn't just the likeness in build and features, but something in the way Eddie moved, the quick expressive face, always seeking a laugh. Although it was a drama, Eddie had clearly been cast to lighten the mood: raising his eyebrows at a barked order from his boss, then colliding with a tea trolley on his way out of the office.

Caitlin came in holding a script and a bottle of Sol. She had landed a small part in a piece of experimental theatre at the Komedia in Brighton, with rehearsals beginning the next day. Roger knew he'd been too preoccupied to offer her the encouragement she expected, and it had become another source of conflict between them.

"Budge up," she said, sitting at the other end of the sofa

and resting her feet against his thigh. He stroked her leg and remembered the time not so long ago when her body had inspired a permanent state of adolescent lust.

On screen, Eddie Randall was chasing an armed robber through the London docks.

"Anything else on?" said Caitlin. "Something made this century, for instance?"

"I'm only watching it because of this guy."

She peered at the screen. "Didn't he used to be in that awful sitcom?"

"Eddie Randall. My uncle knew him in the sixties."

"Really?"

"I met his son the other day."

"Is he an actor as well?" She was interested now.

"He's an insurance investigator, believe it or not."

"Is he?" Caitlin drank some beer. "What's he investigating?"

Roger experienced a twinge of unease. "Just a car we repaired. He thought it might be involved in a fraudulent claim."

"And was it?"

"I've no idea. We simply fixed it and invoiced the insurer."

"What's his name, this investigator?"

"Nick Randall."

She turned to him, frowning. "Wasn't there something in the paper about…?"

"His wife died a couple of weeks ago. Fell off Beachy Head."

"So when did you meet him? Before his wife died?"

Roger shifted uncomfortably. He didn't like the way her questions had taken on a forensic tone. "What do you mean by that?"

He realised he'd snapped at her. Caitlin swung her legs round and retreated to the far end of the sofa. She studied him for what seemed an age.

"Are you involved in something illegal?"

It was the question he'd been dreading. The one that required an all-out lie.

"What?"

"With Kevin Doyle. Something to do with insurance claims."

"Where did you get that idea from?" He could feel his face heating up, sweat prickling on his forehead. He stared at the TV, where an unarmed Eddie Randall had now cornered the robber.

"I'm not stupid, Roger. I notice things."

"Things?"

"A brand new Range Rover in the drive, for starters. Lynn and the kids on an all-inclusive in Antigua."

Roger jumped to his feet. "This is because you're still jealous of Lynn. It's bloody ridiculous."

"It has nothing to do with that."

"No? Well, my business has nothing to do with you, OK? You do all right out of it. That's all you need to know." It was a cheap comment, and unjustified, but he was beyond the point of reasoning. It felt as though all the frustration and anger he felt at Doyle and Nick Randall and his ex-wife - and most all at himself - was just aching to be unleashed on poor Caitlin.

"Jesus, Roger. I don't want to see you end up in jail."

"Don't be so fucking stupid. I know what I'm doing." He stormed out of the room, spraying peanuts across the floor. Caitlin drew her knees up to her chin and buried her head in her arms. She heard gunshots, a cry from Eddie Randall as he caught the fatal bullet, and then the sudden inane chatter of commercials.

✳

Tuesday was sunny till lunchtime, when Nick met Morag outside the offices of CBA Insurance. They walked down North Street under darkening skies, and as they crossed the road towards the Lanes it began to rain.

"Bloody weather," Morag grumbled.

"It's still better than Scotland, isn't it?" Nick said.

"Aye, I guess so."

The Lanes were crowded with a mix of office workers at lunch, an early influx of Easter tourists and kids on their school holidays. Threading a path between beggars, buskers and buggies, they settled on the Bath Arms because it was traditional rather than trendy, and you could hear yourself talk.

The previous morning he'd finally gone through his business post, which had included a sympathetic letter from Morag, suggesting the case could be transferred to another investigator if he needed to take a break from work. He'd rung and suggested a meeting, to which she had agreed on the condition that it be 'semi-social'.

"In the pub, you mean?" he'd said.

"Precisely."

Now he handed her a pint of Guinness and caught her appraising him. "I didn't think we'd see you for a while yet."

"I need to keep occupied. Otherwise I'm just sitting around in an empty house."

"So really I'm doing you a favour here?"

There was the hint of a wicked smile on her lips, and Nick had a sudden flashback of their night together. He gulped down some beer.

"Where are we, then?"

"We checked both vehicles and got nothing." She opened a leather document wallet and brought out a sheaf of paper. "Then we spoke to the other insurers about their policy history. Squeaky clean, or so it appeared."

He grinned. He knew she was bursting to tell him.

"They mentioned a named driver on their policy. We ran his details and found two matches, both recent claims. Spoke to those insurers and came up with another eight claims. Then we find it's the same solicitor in more than half the cases. A guy called Barry Harper?"

Nick shook his head: the name was unfamiliar.

"Oh, he's bent," Morag said. "And that's not all."

"Go on."

"Knight's Accident Repair Centre crop up on one other claim."

"Excellent. Shame it's only one."

"Yeah. Could be coincidence, I suppose."

"No. It's not."

"I agree. But any half-decent lawyer will shred this lot in less than five minutes, and the police won't take a sniff till we've done all the hard work for them." She smiled. "So bring me some lovely evidence."

"Glad to. Any chance of the other insurers contributing?"

"What, so you can bump up your fees?" She waved away his protest. "I'll sort something out, don't fret."

A dozen feet away, alone at a small corner table and using the *Times* for concealment, Alex observed Nick and the plump Scottish woman. She had followed them from the offices of an insurance company, so she knew the woman was a business acquaintance, but the body language suggested something more. These two had had a sexual relationship at some point, Alex was sure.

Just as she could see nothing funny or likeable in the celluloid performances of Eddie Randall, his son's apparent

119

power over women was equally baffling. She couldn't comprehend why it had taken so long for Sarah to walk out. The woman's horrendous passivity had sickened her: she would never have let his infidelity go unpunished.

She remembered how at eighteen, in her first month at university, she had been abused by a fellow student who misread her signals and went too far on a drunken date. Afterwards she had bided her time, apparently unperturbed, even nodding hello when she encountered him at lectures or in the library. And then, six weeks on, she agreed to see him again and fed him a fatal dose of wolfsbane.

That was how you dealt with men who misbehaved. You didn't forgive them. You didn't get ready to go running back.

She felt that she had done Sarah a favour, first by engineering her liberation from an oppressive marriage, then by releasing her from pain forever.

And watching Nick, she saw little indication of a man wracked with grief. He was smiling, laughing, making regular eye contact with the loud Scottish woman. Alex could see his father in him; she could well imagine how Eddie Randall had felt so arrogantly untouchable in the aftermath of his own crimes.

At the beginning of this process, during the planning stage, she had asked herself: was it right to make Nick pay for his father's crimes? It was never more than a brief hypothetical question, but at least now she had an unequivocal answer.

Yes, he deserved to pay. He deserved to suffer.

They all did.

15

"Bloody lousy fucking journalists!" Franks was red in the face, the veins in his neck distended. He looked the way he did after three sets of tennis, or on the brink of orgasm.

"Didn't you used to be one?" Lindsay drawled.

Franks shook the newspaper in her face, inadvertently dislodging an advertising supplement. "I mean, who gives a shit if some pretty-boy footballer has slept around?" He sucked in the excess spittle forming on his lips. "The grotty people, that's who. The lowest common denominators."

"Aren't they usually the people who read biographies of soap stars and soccer players?"

He threw the newspaper down. She didn't understand – or worse still, didn't care – that he needed to vent his emotions. All she had to do was sit and fucking listen, for Christ's sake.

"Here," she said, pouring him a scotch. "Cool down."

He scowled, then collapsed into an armchair and pressed the glass against his forehead. His heart slowed, the pressure in his head began to ease.

Whether he liked it or not, he had to accept the story was dead. The tabloids had become obsessed with the alleged extramarital adventures of a footballing superstar, and consequently there was no interest in Randall or any of his family. It might have been different if Nick had been implicated. Now Franks's best hope was that the police would find the culprit in time for publication.

His only consolation was that Lindsay had agreed to approach Nick. If she was successful it might galvanise him into finishing the book, which was slipping further behind schedule.

She perused his DVD collection and selected *Heat*. "What about this?"

"Whatever."

"I'll do my best on Friday," she said, "but I'm not promising anything, OK? If he takes one look at me and tells me to get lost…"

Howard shook his head. "He won't. He's got an eye for the ladies, just like his dad."

"Maybe I'm not his type."

She knelt down by the DVD player. She was wearing cream linen trousers and a pink camisole top. When she bent forward he noted the weight of her breasts, the silky cascade of hair over her shoulders.

"You'd be anyone's type," he murmured.

She dropped the disc into its tray and turned. "What are you, my pimp?"

"My dear, what a delicious idea."

"I mean it. Are you expecting me to screw him?"

He laughed to buy himself time. *If that's what it takes…* But he couldn't say so to Lindsay: far too prickly. "I'm confident that a beautiful, intelligent woman will charm him into submission."

She pondered this, approaching cat-like on her hands and knees. Something in her expression made him uneasy. She bared her teeth and slapped both hands on his knees. He chuckled, hoping without much optimism that oral sex was in prospect. He'd much prefer fellatio to Pacino.

"Supposing he takes a shine to me, and I decide that I like him – "

"And he's answering all your questions," he reminded her.

She nodded. "Sure. Then do I sleep with him?"

"Are you asking for my permission?"

She bared her teeth again, emitting a low growl, and lowered her head towards his groin. He had a sudden conviction that she was going to bite him and he squirmed, feeling the fledgling erection shrivel and die.

"I don't know," he said quickly. "I don't know the answer."

Her head snapped up, and to his great relief she winked mischievously. "Had you scared," she said.

"No you didn't." But the catch in his voice gave him away.

Long after the call had ended, Roger Knight went on staring at his phone. He was working from home, and had been poring over bank statements when Angela called from the bodyshop. Nick Randall had turned up unannounced, asking about another of the fraudulent claims.

"Are you sure you can't get rid of him?" he'd demanded.

"I don't think so, no." Answering carefully, because Randall was obviously within earshot.

"Has he spoken to George?"

"Not yet."

One small consolation. He didn't want the bodyshop manager getting dragged into this.

"OK. Tell him I'm happy to see him down here, if it's really urgent. And give him directions or he'll get lost." I wish he would get lost, he thought, and almost laughed.

Steady now, Roger. A little local difficulty, nothing more.

He was still brooding when Caitlin walked in, holding a mug of coffee and a blueberry muffin.

"Fantastic. Thanks." He sounded much too grateful, partly because of the call and partly because this represented another attempt at bridge-building.

The latest argument had been sparked by Caitlin's debut at the Komedia. While he'd praised her performance, he'd unwisely confessed to finding the play nonsensical, pretentious and distinctly unfunny. Her fellow artistes, whom he'd been obliged to join in the pub afterwards, had struck him as jumped-up little tossers.

"And your colleagues are delightful, of course," she'd responded. "You prefer the company of animals like Doyle."

Pushing away the memory, he took a sip of coffee and said, "I've got a meeting here a bit later."

She groaned. "Not Kevin Doyle?"

"No. Funnily enough, it's Nick Randall." He tried a smile but it came out wrong.

"The actor's son? The insurance guy?"

"I might be putting some debt recovery business his way."

"Oh." She sounded hopeful, but still looked worried. She knows me too well, Roger thought, even though she knows only a fraction of it. He wondered what she would do if she ever found out.

More to the point, he wondered what *he* would do.

Despite the directions Nick missed the Clayton road and had to turn round in the lane that led to the famous windmills, Jack and Jill. Knight's house was a couple of miles along a narrow road, set in several acres of grass and woodland at the foot of the Downs. Turning into a wide carriage drive, Nick parked between a new Range Rover and a two-year-old Saab convertible. Business must be good, he thought.

Roger Knight opened the door. He was wearing blue jeans and a purple Lacoste polo shirt. His face was slightly flushed, and when they shook hands his palm felt damp.

"Good to see you again," Roger said. "You found it OK?"

"Just about."

Nick stepped into an entrance hall the size of his own living room, with a black and white limestone floor and a wide galleried staircase.

"I have a study through here," Roger said. "Slightly more comfortable than at the bodyshop."

They were crossing the hall when a young woman emerged from the back of the house. Nick immediately recognised her from the picture in Knight's office: medium height, very slim, shoulder-length blonde hair and quite extraordinary green eyes. She smiled at Nick, and as she came closer he noted a smattering of freckles across her nose.

"Before you rush off, can I get you a drink?" she said.

"I'm fine," said Roger brusquely. To Nick, he added, "This is Caitlin."

"Nick Randall." Another handshake, this one cool and soft. Nick had to force himself to turn away from the green eyes. "I'll have a coffee, please," he said. "Milk and one sugar."

Knight seemed irritated by her presence. He nodded briskly and said, "This way."

With an apologetic smile for Caitlin, Nick followed Roger into a large oak-panelled study. He sat down in a functional cantilever armchair that might have been selected deliberately because it was lower than Roger's chair: a clumsy effort to put him at a disadvantage.

"I read about your wife's death. Terrible." Roger sounded sincere, but there was a caustic note when he added, "The newspapers had a field day."

"That's the papers for you."

"I spoke to my uncle's former partner," Knight went on, undeterred. "A man called Ted Wheeler. He remembered your dad pretty well."

Nick only nodded politely, careful not appear too interested. But he recalled Howard Franks taunting him with that name, and felt a cold shiver pass through him.

"I said I'd pay the old scoundrel a visit," Roger said. "Poor sod's got emphysema."

"Sorry to hear that."

"Of course, he smoked like a trooper all his life. Well, they all did back then, didn't they?"

Again Nick made no comment. He opened his briefcase as noisily as possible, signalling a change of emphasis. "The claim for the Renault Espace," he said. "The insurers have raised a number of concerns."

Knight had been affecting a relaxed pose. Now he leaned forward and said, "Such as?"

"I can't say at this stage. But it's likely that the insurers won't be paying your account until my enquiries are complete."

"In that case they'll be in breach of contract, and our lawyers will take the necessary action." This was Roger showing he wasn't afraid of a bit of verbal jousting.

"There's another case I'm investigating." Nick produced a copy of an invoice from his briefcase. "A Mondeo with heavy frontal damage, repaired back in January."

As he passed the paperwork across the desk, Caitlin entered the room with a single mug of coffee.

"I hear you might be doing some work for Roger," she said.

Nick saw Roger flinch. "The debt recovery," he said quickly. "You remember we discussed it last time?"

"Oh. Yes." Nick's uncertain response left no doubt that he was here for entirely different reasons. If Roger was lying to his girlfriend, that was his problem.

"Thanks, love, but we are rather busy." Roger made a shooing gesture with his hands. Caitlin gave him a venomous glare and swept out of the room. He'd pay for that later, Nick guessed, and Roger's red face seemed to confirm it.

After examining the invoice for a few seconds, Roger began typing on his keyboard. "Do you have proof this claim is fraudulent?"

It was a question Nick had anticipated. "The insurers are running some data mining tools to identify patterns in claims behaviour." He smiled. "I'm confident that we'll identify many more. With enough claims, the pattern becomes the proof."

Roger nodded, slowly digesting the information. "Well, I suggest that when your pattern becomes proof, you'll find my company has absolutely no involvement."

"I'm glad to hear that."

Roger took his time reading something on the computer and then gave a curt shake of his head. "This looks like a perfectly normal repair. All the documentation's in order." He sat back and steepled his fingers, looking for a moment like a bad imitation of a Bond villain. "So if there's no other help I can offer you...?"

Nick paused before replying, enjoying Roger's struggle to appear calm. "I think that's all for now." He stood up, having barely touched his coffee. He realised he'd probably asked for it in order to see Caitlin again.

Roger saw him to the front door and said, "Drive carefully!" The sarcasm was only too evident.

Nick unlocked his car and slung his briefcase on to the back seat. He should have been thrilled by Roger's obvious discomfort, but all he could think about were those magical green eyes.

"Caitlin," he said, testing the sound of the word. Then he muttered, "Not good."

Roger's day ended with a disastrous attempt at making love to Caitlin. Afterwards he lay awake, trying to work out why his life was so rapidly falling apart. Following Nick Randall's visit, the rest of the day had been a stand-off. Caitlin hadn't directly accused him of lying to her, but the implication was there in every look and gesture.

He had an urgent discussion with Barry Harper, and they both agreed to put a hold on the new claims. "I'm positive it's a bluff," Barry said. "But we'd do right to be cautious."

Kevin Doyle was less receptive to the idea, but it was only the reaction that Roger had been expecting. "I need that cash," he said. "The finance on the motor's bleeding me dry. And the fucking mortgage."

Not to mention the booze and the coke habit, Roger thought.

"It shouldn't be for long," he said. "The point is, we got greedy. In future we have to be more careful."

Afterwards he emerged from his office to find Caitlin loitering suspiciously close, her bag for the theatre over her shoulder. She marched to the front door.

"The play's not for hours yet," he said.

"I'll find something to do," she said, hurrying out.

The only bright moment was a call from his children in Antigua. After he'd spoken to them, Lynn took the phone and thanked him for funding the holiday. As she said good-bye the kids started chanting, "Wish you were here!"

He laughed, expecting Lynn to scold them, but all she said was, "See you soon."

Caitlin arrived home at midnight, by which time he'd dozed fitfully for an hour or so. He turned towards her as she climbed into bed.

"How did it go?"

"Boozy crowd. They really liked it."

"Good."

She was on her side, facing away from him. He stroked

her thigh, and when she didn't object he shuffled closer.

"I'm sorry," he said.

She said something, but he didn't catch it. He began kissing her shoulders and neck, his hands moving round to cup one of her breasts. He moved against her, willing her to reach back and touch him.

She said, "I can't do this." Her voice was reproachful, as though it should have been obvious. "You've lied to me. You're up to your neck in trouble and you won't admit it."

He rolled away from her, and his shame found an outlet in anger. "It's business, Caitlin. You don't understand."

"Don't patronise me. I know what fraud is. How will your kids feel when you're sent to prison?"

He tried to scoff. "This is really about us. Our relationship."

She turned to face him, and he saw the trail of tears on her cheeks. "We have no relationship. Not while you won't tell me the truth."

The words lay between them, a challenge for him to accept or deny. He did neither. He said nothing, and waited, and then Caitlin turned away from him.

He thought about the practicalities of how it would end. How ironic that for more that a year she'd held on to her tiny flat in Hove, paying the rent from her meagre income until finally, three months ago, he'd persuaded her to give it up.

He thought about Nick Randall, relentlessly building a case against him. Thought about Ted Wheeler, and whether the old man could help him at all.

Thought about his children, lying on the white sands of Jolly Beach. Thought about how Lynn had sounded on the phone.

Thought about incarceration, disgrace, financial ruin. How would he cope?

Fell asleep, the answer still reverberating in his head. He wouldn't.

And when Roger shuddered and began snoring, Caitlin remained awake, her eyes misty with tears. She too had been thinking about the end, about the lie they were both living, but she had also been thinking about Nick Randall.

She'd overheard enough of the conversations with Doyle and the slimy solicitor to gather that Roger was in deep trouble. It was also clear that Nick Randall could be instrumental in Roger's downfall, but the more she considered it, she began to wonder whether he might also be Roger's saviour.

16

Good Friday. It didn't feel like it to Nick. He got up at eight, opened the curtains and scowled at sunshine glinting on a placid picturebook sea. Any other year, in any other situation, he'd have been delighted. Instead he had four empty days to fill. He would visit his wife's grave and sort out the paperwork relating to her death, and perhaps try to catch up with his own work.

And he knew he should do something about Franks, but he had no idea what. It was tempting to ask Roger Knight about this character who knew Eddie in the sixties, Ted Wheeler, but he was worried about compromising the fraud investigation. Having to admit to the favour under cross-examination would destroy his credibility as a witness against Knight.

It was half past nine when the doorbell rang. He opened the door to a smartly-dressed, attractive woman of about forty, dark hair tied up in a braided bun. She was staring wistfully towards the promenade and turned slowly, greeting him with a calm, rehearsed-looking smile.

"Mr Randall? My name is Lindsay Price. I'm here about the biography of your father." The voice American, probably East Coast.

Nick frowned. Not a Jehovah's Witness, then. "You're a reporter?"

"I'm working as a research assistant for Howard Franks."

She took a step backwards, perhaps anticipating a bad reaction. It helped Nick to check his temper.

"I don't mean to be rude, but Franks knows we're not interested in helping him."

"Absolutely. And he's aware that he didn't get off to a good start…" She shrugged, then squinted past him. "Uh, I've just driven down from London. Can I use your bathroom, please?"

It was probably a ploy to get inside the house, but he didn't see how he could refuse. He showed her the way and then waited in the hall, unable to decide what approach he should take.

The toilet flushed and she came out, her jacket now folded over her arm. She was wearing a thin burgundy jumper that showed off an impressive figure. Ten years ago she might have been a *Playboy* centrefold, he thought. She caught him looking and it seemed to boost her confidence.

"Actually, I haven't been totally honest with you," she said. "I work for a law firm in the City. The research is something I do as a favour to Howard."

"I take it you're his girlfriend, then?"

She smiled at the term, and said, "Kind of. It's not an exclusive thing."

He laughed, trying not to betray his shock. "I can see what Howard gets out of it," he said, "but I'm not so sure about you."

He thought she might bristle at this, but she laughed with him. "It's a mutually beneficial relationship." She seemed to be about to add to this, but instead changed tack. "I'm sorry to hear about your wife. Do the police know what happened yet?"

"Only what's been reported in the papers," he said. "I assume Howard reads them avidly?"

"I'm afraid he does." She shrugged, then switched her jacket from one arm to the other. "Look, I don't want to pressure you. If you'd rather I just left…"

She took a step towards the door, and he raised his hands.

"No. I'm being rude. Would you like a drink?"

She let out a sigh as if wilting. "I am so glad you said that. I would love a cup of tea."

Roger Knight cruised at eighty on the M25, U2 blasting from his stereo, delighted to find that the traffic chaos normally predicted for a holiday weekend had failed to materialise. Leaving Clayton just after eight, it took him only forty minutes to reach the A2, heading towards Gravesend.

After finding his number for Wheeler was out of date, he'd spoken to Barry Harper, who warned him that the old man didn't take kindly to visitors. "Losing his marbles if you ask me."

On the phone Wheeler sounded confused and belligerent. Although he claimed to remember who Roger was, he kept demanding to know how he had obtained the number. Finally he consented to a visit, but only when Roger agreed to bring him a gift.

Reaching Gravesend, he took a wrong turn towards Dartford and found himself parallel to the Thames, a line of cranes dipping beneath a brooding sky. A tanker was making slow progress through the grey water.

Eventually he found the address in a row of terraced council houses just off London Road. In a street that generally cried out for refurbishment, Wheeler's house was practically derelict. The roof was spotted with missing tiles, the window frames were black with rot and the render was pitted and stained with rust from the broken guttering. Roger felt glad his uncle hadn't lived to see Wheeler end up like this, and it made him appreciate the extent to which he'd transformed Ray's dubious legacy into something more tangible.

He was standing on the pavement, trying to detect signs of life inside the house, when he became aware of coughing. He turned and saw a decrepit old man shuffling towards him, a cigarette dangling from his mouth and a *Racing Post* folded beneath his arm. Long strands of white hair fluttered from a mottled scalp. The man walked with a pronounced limp, throwing his right foot round in a circular motion and dragging the left behind it. Between each bout of coughing he sucked on the cigarette, his hand clamped to his mouth to hold it steady.

Roger felt his heart sink. His memory of Ted Wheeler featured a strong middle-aged man with a penchant for sharp suits and flashy cars, thick gold jewellery and plenty of Brut. What approached him now was little more than a skeleton in a mangy cardigan and baggy slacks.

Thirty feet away, Ted spotted him and stopped, looking around in panic.

"I'm Ray McPherson's nephew. We spoke yesterday."

Ted stared as if trying to unlock some distant memory, then gestured at the bag Roger was holding. "That the rum?"

So his memory wasn't that poor. "Two bottles of Captain Morgan," Roger said.

Ted sniffed. "And you told no one you was coming here?"

"That's right."

"Good. Keep it that way. I don't wanna be leaving this place till they carry me out in a box, and I ain't doing that before my time, you get me?"

Roger nodded uncertainly. Losing his marbles, all right.

"Come on, then," said Ted. "Better get your arse inside."

After he'd made tea for Lindsay, Nick sat in an armchair and told himself that, no matter what was said, he would stay calm and polite. Lindsay had selected the couch and placed a small notebook on her lap. He watched her turn to a clean page and uncap her pen.

"I assume you know what Franks is alleging?" he said.

"The death of Leslie Jones?"

She nodded, and met his gaze. "I also believe it's true."

There was an uneasy moment. Nick took a deep breath.

"The thing is, I was nine when Dad died. Does Howard really think I'd know what went on —?"

"This isn't about whether you can confirm or deny what your father did."

"No. I know what he really wants," Nick said, his voice rising. "He wants to be able to quote me, or my sister, to lend credibility to the book."

Lindsay was shaking her head. "He values your insight because he's genuinely trying to understand your father. Trying to fathom how a successful, popular actor would risk everything for sex with underage girls."

Nick sat back as if winded. "What?"

Lindsay looked surprised that he didn't know. "That's why Leslie was killed," she explained. "He worked at a club in Soho called Lewds. Eddie Randall had befriended the gangsters who owned it. They held private parties and brought in girls, sometimes prostitutes but also naïve young women who wanted to be dancers or actresses. They thought that sleeping with these powerful men would benefit their careers." She had a mournful, distant look in her eyes. "In June 1968 a fifteen-year-old girl was gang-raped and strangled —"

"Hold on!" Now he was shouting. "Where the hell do you get this from? Where's the evidence? Where's the police investigation?"

Lindsay regarded him with a mixture of pity and scorn. "There was no investigation. The girl came from a poor background, probably homeless, a runaway —"

"What do you mean, probably? What was her name?"

"She was never identified. Just another missing person that doesn't get found."

"This is crazy."

"Leslie Jones knew what they'd done. He threatened to go to the police and your father had him killed."

The doorbell rang. At first it didn't register with Nick: just another sound to add to the white noise of fear and confusion in his brain.

He realised she was looking at him oddly. "Shouldn't you see who that is?"

Coming into the hall, he saw a shadow receding from the door. He opened it and the woman at the end of the path stopped and turned towards him. He recognised the blonde hair, the uncertain smile, the green eyes.

Caitlin.

17

Waiting for him to answer felt worse than stagefright. Caitlin convinced herself that he was out. Perhaps just as well. Probably a bad idea, anyway.

It was a relief to walk away. Then she heard the door open and saw him staring, bewildered. She retraced her steps, nervously twisting her hands together.

"It's Caitlin, isn't it?"

"Yes. After you saw Roger yesterday, I thought... I thought I should..." She let out an exasperated sigh. It had all sounded so convincing in her head.

"Is Roger with you?" he asked.

"No. He's gone to see someone. A friend of his uncle's."

"Ted Wheeler."

She nodded. "But I think it's about you. Did this Wheeler know your father?"

"Probably hoping to get some scandalous gossip about Dad to use against me."

"Oh." She hadn't realised how much he knew. If he was this far ahead of her, it might already be too late for Roger. She turned her head, and thought she glimpsed someone in the hallway. Was that why he hadn't invited her inside?

Nick asked, "Do you know why he might be trying to do that?"

"I'm not completely sure, but..." She faltered, uncomfortable with the lie.

"I'm investigating some fraudulent insurance claims. Roger Knight's garage has cropped up a couple of times."

"I'm sure Roger wouldn't be... he wouldn't do anything that stupid."

"It's possible that he's being used," Nick suggested gently. "Does the name Lauren Doyle mean anything to you?"

"Lauren? That's Kevin's wife." She blurted it out, and saw a flash of celebration in his eyes.

"How do you know Kevin?"

"He's… an acquaintance of Roger's." She shut her eyes, wishing she could retract everything, but it was too late. And Nick's eagerness to know about Doyle gave her an idea.

"He runs a salvage company, Griffin Farm Breakers. I've never trusted him. He's quite capable of doing this behind Roger's back."

"You don't think there's any chance Roger's part of it?"

Caitlin shook her head. Let him believe that and go after Doyle instead.

"But if that's the case," Nick said, "why has he gone to see Ted Wheeler?"

He'd easily trapped her, but at least he had the decency to look sheepish about it.

"OK, that was a bit unfair," he added. "Thanks for coming to see me." He smiled, and that gave her the courage to say what she had intended.

"I wanted you to know, Kevin Doyle's a violent man. He's got convictions for assault."

"That doesn't surprise me," said Nick wryly.

"Be careful. Please."

Once again Caitlin sensed a movement within the house. She shifted sideways and saw a tall attractive woman watching her. The woman held her gaze for a moment, and then stepped out of sight. Caitlin found herself blushing, even though it was a stupid, illogical reaction.

"I'd better go," she said. "Roger doesn't know I've done this. Please don't tell him."

"Of course not."

"He's a good man. Really."

She turned away, unable to make sense of the sudden hollowness she felt. She didn't look back but she could feel Nick watching her, and she pictured the woman standing behind him. His lover?

Having seen the outside of Ted Wheeler's house, Roger prepared for the worst when he stepped inside. He was not disappointed. Although he tried to pick a careful route along the hall, he could feel his shoes sticking to the carpet.

Wheeler shrugged off the dirt and squalor with the explanation that he had fallen out with a neighbour, a woman in her fifties who had cleaned the house for him. "She always done it for free," he said. "She thought I was one of those eccentric old sods with a fortune stashed under the floorboards."

Roger smiled politely, and Ted answered it with a glare. "But I don't have a cent. Not a fucking penny."

"What happened to it?"

"Made some wrong decisions. Trusted the wrong people." His growling delivery deterred Roger from further questions on that subject.

"So the housework's down to you now?" he said cheerily, ducking his head to avoid a cobweb.

"Fuck it. Doesn't bother me."

Wheeler led him into a tiny cramped kitchen, where Roger stood with his buttocks pressed against a grimy plastic table while the old man moved slowly from sink to counter, filling a kettle so old its design had become fashionable again. A scrawny black cat wandered in, gave Roger a cursory inspection and then made for Ted, who growled and aimed a weak kick at it.

"Bloody moggy. Keeps crapping all over the place." He

put the kettle down and launched into a coughing fit, barely covering his mouth above the two mugs on the counter.

"Fucking lungs are packing up," he said when the hacking had subsided. "That and the gammy leg, and the dodgy ticker, and the fact it takes an hour to have a piss."

"Not a lot of fun, getting old," Roger said.

"Nah. Still, better than the alternative, eh?" His face suddenly darkened. "You ain't told anyone where I live?"

"No. We agreed on the phone."

"I'm not messing around." Despite his frail state, the old man spoke with the authority of someone accustomed to inspiring fear.

"Who are you hiding from?" Roger asked.

For a moment Ted looked genuinely scared, as if Roger knew more than he was letting on.

"Made some enemies in my time," he muttered. He began spooning budget brand instant coffee into the mugs. "You know Mickey Leach?"

"He was in business with you and uncle Ray," Roger said.

"Yeah, well, he snuffed it last year. He was eighty-two, living in a nursing home but in pretty good health. Doing all right, he was. Just before Christmas they found him dead."

"What was it, heart attack?"

"Post mortem was inconclusive, but it might have been suffocation."

Roger took a step forward, not sure if he'd heard correctly. He noticed that Ted's wavering hand had spilled coffee on a worktop already littered with crumbs and food stains.

"They said maybe one of the other patients did it, but I ain't so sure." Ted held one of the mugs against the edge of the unit and swept the contents of the worktop into it.

"Who do you think it was?"

"If I knew that, I wouldn't have to be so careful." He shuffled to a cupboard and took out an open bag of sugar. "Your uncle, when did he die?"

"Years ago. Ninety-four. Bowel cancer."

"That's right. Poor bastard was all skin and bones by the end."

Roger nodded, wondering if Ted had looked in a mirror lately.

"That's what I wanted to ask you about. Back in the sixties you, Ray and Mickey all knew Eddie Randall?"

"Yeah. This is about that book, isn't it?"

"The biography by Howard Franks?"

"Yeah. I got word that Franks wants to talk to me, but I'm having nothing to do with it."

"Surely he's only interested in Eddie Randall?"

Roger had to wait through another coughing fit, during which the kettle boiled. Roger said, "Let me get that," and quickly lifted the kettle off the stove.

"I got no reason to help him," Ted explained. "And I ain't about to advertise my existence, am I?"

Roger reached the fridge before Ted and took out a carton of full fat milk. "Is there any dirt to dig?"

The old man chuckled. His red eyes looked watery. "Oh yeah," he said. "There's dirt all right."

"Can you tell me about it?"

"What's it to you, anyway?"

Roger stirred both mugs of coffee and chose the one he felt was least contaminated. He decided on the direct approach.

"His son could put me away. I want something I can use on him."

The old man cackled, appreciating the honesty. "He was

an odd sort, Eddie Randall. Had everything you could want and still wasn't happy. Always searching for the next thrill."

Roger waited, putting off his first sip of coffee.

"He liked girls," Ted said. "Young girls. Sometimes getting a bit rough, you know? Well, one night we had a party at the club, and one of 'em ended up dead."

Roger breathed out slowly. "Shit."

"Yeah. Well, this feller who worked for me tried blackmailing him. Eddie made the mistake of paying up, so of course the blackmailer wanted more. Eddie asked me to sort it for him."

"What did you do?"

Ted stared at him, and now Roger saw the steel in his eyes. "What d'you think I did? I fucking sorted it."

After closing the door, Nick was startled to find Lindsay standing behind him. He was so absorbed with Caitlin's revelations that he'd forgotten she was there.

"Friend of yours?" she asked cheerily.

"Just work." And none of your business, he thought.

As they returned to the living room, Lindsay said, "I could have sworn I heard the name Ted Wheeler just then."

"You were listening to us?"

Ignoring his indignation, she said, "He's one of the men who arranged for Leslie Jones's murder."

"You have no proof of that."

"Have you spoken to Wheeler? Maybe you need to hear it from him."

Nick shook his head. "What has he told you?"

"Actually, Howard's been unable to contact him. His address would be very much appreciated." A glint of humour in her eyes.

"I don't have it."

"It sounds like your visitor does. What was that name? I assume it's Knight as in shining armour?"

She gave a little laugh at her own joke. This was just an amusing foray into someone's life, he realised. Eddie's fate - or his own for that matter - meant nothing to her.

"You can tell Howard I'm not changing my mind. And I don't want to hear from him or his representatives again."

"Suit yourself. But even if you don't give us Wheeler's address, you really should talk with him."

"I think you should finish your tea and leave."

Unperturbed, she tipped her cup and drank delicately, then picked up her handbag and jacket. She moved close to him, and he took an involuntary step backwards, fearful of contact. She regarded him with pity.

"Seems to me you're in denial, Nick. Sooner or later you have to face up to what Eddie was."

What Eddie was. The phrase made his stomach contract. He didn't trust himself to respond, but stood in grim silence as she strolled out, a triumphant smile on her face.

"She was a dirty little cow, all right. Mickey swore she was a virgin, but I ain't so sure. Might not have been fifteen, for that matter. How can you tell once they're all dolled up? Long as they got tits and hair, that was good enough for me."

A cackle, which led to a coughing fit. Roger regarded him with distaste, trying to decide whether Ted Wheeler had become this despicable as his body aged and rotted, or whether he'd always been this way and Roger had simply been deceived by outward appearances. He was reluctantly inclined towards the latter.

He steeled himself and asked, "How did she die?"

"Eddie had this idea from some film he'd done. One of them satanic horror movies. We're all off our heads, you gotta remember. Sounded like a laugh, and the girl was up for it. Didn't say no."

Roger only nodded. There was no point asking whether she could have refused.

"We acted out this ceremony. Stripped her naked, tied her up. Might've done some stuff with candles, dripped it on her body. Mickey wanted to paint blood on her, but we couldn't get hold of any. And by that time we just wanted to fuck her."

Roger felt nauseous, watching this decrepit old man become animated as he discussed the rape of a school-girl. Kept pushing away thoughts of Sally and Bridget, and what he'd do if someone like Wheeler ever got his hands on them.

"Then someone had the idea of putting his hands round her neck."

"Eddie Randall?"

"How the fuck should I know? I wasn't taking notes. Anyway, when we finished we realised she wasn't breathing. Might've been heart failure or something. We tried to bring her round but it was too late. Nothing we could do."

"How many men... had sex with her?"

Ted searched his memory. "Four or five, I suppose. No more than that." Seemingly unaware of the effect he was having, Ted tapped a grubby finger against his mug as he gathered his thoughts. "Thing is, Eddie was the only one with a reputation to protect. That's why Leslie blackmailed him."

"And how did he know about it?"

"Saw us carrying the body out. We thought all the staff had buggered off for the night, like they was supposed to.

Nasty little troublemaker, he was."

"And the girl? What happened to her?"

He chuckled, as you would at a fond reminiscence. "Mickey kept a boat at Newhaven. We wrapped the body in chickenwire, dumped it a couple of miles out."

Roger said, "Charming," but the sarcasm was lost on Ted. He seemed proud of their ingenuity.

"Just one of those things. We weren't gonna get banged up for it."

Roger set his mug down on the counter and prepared to leave. Viewed from his current predicament, it had been a successful visit, but right now he felt sullied by the knowledge he had acquired.

"Shame, really," Ted concluded, still lost in the past. "Pretty little thing, she was."

18

When Lindsay returned from Brighton empty-handed, it only hastened Franks's desire to be rid of her. He intended to savour the moment, though: perhaps book a table at the Ivy and tell her during the meal. There was always the chance she'd make a scene and get him in the papers.

It annoyed him that his good idea had failed to produce a breakthrough. Perhaps it was bad timing so close to Sarah Randall's death, but he'd expected Nick to be influenced by Lindsay's appearance. He'd even gone so far as to recommend which top she should wear, a thin sweater that emphasised her breasts. In Franks's opinion, if big tits weren't going to work, nothing would.

The only scrap of good news was confirmation that Ted Wheeler was still alive. Howard's contacts in the media had been trying to track him down for months. Last year he'd managed to trace Mickey Leach to a nursing home in Bedford, but the old man refused to say a word about his connection to Eddie Randall, probably afraid of incriminating himself. He'd died shortly afterwards, which left Ted Wheeler as the only living member of the criminal fraternity with links to Eddie.

Lindsay's account of the conversation left him confused, however, and it had led to a heated exchange on Friday afternoon.

"Let me get this straight. Nick doesn't know where Wheeler is?"

"No."

"And yet his visitor does know?"

"I think it's her boyfriend who knows. A man named

Knight."

"And you think Nick's investigating him?"

"That's how it sounded."

"But you didn't think to ask for Wheeler's address?"

"Nick doesn't have it."

"Not Nick. The visitor."

Lindsay groaned. "She didn't even come inside. What was I supposed to do, run down the street after her?"

"Yes, if need be," Franks said. As a journalist he'd gone to far greater lengths.

Lindsay threw her hands up in despair. "I don't believe you. I do this as a favour and all I get is criticism. I wasted half my day on this."

"More than that, you wasted a precious opportunity."

"You bastard. You might show a bit of gratitude."

Franks had already given up on the prospect of sex this evening, so he didn't hold back his contempt. "I thought you were capable of carrying out a simple task. I was obviously mistaken."

Lindsay bunched her fists, shook them impotently at him and stormed out of the house. In truth it was a relief to see her go, although there was a casserole in the oven which he'd lovingly prepared while she was away. Far too much to eat on his own, so it would go to waste.

Unless he could reach Fiona, of course. Or Penny. Or Geraldine.

It was all going down the toilet. Lately Kevin hadn't been sleeping well, and every morning his first thought was always the same: would the cops show up today?

They'd had such a good thing going with the insurance scam. It was unlike anything Kevin had ever done. A clean white-collar crime: low profile, low risk, and a nice big wodge of cash in your hand every few weeks. It more than made up for the long days he spent sitting in the salvage yard, fiddling with paperwork and pretending he knew what he was doing.

And all because Lauren couldn't bluff out a smartarse question from some bloody insurance investigator. Ever since then their relationship had gone sour, and he'd started hitting her again. A couple of years back he'd fractured her arm and her old man threatened to go to the police. Kevin had sworn he'd never touch her again, and it was a promise he'd been able to keep until now. Until this.

They still had sex when he wanted it, but he knew she was probably scared to refuse, and that pissed him off as well. Just because he had a temper, it didn't make him a rapist.

His other bugbear was Knight. Thought he was the brains of the operation. Thought he knew best. Always wanting to take the safe option, to wait and see. Kevin had had enough of it. No matter what Roger said, Nick Randall was the problem. Scare him off and you'd solve the problem. At worst, you'd buy yourself some time.

In case it all went badly wrong, Kevin had started gathering some cash together. He'd considered torching the salvage yard, or maybe his own house. Get a big insurance payout and disappear with it. Fuck Lauren, fuck Roger. Just take off to the States or Australia and start all over.

On Good Friday he and Jim Harvey had a night out in Brighton. Kicking off in one of the bars in the Kings Road Arches, they got nicely stoked up before moving into town. After a burger in North Street they ended up in Wetherspoons, having put away eight or nine pints each.

Jim had a thing about posh students with plummy voices and natural coloured hair. He got chatting to a group of them, celebrating an eighteenth birthday. Kevin joined him, flashing his money around, but not at all sure it would guarantee him a shag.

At closing time they spilled on to the street. He suggested they go to a club, but he could tell the girls would take some persuading. Jim just wanted to drag one of them into a dark alley and have done with it.

While they were working on the girls, a couple of young guys wandered over and got involved. Some nerdy little prick told Kevin to leave them alone, and Kevin laid him out with one punch. His friend started to move but Jim was on him, a couple of quick blows to the face. By now the girls were screaming.

There was the usual police presence round the clubs at the bottom of West Street, and at the sound of sirens Kevin and Jim fled through the Churchill Square shopping precinct. From there they made their way to the seafront and stood by the railings overlooking the beach, watching the pier lights sparkle on the water.

"Fucking good night," Kevin said. He kept replaying his moves, superimposing Nick Randall's image over the weedy student.

"Yeah," Jim agreed, a little morosely. "Could have done with pulling, though."

"They weren't up for it."

"My one was."

"Bollocks."

"Fuck off."

"Yeah, well. Think I'll go home and give Lauren one up the arse." Kevin could feel the adrenalin still pumping, the taste for violence coursing through his veins. He felt powerful, in command of his own destiny.

He said, "Tell you what, how'd you fancy something a bit

different tomorrow night?"

"Like what?"

"That insurance guy. We pay him a visit."

Jim's eyes were shining. "Why not tonight?"

"Too pissed. Gotta do it properly." He felt a warm glow at his own good sense, and almost wished Roger were here to witness it.

"What're we doing then, knock on the door and chin him?"

Kevin shook his head, then had to grab the railing to steady himself. "Better than that," he said. "Give him a real fucking fright."

19

Saturday morning, Roger decided he'd had enough of walking on coals. He found Caitlin in the garden, stabbing at weeds, and suggested they go out for lunch. They might stand a better chance of civilised conversation on neutral territory.

To his surprise, she seemed happy to accept. He waited for her to clean up and then they drove to one of his favourite pubs, The Yew Tree at Arlington. The weather was beginning to clear after some light showers, and the Sussex countryside was green and lush.

In the car they listened to Jonathan Ross on Radio Two, sharing laughter for what seemed like the first time in weeks. He was turning on to the Berwick road when Caitlin said, "Do you think it's run its course?"

For a second he thought about playing dumb, but instead he answered truthfully. "Maybe."

"That's what I think. But we don't have to be silly about it, do we?"

He glanced at her. She was frowning, looking much older and wiser than the image of her that remained in his heart.

"No. We don't."

"Good." There was satisfaction in her voice, as though a major hurdle had been cleared.

They found a table in the bar area and ordered lunch. Caitlin insisted on an orange juice and offered to drive home, a gesture of goodwill he was happy to accept. He suggested a toast to her final show at the Komedia and they clinked glasses. Then Caitlin said, "You won't mind if I stay a few more weeks, just till I get myself sorted?"

"Who said you need to move out?"

"If that's what we decide."

"Of course. Stay as long as you want." He drank some beer, agonising over what to say. He knew he couldn't match her brutal honesty. "Do you want to leave?"

She thought about it, and nodded. "I've missed having my own place."

"Is this to do with the insurance claims? Nick Randall?"

She seemed to blanch at the mention of his name, and in that moment Roger abandoned an impulse to tell her everything.

"Well, yes and no. I suppose it clarified a few things."

He nodded, pretending to understand. He couldn't believe she would regard him as a criminal because at heart he didn't believe it of himself. He'd managed to justify the insurance claims as a kind of bureaucratic sleight of hand, rightful compensation for the unprofitable labour rates forced on him by the insurers over many years.

"What did Ted Wheeler tell you?" Caitlin asked. It was the first time she'd mentioned his trip to Kent.

"Not much," he said. "A few anecdotes about Eddie Randall."

"Anything useful?" There was a sardonic twist in her voice.

He sighed. "Maybe." Last night he had dreamed of the murdered girl, only this time it was Nick who lay choking her, while he and Kevin Doyle stood and watched, doing nothing to intervene.

"I can't pretend I know all the details," Caitlin said, "and really I don't want to know, but I'll tell you this." She looked him in the eye. "Whatever you've got in mind to stop Nick Randall, it won't work."

He held her gaze for a long time. He knew she was

sincere, which was more than could be said for Doyle or Barry Harper. She had just confirmed the uneasy conviction he'd been harbouring ever since he first considered trying to blackmail Randall with his father's secrets. Nick had too much integrity to falsify his reports, no matter what Roger threatened him with.

But what else could he do? Let Kevin have his way?

"You're so miserable these days, Roger. That's one of the reasons I have to leave."

He snorted. "Because I'm such a grumpy sod?"

"Because you're trapped. You're desperate for a way out."

He repeated, "A way out?" Did she mean their relationship?

"Listen to me." She leant forward and took his hand, toying with the wedding band he had never discarded. "If you're doing something illegal, get out of it. If you've made some money, find a way to give it back. If other people are involved, get them out of your life."

He couldn't help grinning. She was so earnest, so moral. Suddenly the young woman was back, the one who'd enchanted him, and it tore at his heart that she had returned only because the relationship was over.

"Next," she went on, "get on a plane to Scotland. Stay with Lynn if you can, otherwise book a hotel and work on her, persuading, pleading, promising, until she agrees to come back. And if that means selling everything in Sussex to become a crofter –" at this they both laughed, "– then do it. Do whatever it takes."

She waited for him to speak, and at that moment their meals arrived. When the waitress moved away he picked up his beer and toasted her.

"Excellent advice."

She raised her glass in reply. "But will you take it?"

He paused. *Honesty*, remember. Honesty.

"I don't know," he said.

Saturday night in Kingston on Thames, the lumpen proletariat roaming the streets in drunken hordes. Alex drove fast on the ring road, jabbing her horn when a lazy crowd ignored her right of way at a crossing. What joy to floor the accelerator and take them out like bowling pins.

She resisted; far richer delights lay in store. The endgame was approaching. The numerous strands of Project Randall were being woven into the garrotte that would choke the life from her victims.

Joining the M25, she picked up speed and made use of the adrenalin coursing through her body. A couple of hours ago she'd taken some dexedrine in anticipation of the long night ahead. As the pace of her plans increased, sleep became an unwelcome intrusion.

She was passing Gatwick when her phone rang. She checked the display and smiled.

"Lover," she said.

"Where are you?"

"Arundel," she lied smoothly. "Client meeting."

"It's Saturday."

"Sometimes I have to work weekends. Same as you."

"You know I've only got a couple of hours, maximum?"

She made a purring noise, the kind of thing that rendered men insensible with lust. "That's plenty of time," she said.

"Oh Jesus, I can't wait. I'm nearly finishing myself off here."

"That would be an awful waste." Emphasising *awful* like some trashy actress, and didn't he just lap it up. She heard him groaning.

"Hurry, please. I want you so much."

"Patience, my darling. Good things come to those who

wait…" She cut the connection and added, "But it depends on your definition of good."

In his dream Nick was on the cliffs near the Belle Tout lighthouse. A full moon blazed a path across the sea. Someone was pushing against him, forcing him towards the edge. His bare toes dug into the grass, but it wasn't enough to resist. Soon he would plunge to his death.

At the last moment he managed to turn and face his attacker, and the shock caused him to lose his balance. There was a loud crack as the chalk gave way beneath his feet. He opened his mouth to scream —

And woke, certain the noise had been real. In the stillness of the bedroom all he could hear was his thudding heart. He moved up on to his elbows and forced his breathing to slow down. Eyes wide open in the dark, waiting for the sound to be repeated.

Probably just a cat, or a fox prowling the dustbins for food. But he stayed frozen for a long minute, watching the digital clock move from 2:36 to 2:37. Then realised he was holding his breath and let it out in a rush. He remembered the dream, but couldn't picture the face he'd seen. He told himself he was being stupid and relaxed back on the bed.

And heard something else. A scraping, sliding noise.

From inside.

Now he sat up straight, wondering if he dared use the phone. What kind of response time could he expect on a Saturday night? And what if it was nothing? He decided he had to investigate first.

He got out of bed and quickly pulled on some shorts. Searched the room for something he could use as a weapon, but found nothing.

He crept on to the landing and paused at the top of

the stairs. There was a moment of agonising indecision. Should he make a noise in order to frighten the intruder off, or move stealthily and hope to surprise him?

Neither option was particularly appealing, but he couldn't just stay where he was and let the bastard ransack his house.

He took the stairs slowly, keeping close to the edges so the boards wouldn't give him away. A couple of times he heard movement in the living room: the gentle clatter of items being discarded. Fucker's going through my CD collection, he thought.

At the bottom of the stairs there was an occasional table that Sarah had bought for the hall. There was a bronze figurine on it, and while the figure itself was delicate, the base was quite hefty. Since he had nothing better available, Nick lifted it up and slowly approached the living room door.

He was reaching for the handle when his vision disappeared. He felt rough material against his face and then a heavy arm around his neck, crushing his windpipe. He tried to raise the figurine but it was knocked from his hand.

Movement in the living room, someone hurrying.

A gruff male voice: "You got him?"

"Yeah."

Two of them. One lurking in the shadows while the other searched the house.

Nick tried to break free but he was punched twice, hard, in the stomach. He felt himself gagging against the hood, unable to breathe. A rush of cold air hit him as the front door opened, and his heels scuffed on the carpet.

"Come on. Let's get him out."

He panicked, began writhing madly, choking and spluttering, but a blow to the head sent him reeling. Possibly he blacked out for a second, then felt himself being dragged towards the door.

Suddenly there was a blaze of light and the glassy shriek of a car horn. Nick felt his assailants react with the same shock.

"What the fuck…?"

"Come on."

He was dropped unceremoniously on the path and hit his head against the decorative stone that marked the tiny lawn. At the same time the car horn ceased, and he wondered if he'd imagined it. He grabbed at the sack over his head. Heard car doors slam, the gunning of an engine.

He got up just in time to see a car race away without lights: something fast and sporty, maybe a BMW. Then another car, parked across the street, pulled out and set off in pursuit. Both turned on to the seafront road, tyres squealing, and were gone.

Alex followed the BMW into Brighton. The driver put his lights on, then accelerated up to seventy approaching a large traffic-light controlled junction. It sped through on red, just missing a car preparing to turn right. Alex slowed to let the other car cross and saw the BMW's passenger turning in his seat, obviously hoping to witness a collision.

She considered pursuing them, but quickly decided against it. With the clubs chucking out around now, the city centre would be full of police. No point risking unnecessary attention.

Instead she turned left, away from the seafront. She wondered if Nick had noticed her registration plate, but judged it unlikely in all the confusion.

She had parked opposite his house at just after two am, intending only to collect her thoughts at the end of a productive evening. A little later she'd seen the BMW pull up, and watched two burly men pull on face masks and disappear around the side of the house. At that point she considered phoning Nick, but curiosity got the better of her.

For the next few minutes she waited, calmly aware that her prime target might end up dead. Against this possibility she had to weigh up the risks of intervention. If she were herself injured or captured, all her plans would be ruined.

When the front door opened, and it was clear the men were intent on abducting him, she saw a chance to prevent it and remain anonymous. The only drawback was that it gave her no clue as to who was responsible. Clearly Nick had made other enemies, which was interesting in itself, but also a complication she could do without.

She spent the journey home considering her response to this latest challenge. There was no question of stopping. It was merely a choice between continuing as planned or forcing the pace.

In the end, she decided: *force it.*

20

"Men!"

"What?"

"Ohh, sometimes I could strangle the lot of you!"

Diana picked up Chloe and walked out of the kitchen, leaving Nick and Pat to exchange a bemused glance.

"It's not you," said Pat. "We're going through a bit of a rough patch at the moment, what with everything…"

Before he could elaborate Diana marched back into the room, having deposited Chloe in her bouncing cradle. Both men watched as she balled up her apron and hurled it at Nick. He ducked to one side and caught it neatly. "Does this mean you're withdrawing the invite to Sunday lunch?"

She almost cracked a smile, turning away so he wouldn't see it. She opened the fridge and took out a bottle of wine.

"Uh oh," said Pat.

"And you can piss off," Diana snapped.

Pat looked sheepish. "My cue to play with the kids, I think."

Diana poured two glasses of wine and handed one to Nick, then sat down opposite him.

"I can't believe you didn't go to the police."

"I've explained that."

"They were trying to kidnap you, for God's sake. You might have been killed."

"I don't think so. Probably a beating." Nick congratulated himself on sounding far more confident than he felt.

"So what's to stop them trying again?"

"I'm more interested in what stopped them last night."

He'd explained the surreal intervention that had thwarted

159

his would-be abductors, but he had no idea who had saved him, or why. In the confusion he hadn't even managed to get the make of the second car.

The oven bleeped. Nick glanced at Diana, then at the apron on the table, and said, "Let me do that."

"Sure you know how? It's not a microwave."

He laughed sarcastically. He'd been dreading this conversation, but now he felt the worst was over. Last night he'd gone inside, inspected his various bumps and bruises, taken some painkillers and then located the point of entry: a window in his downstairs toilet. He fetched the Yellow Pages and sat down, knowing the first call ought to be 999.

Then he thought about the media, Howard Franks pouncing on any chance to re-ignite the story. So he vetoed that idea and called an emergency glazier, who finally arrived at four o'clock and communicated his feelings with a sniff. "Take much, did they?"

"Not really," said Nick. All he wanted now was to get to bed.

"Still, look on the bright side, eh?" the glazier said.

"What?"

"You can stick in a nice big claim. Make up for all that premium you been paying for years."

Eight hours later, basting roast potatoes in his sister's kitchen, Nick smiled as he recalled the comment.

He saw Diana working up to something. "Is there any chance this could be connected to Sarah's death?" she said at last.

"More likely it's a case I'm working on." He hadn't told Diana that he'd recognised one of the voices: Kevin Doyle. But it was nothing he could prove in court.

"Someone did this because of an insurance claim?"

"There's big money involved."

Diana shuddered. "Why can't you get a safer job?"

She stood up and opened her arms to embrace him. There were tears in her eyes. "First Sarah. Now this." She stepped back, a hand on each of his shoulders, and looked him directly in the eye. "What have you done to deserve such bad luck?"

For once he didn't have a glib answer. But a song popped into his head: *Someone's Got It In For Me.* Then a thought so unexpected that he felt the colour drain from his face.

"What's wrong?"

"Nothing. I just need to sit down."

"Are you all right?"

"Yeah. Fine." He took a sip of his wine. "You ought to make up with Pat."

"He doesn't deserve it," Diana grumbled.

"Go on. I don't want to eat lunch in a war zone."

Reluctantly she left the room, and he returned to the question that had accompanied the song. What if someone *had* got it in for him? What if that was why Sarah had died?

He considered it from various angles, trying and failing to identify anyone who might go to such terrible lengths, and then he realised just how staggeringly egocentric he was being. What would Diana say? *You think the world revolves around you. Arrogant little sod.*

No. He dismissed that idea and stood up. Time to forget his troubles and play Favourite Uncle for a while.

It was an agitated Kevin Doyle who rang Roger at ten o'clock on Sunday morning, saying he was on his way over. Roger retreated to his study and prepared for the worst.

Since their lunch the day before, he and Caitlin had been friendlier than at any time for weeks. Nevertheless she had insisted on moving to a spare bedroom, confirming that the relationship, if it continued at all, would do so on a platonic basis. Last night she'd finished her run at the Komedia and afterwards had gone clubbing with the rest of the company. When Doyle rang she was still in bed.

Ten minutes later Roger heard a car pull up outside. He opened the front door and registered Kevin's appearance: wild-eyed, unshaven, jittery.

"Christ! What have you been taking?"

Kevin shouldered his way past without speaking. Roger watched him stalk into the study and counted to ten.

"You look like you've been up all night."

"I fucking have, that's why." Kevin sprawled in a chair and threw his feet on to the desk, one soiled trainer perilously close to a photo of the children. He pinched the bridge of his nose and frowned as if trying to unblock a memory, or perhaps chase one away.

"What have you done?"

"I was fed up, just sitting on our arses. Me and Jim, we thought if we could really scare the shit out of him…"

"Nick Randall?"

Kevin grunted affirmation. He started scratching his scalp with manic intensity. "We broke in. We were gonna have him away —"

Roger threw himself forward in his chair, banging his knee on the desk. "*What?*"

"Bung him in the car, take him down to Worthing or somewhere. Give him a kicking and leave him on the beach. Tell him to drop the investigation or next time he'll end up dead."

Roger put his head in his hands and said, very quietly, "And what happened?" Thinking: *they killed him.*

"There was someone spying on the house, at three in the fucking morning. Leant on the horn, flashed their lights.

We had to drop him and leg it."

"So who was it?"

"I dunno. They followed us into town, then disappeared. Jim reckoned it was a bird."

Roger didn't understand at first. "A woman?"

"What I'm thinking is, maybe the pigs are watching him."

"You'd better pray that's not true." And so had I, Roger added to himself. He brooded for a minute, and then said, "No. They'd have arrested you there and then."

"So who, then?"

"I've no idea." He had another thought. "What car did you use?"

"My beamer, but I swapped plates with an old 3-series at the Farm." Despite everything, Kevin had the gall to boast of his ingenuity.

You fucking moron, Roger thought. And in that moment his decision was made, nicely anticipating Kevin's next question.

"So what now?"

"We shut it down. It's over."

"No way. I ain't having that." Kevin's foot twitched; the picture fell off the desk and smashed.

"Get your feet off there," Roger snarled. He waited for the other man's sullen gaze to meet his. "And another thing. You're fired."

"Fucking…" Kevin's mouth hung open in disbelief. "What am I gonna do for money?"

Roger unlocked the filing cabinet behind him and produced a thick brown envelope. He tossed it to Kevin.

"Fifteen grand," Roger said. "We'll call it severance pay, and think yourself lucky. You don't deserve a penny."

Kevin peered into the envelope, muttering under his breath, and then suddenly launched himself across the desk. His outstretched fist caught Roger on the chin, while his other hand went for his throat. Roger cried out, raising his hands in a feeble attempt to fend him off.

Under the weight of the two men, Roger's chair toppled backwards and they both fell heavily into the narrow space behind the desk. In the desperate tangle of limbs, Roger managed to prise Kevin's hand from his throat, only to let out a winded exclamation as Doyle punched him in the chest.

"Piece of shit!" Kevin spat. Expecting no more resistance, he began to rise, reaching across the desk in search of a weapon. "Fifteen grand!" He snatched up another framed photo, broke it on the corner of the desk and pulled out a shard of glass. "I want a better offer or I'll cut your fucking face to shreds."

Turning back, jabbing the glass to show he meant business, he expected to see Roger wide-eyed and submissive. Instead he found himself staring at the snout of a Browning pistol.

"Where the fuck d'you get that?" Trying not to betray the fear in his voice, Kevin stood up and slowly backed away.

"Unlike you, I take the time to prepare."

"You wouldn't…"

Roger smiled. There was a glint in his eyes that Kevin had never seen before. It matched the certainty in his voice. "Wanna try me?" he said.

Feeling like Clint Eastwood, and talking like him now.

As Roger stood up, Kevin retreated further. Roger nodded towards the envelope.

"Take it."

Kevin snatched up the money and stuffed it inside his jacket. Suddenly the door opened and Caitlin was there, frowning first at Doyle's broad back, then seeing past him. Before she could speak, Roger cried out "Caitlin! Get away!"

Kevin turned, a second too late. Caitlin ran to the foot of the stairs and called, "Shall I ring the police?"

"No," said Roger. "It's done with." The macho tone produced a certain guilty pleasure. He'd owned the gun for years, and had intended to hand it in when possession became illegal. This was the first time he'd ever threatened someone with it, and the sense of power made him dizzy.

He followed Doyle to the door. In a last act of petty defiance, Kevin spat on the tiles. Roger ached to fire the gun, just a warning shot, but didn't trust himself to shoot straight.

"You ain't heard the last of this," Kevin said, kicking the door shut behind him.

For a moment Roger and Caitlin faced each other, neither saying a word. Caitlin hurried to the window and watched the BMW speed away. Only then did she confront Roger.

"What the hell is going on?"

He shrugged. His legs felt like they could crumple at any second and there was an unpleasant weight in his stomach.

"I took your advice," he said. His vision blurred, and he felt sweat prickling on his forehead. Still holding the gun, he rushed to the toilet across the hall and was violently sick.

21

Devil's Dyke is a popular beauty spot high on the South Downs north of Brighton. Its name derives from a curious indentation in the hill, said to be an attempt by the devil to cut a channel through the Downs and allow the sea to flood the Sussex Weald. As a place where evil had been thwarted, it seemed an appropriate venue for Caitlin and Nick to meet.

Fortunately he arrived promptly, before she could lose her nerve and drive away. She'd been having second thoughts since the night before, when in a burst of courage she had called and asked to see him. She was glad he had suggested they meet on neutral ground.

His own greeting was an uncertain smile as he parked alongside her car. It was a glorious spring morning, and Easter Monday; the car park was rapidly filling with an assortment of walkers, cyclists and hang-gliders.

"I thought we could go for a walk?" Caitlin said, and then blushed. It sounded like she was suggesting a date.

"Lead the way," he said, and they set off along the top of the hill.

They discussed acting for a while, shaking off their nerves in small talk. She wanted to know if he'd ever considered a career in showbusiness.

"Not really. I just never felt the calling. It is a vocation, isn't it?"

"Absolutely. No way you'd put up with the rejection and heartbreak if you didn't feel you were destined to do it."

He looked at her closely. "I guess I wanted an easier life."

There was a sardonic edge to his voice, and it returned

them neatly to the present situation. She was dreading having to tell him, and almost wished he would demand the answers from her.

Delaying the moment even further, she said, "I hope I didn't interrupt anything on Friday…"

Nick frowned. "Not at all." He explained that Lindsay was working for Howard Franks.

"So I guess he hoped you'd succumb to her feminine charms."

"I suppose so. I hadn't thought of it like that."

Caitlin gave him a sceptical look. "She was stunning."

Nick grunted. "Was she? It was all I could do not to throw her out. In fact," he added, "I wish she hadn't been there. I had a lot of questions for you."

She let out a long sigh. "Now I expect you have even more?"

They stopped and admired the view to the south, across Brighton and along the coast towards Selsey, the sea beyond sparkling in the morning sunshine.

Nick said, "I take it you know what happened on Saturday night?" And before she could respond, he added, "It was Kevin Doyle, wasn't it?"

She stopped and faced him. "How did you know?"

"I recognised his voice."

"Were you hurt?"

"A few bruises."

"Have you told the police?" she asked cautiously.

"No."

"Can I ask why not?"

He turned to her. "I'm not sure I know myself," he said. "Tell me what happened."

So she took a deep breath and described Doyle's brief visit yesterday, omitting to mention that Roger had ejected him at gunpoint. She told him that Roger had been appalled by what Kevin had done, and had vowed to end his part in the insurance fraud.

"What will happen if he withdraws the claims?"

Nick shrugged. "That depends on several factors: the amount of money involved, the attitude of the insurers. They don't always welcome the publicity. On the other hand, they may choose to push for prosecution."

She was pensive for a while, wondering how she had ever thought her actions could protect Roger. It was out of Nick's hands by now, she realised, even if he wanted to help. But the payoff, the chance to do something for Nick, still remained.

After a few moments of companionable silence she produced a crumpled Post-it note and handed it to him. "Ted Wheeler's address. I took it from Roger's office."

"Does he know about this?"

"No. None of it."

He looked at her sharply, and she felt a ripple of shame at her dishonesty. Then she realised he was trying to gauge the extent of her feelings for Roger.

Nick said, "If he's determined to go straight, surely he has no interest in my father's indiscretions?"

"He hasn't. This is for you."

"What did Ted Wheeler tell him?"

"He hasn't said much about it. But I don't think it was a pleasant conversation."

Nick nodded grimly. "I'm sure it wasn't." He checked his watch. "What have you got planned for today?"

"Me? I don't know. Why?" *Stop gabbling, idiot.*

"I might as well go and see him now. Want to come along?"

✳

After Saturday night Alex knew she was taking a risk by continuing to keep Nick Randall under surveillance. On the other hand, she wouldn't forgive herself if the would-be abductors decided to try again.

To minimise the risk of identification she'd rented a different car, a green Honda Civic with high mileage and sluggish acceleration. She'd been stationed in Wish Road from eight in the morning, and when Nick emerged two hours later and drove to Devil's Dyke, she assumed he was intent on a solitary walk. Intriguingly, he was joined by a woman in a silver Corsa, and they set off together along the ridge of the Downs.

Alex used the time to stretch her legs, making a few unhurried circuits of the car park. Less than half an hour passed before they returned, but this time the woman climbed into Randall's car and they drove away together. Alex quickly decided she had to gamble on following them.

She was glad she did, for the Audi joined the A27 and remained in the slip road leading to the A23. Wherever they were headed, it wasn't back to Nick's.

Once on the dual-carriageway it was relatively easy to maintain a safe distance from Nick's car, which for the most part was travelling at seventy to eighty miles an hour: a little pedestrian for Alex, but her growing sense of excitement more than compensated.

Back in the car park, a wonderful possibility had occurred to her. Now, as the Audi reached the junction for the M25 and selected the anti-clockwise route, she hardly dared to believe she could be right.

"Go on," she urged. "Take me to him."

✳

On the drive to Kent Nick tried not to think about what

Ted Wheeler might have to say. Having Caitlin in the car certainly helped. He found himself wondering how events had led to this: the girlfriend of a fraudster accompanying him on a visit to a criminal acquaintance of his father's. Bizarre.

As on their walk, the conversation was easy and the silences felt natural. But there was something he wanted to ask her, and he knew it would gnaw at him until he got an answer.

"Did Roger tell you about the mystery driver who scared Doyle away?"

"Yes. It didn't make a lot of sense."

Nick glanced quickly at her. "Nor to me. I had wondered…" He chuckled nervously. "Was it you?"

"Me? No, I spent the early hours of Saturday in the Funky Buddha, getting pleasantly ratarsed."

"Whoever it was, I'd like to thank them."

"Actually, Kevin thought it might be the police." She sounded embarrassed. "I mean, after your wife died…"

"You think the police are watching me?" Saying it aloud, it didn't seem so ridiculous. DCI Pearce had assured him he was in the clear, but perhaps he'd been naïve to believe her.

"It's unlikely," Caitlin said. "Surely they'd have arrested Kevin?"

"Maybe." He couldn't believe it hadn't occurred to him. He found himself checking the mirror, and heard her gasp as the traffic in front slowed down. He looked back just in time to brake.

"It's a silly idea," she said. "Forget I said it."

"Sorry. Paranoid."

But now the idea had been planted, it wasn't so easy to dislodge. And it raised another uncomfortable question.

Just who could he trust?

Following Lindsay's unsuccessful visit to Nick Randall and their subsequent falling out, Howard Franks had made no attempt to contact her. By Monday he was reconciled to the fact that the relationship might have ended, and he actually found his attitude towards her softening. OK, she had been fiery and a little too independent, but she had a magnificent body, and the sex – when she made the effort – was as good as anything he'd experienced.

It was therefore with mixed feelings that he greeted her call, just before midday on Easter Monday.

"Hi, Frankie." She knew he hated her pet name for him.

"Good morning, Lindsay."

"Ooh, very formal. Do I take it I'm not forgiven?"

"I seem to recall it was you who stormed out."

Her laughter was high and mocking. "Come on, lighten up. Isn't it a beautiful day?"

"If you say so." He wasn't sure why he felt so sullen. Perhaps a reaction to her infuriating exuberance.

"Are you very busy, sweetheart?"

"As always." In fact he'd woken late, taken a stroll in Queens Wood, bought a handful of newspapers and was now lying on the chaise longue in his study with a pot of coffee and a plate of chocolate digestives.

"I'm gonna come over later. If the weather holds I thought we could barbecue."

Franks pulled a face. He regarded barbecues as a crude and carcinogenic form of cooking, strictly for the underclass.

"I know what you're thinking," Lindsay trilled. "But it'll

be fun."

Fun, Franks thought, would be the chance to take you from behind one more time.

He said, "We'll see," making sure to sound as brusque as possible.

"OK, Grumpy. See you soon."

After the call ended, he decided to treat this as a positive development. A farewell fuck would be quite welcome, and afterwards he could tell her what he really thought of her.

He'd better start rehearsing.

In the street where Ted Wheeler lived, half a dozen unruly kids were playing football. They scattered as Nick approached, scowling and muttering curses. He drove on a little further and parked.

"Shall I stay here?" Caitlin asked as he released his seat-belt.

"What, to guard the car?" He grinned. "No, I'd be glad of the moral support."

A few minutes later, as he knocked on the battered front door for the fifth time, he apologised for having dragged her on a wild goose chase.

"Oh well," he said. "The least I can do is treat you to lunch on the way back."

There was a noise as the letterbox flap opened and an elderly voice growled, "Why doncha fuck off?"

Nick snorted. "Ted Wheeler, I presume?"

"Never 'eard of 'im. Who wants to know?"

Nick crouched so that he was level with the letterbox. He could just make out a pair of rheumy, bloodshot eyes.

"I'm Nick Randall. Eddie Randall's son."

"I know who you mean. Move away, let me see your face."

Nick did as he was told, and a moment later they heard

the sound of bolts being drawn back. The door opened and Ted Wheeler stood there, a cadaverous old man leaning on a stick, wrapped in a oversized green cardigan with what appeared to be several baked beans stuck to it.

"Thought you'd turn up one of these days." He nodded at Caitlin. "Who's the bird?"

"This is Caitlin, my… er…"

"Girlfriend," Caitlin chipped in, with a smile.

Ted noted Nick's surprise, then grunted. "Wouldn't be so shy about it," he said. "She looks all right to me."

And without another word he turned and shuffled away, which Nick took as an invitation to follow. Stepping aside to allow Caitlin in first, he heard shouts from the footballers and saw they were harassing a Honda Civic trying to make a three-point turn.

Inside the house, Caitlin wrinkled her nose with distaste. "Urine?" she mouthed.

Nick sniffed, then nodded. In the course of hundreds of investigations he'd experienced far worse. "Five minutes and you won't notice it," he whispered.

Ted Wheeler was in a shabby living room, where an ancient TV was showing a Disney movie. The old man picked up a remote control and muted the sound. His hand trembled as he set it down.

"Who told you where I lived? Roger, was it?"

"Roger Knight? Yes."

"Bastard." Ted's eyes seemed to fill with tears. "Not safe, I am. I told him that. I told him."

"What do you mean?" Nick asked. He chose a rickety chair opposite Ted's and gingerly sat down. Caitlin remained in the doorway.

"Mickey Leach, one of my old partners. He died in a nursing home last year. I reckon he was murdered."

"Do you know why?"

Ted gave a wheezy sigh. "Could be all kinds of reasons. I got my own ideas."

Nick grew alarmed at the distant look in Ted's eyes. He didn't want to prolong his visit any more than was necessary.

He leant forward and said, "You know the reason I'm here, though?"

"Yeah. That fucking book."

"Has Howard Franks spoken to you?"

"Nah. Listen, I told all this to the other geezer, Roger. Why haven't you asked him?"

Nick looked at Caitlin, who gave a theatrical shrug.

"I'm sorry," Nick said. "Why don't you just run through what you told Roger?"

Ted eyed him carefully. He opened his mouth to talk but was overtaken by a bout of coughing. When it subsided, he wiped his mouth with the back of his hand and rubbed his hand on the crotch of his grimy trousers.

"Sure you wanna hear it?" he asked.

"I know Franks is alleging that my dad arranged for the murder of a man called Leslie Jones."

"Is he now?" Ted seemed both surprised and troubled, and Nick's heart flared with the hope that it was untrue.

"Is that what happened?"

"Pretty much," Ted agreed. "Did he tell you why it happened?"

"Something to do with a young girl." Nick gulped. He forced himself to add, "A girl who was raped and killed."

Now Ted looked offended. "That ain't right. It wasn't like anyone set out to kill her."

"But she did die in the nightclub?"

"Yeah."

"And was she raped?" Nick could hear a shake in his voice.

In the doorway, Caitlin had her hand over her mouth, her eyes wide with horror.

"Course not. That's bollocks. We just had sex with her, that's all. It was a party." Ted started coughing again, this time with a strange rhythm. Then he stopped wheezing long enough to add, "Wild party!" and Nick realised what it was.

The old man was laughing.

When she saw Nick park the Audi, Alex had to pull in quickly, blocking a driveway. Nick and the woman made for a rundown council house about a hundred feet from where she was sitting. Just ahead of her, a group of teenagers were playing football in the road, darting and leaping across her field of vision.

After an interminable wait, she almost missed the front door opening. She couldn't quite see the figure in the doorway, so she put the car in gear and moved back into the road, scattering the footballers.

Now she saw him: the spindly frame, the skeletal face and lank Brylcreemed hair. It had to be him.

The picture was complete. She had what she needed.

There was a jolt as one of the teenagers threw his weight against the car, shouting obscenities at her. Alex floored the accelerator and the boy spun away, falling to the ground. In her mirror she saw his friends gesturing angrily. She was tempted to reverse back into them, but cautioned herself not to lose control. There was too much at stake now.

She turned into London Road and headed for the A2, keeping to the speed limits until she was on the M25. She felt a rush of elation. Locating Wheeler was a major achievement: it warranted proper celebration.

And she had just the right thing in mind.

Half an hour had passed. Caitlin decided to make tea, partly to get her away from the dreadful story unfolding in the lounge. First she had to clear up the kitchen, which meant boiling kettles for washing up because there was no hot water.

By the time she'd scrubbed three chipped old mugs and carried them in on an ancient teatray, Nick and Ted were sharing a glum silence. When Nick looked up and thanked her, it seemed as though he had aged visibly since entering the house.

Caitlin sat on a sofa so matted with dirt it had changed colour: it might once have been blue. She took a sip of tea and went to put her mug down on the floor, suddenly spotting a dried lump of what could only be cat faeces. She swallowed heavily, praying not to be sick.

"Nice cuppa, this," said Ted, with an unashamedly lascivious chuckle. "You wanna job?"

Caitlin smiled politely, but said nothing.

"I can't work this out," Nick muttered. "You definitely haven't spoken to Howard Franks?"

"Course not. I ain't gonna, either."

"So who told him about Leslie Jones?"

"The man from the nursing home?" Caitlin suggested.

"Mickey?" said Ted. "Nah. He told Franks to piss off."

"You believed him?"

Ted's face darkened, and Caitlin recoiled from the ferocity of his expression. "Yeah, I fucking believed him."

"OK, OK." Nick waited for him to calm down. "Let's think about this. What if it was someone connected to the girl?"

Ted shook his head. "She was a runaway, a little street-walker. Nobody knew who she was, and nobody knew what happened to her, except us lot."

Nick asked, "Who, exactly?"

"Well, me, Ray. Mickey. Eddie."

"And Leslie Jones."

"Yeah. Course."

"And it was Leslie who tried to profit from the girl's death by blackmailing my dad?"

Ted nodded, a little more vigorously than before. He was starting to catch up with Nick's train of thought.

"All right. Let's concentrate on Leslie. Who else knew why he was killed?"

Ted had no trouble with that one. "Me, Ray, Mickey and your old man. And the guys that done the business, but they're both dead: one in prison a few years back, the other in a car accident."

"What if Leslie told someone what he'd seen?" Caitlin suggested.

Nick added, "His wife might have known about the blackmail. Was he married?"

"Oh yeah. Right sour old cow."

"Is she still alive?"

"How the fuck should I know? She ain't exactly sending me Christmas cards."

"Did they have children?" Nick said, and even as he spoke he had the same giddy feeling as when he'd asked Lauren Doyle about the number of gears in her Ford Escort.

"Yeah." Ted spoke slowly, struggling to reach back over so many years. "One of each, I think."

"How old was the boy when Leslie died, can you remember?"

There was an infuriating pause while Ted slurped noisily on his tea and cleared his throat. Then he nodded to himself.

"Something funny with him. Les never used his name. Called him the Spastic."

"You mean he was disabled?" Caitlin asked, and Nick could hear the disgust in her voice.

"Yeah. He's probably ended up in a home, if he hasn't croaked. They don't live as long as normal people, do they?" Oblivious to the offence he was causing, Ted added, "Should put 'em down at birth, if you ask me."

Nick checked his watch. He didn't know how long he could bear to stay here. He felt deflated, certain they'd been close to a breakthrough.

"Jones had a daughter as well?"

"Yeah. Now I do remember Les going on about her, how clever she was, always reading books and that."

"Do you know what happened to her?"

Ted gave Nick a contemptuous glare. "Don't know and don't care."

"How old would she be now? Can you work it out?"

An irritable shake of the head, which presaged another coughing fit. Nick glanced at Caitlin, who inclined her head slightly: we ought to go.

Nick nodded. But he knew he was on to something.

"You believe you're in danger. Isn't it possible that Jones's daughter knows why her father died?"

Ted suddenly went white. Caitlin half rose from her seat, certain the old man had suffered a stroke, but then he blinked rapidly and let out a juddering breath.

"Oh Christ," he said softly. "Oh fucking Christ in Heaven."

"What is it?" said Nick.

"Mickey Leach." He coughed. "Just before he died, he said he'd been having this new visitor. A young woman."

"How young?" Nick snapped, and for once the old man didn't take offence.

"Not a kid or nothing. Young to him." Another snort, which became a cough. "Cracking bit of skirt. You know what he said?" A pause for sad, fond recollection, and then he quoted: "'If I was ten years younger, I'd screw her till the baby pushed me off.'"

22

Nick and Caitlin emerged from the house and walked to the car in silence. As he fumbled for his keys, Nick felt a hand on his shoulder.

"Are you all right?"

He turned and met those bewitching eyes, filled with concern. She trailed her hand down his arm and briefly gripped his hand.

"It's going to take some time to sink in."

Back in the car, Caitlin said, "It sounds like Howard Franks holds the key to this. Are you going to speak to him?"

"I'll have to," Nick agreed. "Though I doubt he'll want to reveal his source."

She dug in her small handbag and produced a mobile phone. "What's his number?"

"I don't have it with me."

Caitlin tutted. She could hear the reluctance in his voice.

"Listen," she said, "I know it's not easy, but you can't turn away from it now."

Nick scowled. "You sound like my sister." He had a thought. "Actually, she'll have Howard's number. He wrote to her as well."

He relayed his sister's number. "Answer machine," Caitlin said, waiting for the signal to speak. Then, "Hi, Diana! You don't know me, but I'm a friend of Nick's. Could you give me a call when you get this, please? It's about Howard Franks." She reeled off her number and ended the call.

Nick was wryly shaking his head. "That'll set the cat amongst the pigeons."

"I only said 'friend'."

"She's my sister. She'll jump to conclusions."

There was an enigmatic smile on Caitlin's face. "Oh well," she said.

By the time they reached the M25 there had been no call, and Nick had abandoned any thoughts of visiting Franks. They drove on until he saw a sign for the services.

"How about if we stop here?" he said.

"When you said treat me to lunch, I didn't realise you meant McDonalds."

He laughed. "Neither did I. You don't mind, do you?"

"Course not. I'm dying for the loo. There was no way I'd have used Wheeler's."

The services car park was busy with holidaymakers taking advantage of the good weather. Oblivious to the noise and bustle, and the thunderous pounding of traffic on the motorway, Nick could only hear Ted Wheeler's voice.

"This idea that someone's after revenge," he said. "If you had a grudge against my dad and the others for what happened, there'd be no better source of information than Howard Franks. He's a former journalist. He has contacts all over the place to help him find people."

Someone's got it in for me.

An idea came and went in an instant, as Caitlin said, "He hasn't found Ted Wheeler."

"No. And Wheeler's still alive."

"What are you saying? Franks is connected to the deaths?"

Nick stopped short.

Someone's got it in for me. He recalled what he'd thought – and dismissed as egocentric.

He didn't dismiss it any longer.

Caitlin said, "I'm going to the Ladies. Will you be all right?"

181

"Uh, yeah. I'll wait here."

He made for a quiet corner by a display of tourist leaflets and took out his phone. DCI Pearce's mobile number was in the memory.

"Melanie Pearce."

"Melanie, it's Nick Randall. Sorry if you're off duty."

"Gardening, for my sins." She groaned. "Love the result, hate the work that goes into it."

"I've just had an idea. About Sarah's death."

Pearce's voice solemn now. "Go on."

"You know the witness saw her with someone on the cliffs. Is there any chance...?" He hesitated, a voice in his head now ridiculing the idea. "Could it have been a woman?"

"You think Sarah was with a woman?"

"Possibly. I just need to know if it's feasible."

Silence. Nick thought he'd lost the connection. He watched Caitlin emerge from the Ladies. She'd tidied up her hair, and perhaps added a little bit of make-up. He was struck by how beautiful she was. She seemed to stand out from everyone around her.

Pearce's voice came as a shock. "When we were checking CCTV we picked up a black Focus on the road near the hotel. We ruled it out because we could see the driver was female."

"Oh God." It came out as an exhalation.

Caitlin mouthed, "Diana?" and he shook his head.

"What makes you think it was a woman?"

"It's complicated. Can I see you tomorrow?"

"Of course. And I'll get someone to check out the car."

When he ended the call, he said, "No appetite, but I need a strong coffee."

"Not more bad news?"

"I think I know why Sarah died."

"Your wife?"

Nick nodded grimly. "And I think Ted Wheeler's quite right to be scared."

Lindsay arrived just when Howard was getting comfortable at his desk. As always when he'd finally begun to work, any interruption prompted huge resentment.

He opened the front door. Lindsay was wearing jeans and a FCUK t-shirt, and holding a Waitrose carrier bag. She pecked his cheek and marched towards the kitchen.

"Got some steaks," she said. "In case you didn't have any."

"You're still talking about a barbecue?"

"Why not? It's great weather for once."

Franks peered outside. "They forecast showers."

"Ah, don't be a killjoy."

He shut the door and followed her into the kitchen. She put her shopping in the fridge and took out a bottle of Australian Shiraz.

"Are you staying?" he asked ungraciously. His first thought was how he'd get rid of her if she drank too much.

She seemed unoffended. "I can have a couple of glasses."

"You don't mind if I just finish off what I'm doing? Only I'm in the middle of something."

"Surfing for porn?" Her tone was light, but it clearly wasn't meant as a joke. He assumed an expression of haughty offence.

"Working on the book."

"Don't look so hurt. How's it going?"

"Progressing nicely, thank you."

"I'll get to work like a dutiful little housewife, then. Rustle up a salad."

Franks nodded. He hated this, when he couldn't be sure

if she was teasing. His "Thank you" sounded formal and pompous.

She held the wine bottle by the neck and waved at it. "Shall I bring you some, or would you rather stay clear-headed?"

"A glass would be nice."

Lindsay winked. "Maybe I'll crawl under your desk and surprise you!"

"Really?"

"We'll see."

She turned away, put the wine down on a worktop and opened the fridge again. He watched her for a second, admiring the curve of her buttocks in the tight denim. He'd miss her body, but that was all.

Climbing the stairs, he reworked a bit of the speech he was planning to deliver later, when he'd got what he wanted.

All these snide comments you seem to think are so funny, and yet like most Americans of my acquaintance, you possess no real wit or repartee. The truth is, Lindsay, I don't find you remotely amusing.

The burger bar was crowded and noisy. Caitlin offered to get a takeaway but Nick felt they might as well stay where they were. He emptied five sachets of sugar into the coffee and picked up the little red stirrer. "I never know which end to use," he said absently. "Why can't they just give you a bloody spoon…"

Caitlin chuckled. This was the first time he'd seemed anything like normal since he finished speaking to DCI Pearce. She was still waiting for the right moment to ask him about it.

Gripping her chicken burger in both hands, she said,

"Promise not to watch me eat. I make a terrible mess."

"Me too. Squeeze the wrong place and… plop!"

She smiled, saw the sadness return to his face, and said, "Tell me about the phone call."

He pulled a face. "I'm almost starting to doubt it now. You see, the police thought my wife might have been having an affair. A witness saw her with someone on the cliffs, but the description was too vague to be of any use. Jeans, a jacket, and a woolly hat."

"Do you think that was intentional? The hat, I mean. From a distance it's impossible to say anything about hair colour, the shape of your face…"

"Your gender."

"You think she was with a woman?"

"It's got to be worth checking." He told her what DCI Pearce had said about the Focus spotted on CCTV, and added, "It could be the same woman who visited Mickey Leach."

"Oh my God." Caitlin chewed slowly, working over the implications in her mind. "If you're right, and she did go to Howard Franks for information, he'll be able to tell you who she is."

"I hope so." He checked his watch, wondering where his sister had got to, and at that moment his phone rang. Diana.

"What's happened?" she said. "I took the kids swimming and got home to find a strange message…"

"That was Caitlin," said Nick wryly. "She's with me now."

"Okaaaay." Diana wrestled with her curiosity. "I don't suppose you can elaborate for me?"

"Not really. I just need Franks's phone number."

"But we agreed not to speak to him."

"I know, but things have changed. Please, Di."

She grunted. "Hold on."

He glanced at Caitlin and raised his eyebrows. "Fairly painless interrogation."

"She'll wait till I'm not around," Caitlin said.

Diana came back. "You're in luck. I thought I'd thrown it away." She gave him the number and then said, "I want a full explanation, Nick."

"Yeah, I know –"

"Not just Franks. This woman. It's none of my business, but don't you think it's a bit soon?"

He caught Caitlin's eye and felt himself blushing. "I'll ring you later," he said, quickly ending the call.

"What did she say?"

Nick shook his head. "Are you ready to go?"

"You look embarrassed." They stood up, and as she moved past she nudged him in the side. "You can tell me later."

He grinned. "That's what she said."

Howard was doodling on a notepad when the phone rang. He had his manuscript up on the screen in case Lindsay walked in, but he had little interest in writing.

At first he thought he was hearing things. Or maybe it was a practical joke. "Nick Randall?"

"I need to ask you something."

Franks felt a tingle of excitement. "You've reconsidered?"

A noise from Randall, possibly a snort. "Not exactly."

"Then why should I help you?" He sat up straight, preparing for combat.

"Listen," Nick said. "I don't have time to argue. This is important."

The reception on the mobile phone wasn't particularly good – Franks thought he could hear traffic – but Nick's

186

voice had a genuine note of concern about it.

"Very well," he said. "What is it?"

"The allegations about Dad. Leslie Jones's murder…" Nick sounded breathless, obviously keyed up about something. "I need to know where you got your information."

Franks threw back his head and laughed. "So that's your game, is it?"

"There's no game —"

"Too many years as a journalist, Mr Randall. You think I'm going to roll over for you? Well, forget it. What are you doing, negotiating a deal with a ghostwriter?"

Silence. Franks wondered if Nick had ended the call. He hoped not. He had plenty more to say yet.

When Nick spoke again, his voice was almost too quiet to make out, and its solemnity made Franks uncomfortable. "I need to know because I think you're in danger."

Franks forced a laugh, but it didn't sound convincing. "Are you threatening me?"

"I'm warning you, for Christ's sake! How did you find out about Leslie Jones?"

Franks hesitated. It went against his nature to supply information without getting something in return, but Nick's tone was disquieting. Besides, he told himself, he needn't be too specific.

"It was someone with a link to the studios. A member of the production staff."

"Dad wouldn't have confided in anyone at a studio."

"You do accept the allegations, then?" Franks couldn't resist gloating, but Nick completely ignored the question.

"Did you speak to this person first-hand?"

"Well, I can't…"

"Yes or no?" Nick was shouting. Franks thought he heard another voice in the background, urging him to calm down.

He said, "Actually, her daughter told me."

"Her daughter? Who is she?"

"You know I can't tell you that."

"OK, OK." Nick took a deep breath. "Just tell me this: did you find her or did she come to you?"

"I don't see the relevance," Franks said, "but she approached me after reading an article about my book."

"It's your researcher, isn't it? Lindsay?"

"Look here, I'm quite willing to have a sensible discussion, but —"

"I'm right, aren't I? What sort of car does she drive?"

Now Franks was utterly perplexed, and could only repeat, "What car…?"

He heard Nick shout, "Is it a Focus?" and then the line went dead. At first he thought the signal had been lost. He made to dial 1471 to retrieve the number but there was no dialling tone.

Sensing movement, he turned and saw Lindsay crouching by the door. She held the phone plug in one hand and a pair of garden shears in the other.

"Lindsay? What are you doing?"

"These?" She hefted the shears. "Found them while I was hunting for briquettes. Ideally they need sharpening, but I'm sure they'll do the job."

Franks was pointing dumbly at the phone. "Why did you…?"

"Disconnect you?" she said cheerily. "Because if you're going to find out the truth, I'd rather you heard it from me."

23

"Funny," Nick said.

"What?"

"Got cut off." He stared at the phone's display, wondering if he'd inadvertently disconnected it.

"I'm still trying to catch up here," said Caitlin. "You think the woman who came to your house is the one…?" She left the question incomplete, and for that Nick was grateful.

He redialled and listened, the frustration growing on his face. They were in the car park, standing each side of his Audi.

"No answer," he said at last.

"That's a bit odd, isn't it?"

"He thinks I want the information to write a book of my own."

Caitlin, opening her door, caught the look on Nick's face. "The other possibility…"

"… is that she's there with him."

"You don't think she'd do anything?" She left the question hanging a moment. Then, "Where does he live?"

"Uh? North London, Highgate. I'll have to ring Diana again."

"Come on, then." She marched around the car and held out her hand. "I'll drive."

"You're not insured," he said.

"Doesn't matter. You've got calls to make." She snatched the keys from his hand and climbed into the driver's seat. "Quickly!"

*

Lindsay approached the desk, holding the shears in both hands. Franks sat rooted to his chair, wishing he'd paid more attention to Nick's call.

"What are you doing? Go back downstairs."

Lindsay laughed, a sound that Franks had never much enjoyed and now found chilling. She reached the desk and held the shears out, the blades pointed at his chest. He debated whether he could disarm her and she anticipated his thoughts.

"Not a chance, Frankie."

Her voice sounded different, strange, but he couldn't work out why. He puffed out his chest and said, "I demand an explanation."

She chuckled. "You really can't help yourself, can you?"

"I thought we had a relationship."

"That's rich. What you mean is, you thought you were exploiting me for information and sex."

He said nothing, but his expression gave him away. The change in her voice was still troubling him.

"The thing is, Mr Smartarse Biographer, it was the other way round. I was exploiting you."

"But why?"

"My father. Funny how everyone's so interested in him now, when there's money to be made, reputations at stake. Nobody gave a toss when he was killed."

Franks shut his eyes, cursing his own sloppiness. He should never have accepted her story at face value. Normally he'd try to verify any information, especially when it was offered to him on a plate, but on this occasion lust had won the day.

"Leslie Jones?"

"Give the man a prize."

And now he had it: the American accent had gone and

in its place a featureless Home Counties tone. Perhaps a hint of South London roughness, burnished by education and travel.

She stepped back, flicked the shears to her right. "Into the bedroom."

He gripped the sides of his chair. "Please," he said. "I can help you. We can really make Randall suffer for this."

"Oh, I did that when I killed his wife." She spoke so casually that it took a few seconds for him to comprehend. "Right now, I'm more concerned with making you suffer."

"What have I done?"

"Raped me, for a start."

"What? That's preposterous. Everything we did was consensual."

"One more chance," she said. "The bedroom."

Truculently, he said, "No. I've nothing to apologise for."

He saw her look away and followed her line of vision, realising too late it was a bluff. He tried to raise his hands as the shears swung at his head, but he wasn't quick or strong enough to deflect the blow.

They were slowing down at the approach to the Dartford Tunnel when Nick's phone rang. It was Melanie Pearce, and she sounded excited.

"I've had someone look at the Focus. The CCTV was clear enough to read the plate, but I'm afraid –"

"Registered with false details?"

"Afraid so." She sounded suspicious. "You seem to know more than I do."

Nick quickly ran through the situation with Howard Franks. When he finished, Pearce said, "I also rang the witness. He's pretty sure Sarah was with a man, but then admitted that was largely because of the height difference."

"The woman I'm picturing is tall and broad-shouldered."

"You've met her?"

"That's another story," said Nick. "Do you think I could be right?"

"Using an untraceable car suggests pre-planning. You need to see the CCTV as soon as possible."

"OK. We're about to go into the tunnel so we might lose you. There's one other thing."

Pearce groaned. "Go on."

"I spoke to Franks about half an hour ago, but the call was disconnected and now I can't get through. I'm worried this woman, Lindsay, might be there."

Pearce didn't hesitate. "Give me his address. I'll get a car sent round."

Nick read out the address. "Take care," said Pearce. "Don't approach the house till the police arrive."

"They'll be there long before us," said Nick. He ended the call and added sadly, "I hope."

Caitlin glanced over, then gave his leg a friendly squeeze. "We've done our best," she said.

When Franks regained consciousness he found himself stripped naked and lying spread-eagled on the bed, his hands and feet securely bound to each corner of the frame. In a bitter irony, the restraints were a set of silk ropes he'd purchased for use in sex games with various lovers – games in which Lindsay had refused to participate.

She had also stuffed a handkerchief in his mouth and run packing tape over it. He had to swallow constantly to suppress the gag reflex. He knew if he vomited he could choke to death.

His head was throbbing from the blow with the shears, and he could feel blood trickling over his ear. He struggled to lift his head a few inches from the mattress and saw he was alone. He listened intently, praying she'd thought better of her actions and fled the house. Found himself compiling an inventory of the precious items she might have stolen.

Then the sound of movement downstairs brought him back to reality, and the most precious item of all: himself.

She's not going anywhere, idiot. She hasn't had her fun yet.

He let out a hopeless sigh and stared at the ceiling. How on earth had he landed in a situation like this?

A familiar hissing noise caused him to frown. Furniture polish? The woman was a psychopath. Why would she tie him up and then start on the housework?

It was such a ridiculous image, his body trembled with hysterical laughter. Then it occurred to him that she was wiping away fingerprints, erasing all trace of her presence.

In a frenzy he began pulling on the restraints, ignoring the pain as they bit into his skin and drew blood. He tried to cry out but the gag moved deeper into his throat. He choked, phlegm and bile spraying from his nostrils.

"Afternoon naps. Aren't they refreshing?"

She moved into his eye line and stood at the foot of the bed. She was wearing an apron and rubber gloves.

"Quite a fashion accessory," she said, displaying her arms and flexing the fingers. "Or are they another of your sex toys?"

He shook his head. Perhaps she was some kind of insane puritan.

"Shame we missed out on the barbecue," Lindsay continued. "I'd intended this for after the meal, but Randall seems to have excelled at playing detective. Ah well. I'll take the steaks with me, if it's all the same to you?"

She waited for an answer, and then tutted. "Silly me. You can't speak, can you?" She moved around the bed and he squirmed, contorting himself in a futile attempt to keep away from her.

"It's not pleasant, is it, that feeling in your throat?" She leant over the bed, her face inches from his. "That's what it's like having your filthy cock in my mouth. And I had to *enjoy* it."

She turned and bent down by the bed, picking up something from the floor. He shut his eyes, then decided it was worse not to know.

When he opened them, she was holding the shears.

He started thrashing uselessly, making a terrible crooning noise in his throat, some distant part of his brain registering pity at his lack of dignity. A rush of warmth flooded his thigh as his bladder opened.

Lindsay watched with the expression of detached amusement that he knew only too well. "Good idea," she said. "Savour that last one while you can."

It took him a second to work out what she meant. By then she'd moved down the bed, and he heard a metallic rasp as the blades opened.

He tried to scream as the shears brushed against his belly and closed around the soft, delicate skin of his shrivelled penis.

It took Nick and Caitlin over an hour to reach Franks's home, in a leafy exclusive part of Highgate. Nick thought it might be difficult locating the exact address, but he needn't have worried. An ambulance and a cluster of police vehicles marked the house, blue lights reflecting against the windows.

"Uh oh," said Caitlin.

"Quite," said Nick. "Do you have a feeling we're too late?"

Caitlin parked as close as she could and they got out of the car. A couple of uniformed officers were unrolling crime scene tape around the perimeter of the property. The WPC intercepted them as they approached.

"Other side of the road, if you wouldn't mind, folks."

"Is this where Howard Franks lives?"

"You know him, do you?"

"We're the reason you're here," Nick said. He explained his call to DCI Pearce, and her decision to alert the Metropolitan police. The WPC listened with undisguised scepticism and then went inside the house. She returned almost immediately with a slender grey-haired man of about fifty, who introduced himself as Detective Chief Inspector Phil Clements.

"I spoke to DCI Pearce a little earlier," he said in a soft Welsh accent. "I take it you're Mr Randall?"

"That's right. Can you tell us what happened?"

"I think your phone call saved his life, that's what happened."

Nick found it difficult to conceal his surprise. His own interpretation was that he had sealed Franks's fate, but perhaps DCI Clements hadn't worked that out yet.

"It was an extremely savage attack," Clements explained. "If it was this woman that DCI Pearce described, she left him to bleed to death." He nodded back at the house. "As it was it's taken the paramedics quite some time to stabilise him. They're preparing to move him now."

"Will he be all right?" Caitlin asked.

The detective shrugged. "They expect him to live, if that's what you mean."

"What did she do?" said Nick.

For a moment he seemed reluctant to tell them. "It

looks like she knocked him unconscious and tied him to his bed…" The detective glanced back at the house, and winced. "Then she castrated him."

Part Three

September 2003

A visit to a hospice on a bright, cold afternoon changed Alex's life completely. With secondary tumours ravaging her body, Hilda Jones was rapidly shrinking, bitterness and hostility leaking from her like acid. All she ever talked about was the money.

Hilda's spinster sister had died the year before and left everything to her only niece: Alex. Thanks to the overheated property market her modest bungalow in Dorchester fetched nearly two hundred thousand pounds. For Hilda, who'd never owned property or had any savings, it was a catastrophic blow. By that stage the cancer was too far advanced for the money to be of any use, but it didn't stop her griping about what might have been.

"Could have had one of those luxury cruises," was a typical lament. "I always wanted to see the Mediterranean."

"You hate foreigners, remember?" Alex would say.

"I hate 'em living in Croydon. Wouldn't mind if they was serving me drinks and cleaning up after me."

On her way up, one of the nurses had drawn Alex aside and warned of her decline. Alex was careful to exhibit the right degree of concern, and made sure she expressed her admiration for the palliative care staff.

There was a smell of decay in her mother's room, impervious to the cleaning solvents and the bouquet of freesias that Alex had dutifully supplied. She pulled up a chair by the bedside and regarded what seemed no more than a husk beneath the blankets. She pictured a roaring furnace as her mother's body was committed to the flames. Found herself licking her lips in anticipation.

Two weeks ago she'd happened upon a *Sunday Times* feature on Howard Franks. Her impression was of an arrogant self-publicist, but his intended biography of Eddie Randall had intrigued her. After years of trying to forget what had happened to her father, years of unhappiness, of failed relationships and thwarted ambition, she'd begun to wonder if she should confront her feelings rather than suppress them. Perhaps it was time to do something to correct the injustice.

If she could get close to Franks she'd have a rich source of information about the men who conspired to kill her father. What she would do with that information exactly, she could decide later.

Her mother stirred and made a cracking, stuttering sound. Alex lifted her head slightly and moistened the old woman's throat with a sip of water.

"Billy?" she gasped, her eyes still shut. In her lucid moments she complained about the money. The rest of the time, drifting on morphine dreams, she talked to her son. There was a tiny ragged photograph of him by her bed, taken the Christmas before he died: eight-year-old Billy proudly clutching a new football. No pictures of her daughter, Alex noted.

"It's me, Mum," she said. "Billy's dead."

Hilda sank back into the pillow and was almost engulfed by it. After a couple of ragged breaths she said, "You killed him, didn't you?"

Alex faked incomprehension, but underneath she was running through her options. Who knew? Who would believe it? Would she have to silence her mother right here and now? She glanced round, checking for eavesdroppers at the door.

"Why do you say that?"

"Billy was careful in the water. He was scared of the sea." A single tear leaked from her closed eyes. "Pity he wasn't scared of you."

Alex said nothing. She folded her arms and waited.

"First my Leslie. Then Billy. All I had."

The remark was a clumsy attempt to wound her, but Alex remained impassive.

"Tell me what happened," Hilda said. "Nothing I can do now, is there? I just want you to admit it."

Alex shrugged, smiled a gloating smile. "All right. I killed Billy. I held his head under the water and watched him die."

Hilda didn't speak for a long time. Alex began to think she'd fallen asleep. How easy it would be to press her mother's face into the pillow and have done with it. She hadn't killed for more than five years, and suddenly she realised how hungry she was to experience that power again.

And then the old woman's eyes sprang open, and she uttered the words that opened the door: "You weren't his, you know."

Alex gulped, then hated herself for the satisfaction it gave her mother. "What do you mean?"

"Leslie. He wasn't your dad. We'd only just got together when I found out I was carrying you."

Alex examined her mother's face carefully. The old witch might have concocted the story to torment her.

"Then who…?"

"Ha!" An exhalation of pure disgust. "He was evil. A monster. Just like you."

"What do you mean?"

"Lowest of the low. A man who enjoyed hurting people. And when he wanted a woman, he took her."

Alex hesitated. The information was coming too fast to process. "You mean he raped you?"

"Yeah. And I got you in return. The devil's daughter."

Alex turned away. This time she was struggling to hide her pain and confusion. Hilda was trying to lift her head, a dark intensity in her eyes.

"He's rotting in hell now. And one day you'll join him." Her cracked lips began to quiver. "My Billy wouldn't hurt a fly. You didn't have to… didn't have to…"

She couldn't continue, and Alex in any event was no longer listening. She walked to the window and gazed out over the grounds of the hospice, the oak trees around the perimeter shivering in the wind. A plane rose out of Heathrow, cutting a bloodless incision in the sky.

Leslie and Alex, proud father and devoted daughter. Them against the world.

She spun round and returned to the bed, jostling her mother when the old woman refused to acknowledge her presence.

"Did Dad know? Did he know I wasn't his?"

"Course he knew, silly cow. It was him that made me keep you. Weren't my idea."

"But why? Why would he…?" Baffled, she let the question hang in the overheated air.

"Because he was a good man. Decent. Just never had a chance in life, that's all. There's some that get it all handed on a plate, while the likes of my Leslie…"

Her voice grew weaker as the familiar litany emerged, until she was barely mouthing the words. Alex closed her eyes and experienced a moment of pure delight as the purpose of her existence became clear.

It was Leslie who had made her life possible. And he had loved her like a real daughter, cherished her as nobody

201

before or since had done. That made his death all the more unjust, and Alex vowed right then that everyone associated with it would be punished, and their families made to suffer. This was her mission. Her project.

Her mother died that night. The next day a woman named Lindsay Price sent an email to Howard Franks's publishers.

24

It was after ten o'clock when Nick and Caitlin emerged from the police station in Hornsey, where they'd given lengthy statements and also, in Nick's case, been party to a conference call with DCI Pearce in Eastbourne. Over the course of a long evening Nick helped piece together an increasingly frightening scenario in which the daughter of a small-time 1960s villain had embarked on a mission of revenge against the men she held responsible for her father's death.

Leslie's daughter had been identified as Alex Jones, born February 1959, whose last known whereabouts was West Yorkshire, where she had worked in the microbiology department at the Leeds General Infirmary in the mid-1990s. After that, nothing. But Nick told them he was almost certain Sarah had been befriended by a woman called Alex a few months before her death. The detectives agreed that tracing Alex Jones would be their top priority.

In the meantime DCI Clements intended to hunt down and review what paperwork still existed for Leslie Jones's murder. Other officers were assigned to investigate Mickey Leach's death in a Bedford nursing home. And someone would be speaking to Ted Wheeler.

"Becoming Franks's girlfriend was a masterstroke on her part," Nick said. "It gave her access to everything he knew."

"If that's what happened," Clements said, and then conceded, "although it does seem the likeliest explanation."

"I suppose we should be grateful Franks never managed to find Wheeler."

"Hmm. I don't anticipate much co-operation there," Clements observed. "An old pro like Wheeler won't risk incriminating himself."

Nick had mixed feelings about this. He'd felt duty bound to explain the allegations that Alex, posing as Lindsay, had made about his father, but Clements had greeted them with a degree of scepticism.

"What I can't guarantee," he cautioned, "is that the press won't hear about it."

Nick nodded. "Howard Franks will see to that, I'm sure."

"If he lives to tell the tale."

"If it's not him, it'll be someone else." Nick knew that might sound callous, but by then he was past caring.

Just before they left there was an update from the officer who'd accompanied Franks to hospital. Clements took the call and turned to Nick with a glint of humour in his eyes. "He's going to make it. Whether he'll have much in the way of manhood is another matter. Is he the kind of guy who'll miss it?"

"Is there a kind who wouldn't?" Caitlin said, and both men laughed.

The journey home began in silence. Nick put on a CD of Leonard Cohen covers. Caitlin listened to a couple of tracks, then screwed up her face. "What on earth is this?"

"Nick Cave's version of *Tower of Song.*"

"You have a bizarre taste in music."

"It is a slightly strange interpretation." He realised he felt a little hurt, accompanied by an absurd thought: is this our first row? He skipped to the next track. "Try this," he said. "John Cale, *Hallelujah.*"

"I've heard this," she said after the first verse.

He risked a glance and saw her nod appreciatively. "Better?"

"It's beautiful."

There were queues on the M25, and Nick remembered with a jolt that it was Easter Monday. Joining the M23, they watched traffic streaming northbound, holidaymakers returning home from a day at the coast. Cars full of people with enviably normal, straightforward lives.

"You can't be sure," Caitlin said when he voiced his thoughts. "People can live in all sorts of turmoil and you'd never know it to look at them."

He conceded the point, wondering to what extent she was speaking from experience. He knew she had phoned Roger from the police station and explained a little of the day's events.

At Pease Pottage she dug in her handbag and brought out her mobile. "I'd better call him."

Nick nodded and turned the volume down. "I can't really drive with my fingers in my ears. Well, I could try…"

She gave him a playful punch. "We won't be whispering sweet nothings".

"If you say so."

"I do." She sighed. "Been through that and come out the other side."

The tone of her voice changed when Roger answered, becoming flat and emotionless. He seemed to do most of the talking, Caitlin only punctuating with "Mmm" and "No", and several times, "I'm not sure". Then a final "Right", that sounded sorrowful.

Afterwards she said, "He kept asking when I'd be home."

Nick looked at the clock. "Maybe twenty minutes."

She sighed. There was a long pause, and he sensed her running through the words before she said them aloud.

"I don't know if I can deal with him tonight. There's so much he'll want to know…"

"Would you rather stay at my place?"

"Do you mind? Otherwise I've got some friends in Kemp Town."

"No. You're welcome."

"You have a spare room?"

He smiled wryly. "I have a spare room."

"Or the sofa would do. If it's a problem."

"I've got a spare room."

Alex made straight for the flat in Kingston and cleaned up, then collected the bag she kept packed for just such eventualities. It contained all she would need for a few days away, lying low and waiting out the storm of police activity that was bound to follow. The flat was rented in a false name and she remained confident that it could still be used, but it seemed prudent to wait at a distance and be sure.

Besides, after today's events she would have to reappraise her enemy. Nick had somehow made the connection that she was Lindsay. She couldn't rule out that he would also link her to Sarah's death. And there was the question of what Ted Wheeler might have told him.

It wasn't all bad news, of course. There was the immense satisfaction she'd gained in emasculating Howard Franks. And Nick had also led her – unwittingly, she was sure – to Ted Wheeler.

Even so, she knew her next move was unwise. If Nick proved to be one step ahead rather than a step behind, armed police could be waiting for her right now. And because she had to hurry, there was no time for reconnaissance. She might be driving straight into a trap.

Nevertheless, she felt the prize more than warranted the risk. This was the one target that had remained frustratingly elusive. The man who, after Eddie Randall, bore the greatest responsibility for her father's death.

This time she parked in the next street and made her approach on foot. The road was quiet, but not suspiciously so; there was a couple chewing each other's faces off in a doorway. She watched them carefully, decided they were genuine.

The weather had deteriorated during the day, so her thick jacket and beanie hat didn't look out of place. Waiting at the front door, she presented few distinguishing characteristics to any witnesses.

The target was slow to answer. She heard him grumbling as he reached the door and pushed open the letterbox flap.

"Who is it?"

"My name's Caitlin. I need to warn you about Nick Randall."

"Nick…?" He sounded confused.

"Nick Randall," she spoke quietly to the letterbox. "We came to see you this afternoon."

"You're the bird from earlier?"

"Yes. Can I come in? I think you're in danger."

She heard a bolt retracting, and the door opened a fraction. Ted was muttering to himself, puzzling over something.

"You know full well I am. It's that bloody —"

Too late, the penny dropped. He tried to slam the door but she threw her weight against it. He didn't stand a chance, falling backwards and crying out in pain.

She stepped inside, wrinkling her nose at the smell. Wheeler was on his knees, clutching one of the spindles on the staircase and trying to haul himself up. Alex closed the front door with a deft backheel and pulled the hammer from her pocket. As with Franks, the time for subtlety was over.

"So you're Leslie's kid?" Wheeler said, his old man's voice weak and gasping.

She thought of how her father had died and a wave of savage aggression took control. In a second she had brought the hammer down once, twice, and was rising for the third blow when she forced herself to stop.

Before he died, he would answer her questions.

Although Nick was exhausted when they reached home, he didn't feel he could suggest going straight to bed. He suspected Caitlin was equally reluctant to raise the subject, so they drank some coffee and yawned, watched a little TV, yawned some more.

And then out of nowhere Caitlin said, "That night Kevin Doyle broke in, he thought it was a woman who interrupted them."

Nick nodded. "I was thinking the same thing. Alex Jones."

"So she's been watching you."

"I've got to assume so."

She shivered. "It's scary. I mean, no one's safe until she's caught."

"I'm trying not to think about that. Not now, anyway." He yawned again, and so did Caitlin.

She stood up. "I really have to go to bed. I'm shattered."

"Me too. Come on."

She helped him check that all the doors and windows were locked, and then followed him upstairs. He showed her into the second bedroom.

"If you need a change of clothes, a t-shirt and underwear, there are still some of Sarah's…"

"I'll be fine. Thanks."

"OK. There's a spare toothbrush in the bathroom. I think." He shoved his hands in his pockets and stood uselessly for a moment, feeling like a teenager again.

She took a step towards him and examined his face. "Are you all right?"

"I don't know," he admitted. "I've been thinking about Sarah. Before today I thought the worst thing was not knowing why she died. If I could just understand the reason…" He gave a hollow laugh. "And now I know she was probably killed because of me. It was my fault."

"No. You mustn't see it like that." She reached out and gently stroked his arm. His instinct was to shrug it off; it felt too dangerous to succumb to her comfort, as though he would be taking advantage of her. But then he opened his arms and they embraced, hugging each other tight.

Feeling her warmth, breathing the scent of her skin and hair, he knew he didn't want to let her go. He wanted to undress and lie beside her, holding her close for the rest of the night. But he couldn't assume she wanted the same thing, and the part of him that might have chanced it – what his sister called the charmer - could not summon the audacity to make the move. She had helped him enough, hadn't she?

Reluctantly he broke contact. "I want to thank you," he said. "I'm sorry for what I put you through today."

"Don't apologise. We're in this together now."

She kissed him quickly on the lips. "Now vamoosh. I need some sleep."

Feeling a little heartsick, he shut his bedroom door and lay down, running through the events of an extraordinary day. There was something nagging at him, he couldn't quite get it and knew he wouldn't sleep until he did.

Wheeler. Something to do with Wheeler.

He felt himself becoming drowsy, pushing away memories of the old man's face, the dreadful way he laughed while discussing the death of a young girl. A death that his own father might have caused.

Then Caitlin, tonight, arriving at the same conclusion about Alex.

She's been watching me.

Not just watching. Following.

His body jerked, and he realised he'd been asleep for a few seconds. He tried to fight it but couldn't. Didn't want to. In the morning he'd put it together. He'd speak to DCI Pearce. Had to tell her about Alex, discuss the implications.

Tomorrow.

While Nick slept, Alex Jones drank a celebratory vodka in a modest hotel room in Cromer, on the Norfolk coast. She booked in under a false name, went straight to her room and had a long, hot shower. Then she turned on the TV and caught the late evening news. There was a brief report that the writer Howard Franks had been wounded in an assault at his London home. No other information. No appeal for witnesses. No details of the suspect.

She wondered what to make of this. Was it possible the police doubted Nick's story? Did they have other leads to follow before releasing any more information to the media?

Either way, she couldn't let it trouble her. Tomorrow she'd make some changes to her appearance, have her hair cut short. For now, she knew beyond doubt she was safe. It was time to relax and consider her achievements.

Killing Ted Wheeler had been almost pathetically easy, which had diminished the pleasure slightly. The challenge had been to make him talk without any noise alerting his neighbours. She'd turned up the TV as loud as she dared, so that Ted's last moments on earth were accompanied by the tired clichés of *EastEnders*.

Between questions she used a cushion to muffle his screams. A couple of times she held it in place too long and he blacked out. She had to keep reminding herself that he was old now. Weak and puny.

It took half an hour to satisfy herself that he'd told her everything. She learned that Nick had located Wheeler through Roger Knight, the name she'd first heard when she was at Nick's house, posing as Lindsay. What she hadn't known was that Knight was a nephew of the late Ray McPherson, and now ran a car bodyshop in West Sussex.

After telling her about Knight, Wheeler spat blood and a tooth on to the carpet and said, "Your dad, he shouldn't have gone after Randall. You must see that."

Alex smiled a ghastly smile. "You'll forgive me if I don't."

"He worked for me. I couldn't let him pull a stunt like that. If he was a bit strapped for cash he should've come to me. I'd have seen him right."

"I'm sure you were a generous employer."

Ted shook his head and groaned. If he was ever going to throw himself at her mercy, now would be the time. Instead he said, "Ah, fuck it. Just get it over with."

By this time she was ready to oblige. She'd had enough of him, enough of his filthy home, the stench of cat shit and cigarette butts, of blood and sweat and decay. She lifted him into a sitting position on the threadbare carpet and moved behind him, placing one arm around his neck.

Wheeler refused to show any fear. He coughed, spat into his lap and said, "Mickey Leach said you was a decent bit of skirt."

"How charming."

211

"Yeah. You ain't my type, though." And he let out a wheezy cackle. "I like 'em young."

For a moment Alex laughed with him. Then she broke his neck.

When she was satisfied he was dead she lifted the body into an armchair and lowered the volume of the TV. Three hours later she was in Cromer, a location she had selected for sentimental reasons. After all, it was here she had first learned what she was capable of.

She even said a prayer for Billy before falling into a deep, untroubled sleep. She had much to thank him for.

25

Nick woke at seven and immediately resumed his train of thought from the night before. This time he had it instantly. He leapt out of bed and ran downstairs, searching his wallet for DCI Clements's card. The detective had said he could use the mobile number at any time.

Clements answered on the third ring, sounding alert. Nick could hear barking.

"Quiet, Sammy," the detective said. And to Nick, "Best part of the day, taking the dog for a walk."

"I've just realised something," said Nick. "I think Alex Jones has been following me. If she has, she might know where to find Ted Wheeler."

He relayed Wheeler's address from memory and Clements said he'd ring Kent police and get an officer sent round. "You won't be happy till half the forces in England are involved in this," the detective said ruefully before he rang off.

Hearing movement upstairs, he put the kettle on and found some mugs. He was prising slices from a frozen loaf of bread when Caitlin wandered in, wearing an old towelling robe of his.

"Early bird, aren't you?" she said.

He explained the reason for calling Clements. "Sorry if I woke you."

"It's OK. I couldn't really sleep, to be honest."

She asked if she could have a shower, and while she was gone Nick had toast and coffee, then made some for Caitlin.

"What will you do today?" she asked. They were both

leaning against kitchen units. She seemed no more keen than he was to sit down and eat a formal breakfast together.

"A meeting with DCI Pearce this morning. Then I need to try and explain all this to Diana. What about you?"

"First I have to see if my car's still intact."

"Oh God." Nick had forgotten they'd met at Devil's Dyke. "I'll give you a lift up there."

It wasn't quite eight o'clock when they left the house, the air cool and fresh, promising a perfect spring day. He parked next to her car and they got out.

"I hope this won't cause too much trouble with Roger," he said.

"It can hardly have made things worse."

At the moment of parting, they hesitated. The emotional intensity of the previous night had subsided, leaving only friendship and slight embarrassment. Finally she gave him a friendly pat on the arm and got into her car.

He watched her drive away, imagining the kiss they should have shared, and tried not to feel forlorn.

Roger was in bed when he heard the car pull up. Last night the phone had rung in the early hours, startling him awake. He'd grabbed it up, wondering what sort of trouble Caitlin was in, only to find it was his daughter, Sally, thrilled by a huge thunderstorm in Antigua. She'd forgotten about the time difference, and he didn't have the heart to scold her.

She was trying to describe the intensity of the rain when Lynn took the phone and said, "Roger, I'm sorry. I didn't know she was going to call. What time is it there?"

"Half past one. Don't worry."

They chatted for a couple of minutes. He wished her a safe journey home, and then said, "I was thinking of coming up to Scotland for a few days, maybe next week. I'd really like to see the kids."

Lynn sounded cautious. "They'll be back at school."

"I know. And I don't expect you to put me up. I'll stay in a hotel."

"Will the lovely thespian be with you?"

"No." He said it more emphatically than he'd intended.

There was a pause. Then she said, "I'll call you when I get back. Sunday, OK?"

Afterwards he'd lain awake for a couple of hours, made himself a hot chocolate and sat in bed, wondering where Caitlin was, or more precisely wondering what she was doing. He couldn't understand why he felt jealous rather than relieved, and then had to remind himself there might be nothing to be jealous or relieved about.

Now, at eight-thirty, the front door opened and he listened to her moving about downstairs. He was trying to summon the will to get up when there was a tap on the door and she came in. She was wearing the same clothes as yesterday, and her face looked tired and drawn, a little of the sparkle missing from her eyes.

"Hi," she said, and waited. It felt like the opening move in a chess game.

"Are you late or early?"

She frowned, not getting his meaning at first. "Oh no, I've been to bed. I stayed in Nick Randall's spare room."

He digested the information slowly. "Do you want to explain what happened yesterday?"

She sat down on a corner of the bed and began absently stroking the duvet. "I went to see Nick about the insurance claims."

"What have you told him?"

"That you're no longer involved. That you were nothing

215

to do with the break-in."

"He knows that was Kevin? Oh fuck." He stared at the duvet for a long time. "I suppose he'll go to the police?"

"I don't know. He's got rather a lot on his mind right now."

Roger nodded. He had struggled to make sense of their conversation yesterday afternoon. "You said something about Leslie Jones having a daughter?"

"That's right. Alex. Nick thinks she's trying to track down the men she blamed for her father's death. It's possible that she murdered Nick's wife."

He gasped. "No wonder Ted Wheeler was scared." He reached over and took her hand, startling her.

"Roger…"

"Come to bed."

"What?"

"Please." He could hear himself pleading, and it sounded pathetic. He tried to pull on her arm and she wriggled free.

"No." She stood up. "It's over. You know that."

"Just this once." It wasn't even what he wanted, but he was trying to goad her into a response, seeking a reaction to justify the resentment that had been simmering throughout the night. "Or are you screwing him already?"

She blushed, but held his gaze. "It's none of your business." At the door she turned and said, "I'll pack my stuff and get out of your life."

She was gone before he could reply. He immediately felt chastened, his anger forgotten, but pleading with her to stay would sound no less contemptible than the accusation he'd just made.

Nick reached the offices of Eastbourne CID at nine o'clock and was shown into DCI Pearce's small drab office, which she had attempted to brighten with half a dozen professional portraits of her grandchildren, twin boys with golden hair and mischievous smiles. She was telling him about a recent bout of chicken pox when her phone rang.

Pearce listened intently, a frown deepening on her face. He felt a tingle of anxiety in his stomach. Then she said, "He's with me now. I'll put you on speaker."

"Nick? Phil Clements. Kent police have just been on. They sent a patrol to check on Ted Wheeler. No one answered the door, but an officer saw what appeared to be a man asleep in the living room. When they tried the front door, they found it was unlocked."

"Oh shit," said Nick softly.

"His neck was broken," Clements went on. "There were also signs he'd been tortured."

"Tortured?" Pearce repeated, shaking her head in disbelief.

A grunt from Clements. "Alex Jones is number one suspect, of course. Do you have any idea what information she was after?"

"Ted was one of the men who arranged for her father to be killed," said Nick. "I'm sure that was a good enough reason for her."

"You don't think he knew anything of value to her?"

Nick considered the question. "Unless there are other targets she's trying to trace."

"We'll probably never know," Clements said gloomily. "But I hope you're keeping an eye out."

"That's something I intend to discuss with him," said Pearce.

"OK. One more thing. You realise the media will go nuclear on this?"

Nick turned to Pearce, who met his gaze and nodded sadly.

Clements said, "I've got a meeting with my superintendent this afternoon, and Kent police are sending a couple of their officers. I expect they'll want to put out an appeal to find this woman. As DCI Pearce will tell you, the public are often our best hope in cases like this."

He sounded almost apologetic, knowing the impact such a story would have on Nick and his family.

"I realise you may have no choice," Nick responded. "All I'd say is that as far as I'm aware she doesn't know we've made these connections. It's about the only advantage we have. If she comes after me, she won't know I'm expecting her."

It sounded braver than he actually felt, and he could see Pearce didn't approve. "The last thing we want is any more casualties," she said.

"OK, but what if we splash this over the papers and she goes into hiding? All she needs to do is lie low for six months, maybe even a year or two. You won't have a chance of catching her."

There was a gruff laugh that sounded like static. "My argument exactly," said Clements. "But I can't guarantee it'll convince my boss."

"With the best will in the world, it'll leak out anyway," said Pearce. "I reckon we've got two or three days at most."

"Then we'd better hope that's long enough," said Nick, and in the same moment he thought, *Be careful what you wish for.*

Caitlin was in tears as she packed a suitcase, wondering why she'd been so foolish as to expect any other reaction from Roger. Of course he'd be jealous. Of course he'd lash out.

In return, she might have told him that she was attracted

to Nick, and she had wanted to spend the night with him. What stopped her was not only the fear of rejection, not only consideration of Nick's recent widowhood, but a genuine sense of loyalty towards Roger: a conviction that she shouldn't begin a relationship with another man while Roger was still providing her with a home.

Well, she wouldn't be made to feel guilty any longer. She'd rather have a sleeping bag on Paul and Maria's floor than spend another night here. This afternoon she'd go into Brighton and find a bedsit to rent, then sign up with some employment agencies. It was time to grow up, she thought. Thirty-two years old and she had no partner, no kids, no home, no career: just years of disappointment and rejection at the hands of producers and casting directors.

It all had to end. She'd throw away those silly pipedreams, get a job in an office and try to save for a deposit on a place of her own.

Shouldn't take more than ten or fifteen years, she thought with a bitter smile.

There was a quiet cough and she spun. Roger was in the doorway, leaning against the frame. She had no idea how long he'd been there.

"I'm truly sorry," he said. "I know I messed up. I had all day on my own, not knowing what you'd say to Nick, not knowing what was going on… It sent me a bit crazy."

She nodded, but her face was resolute. She resumed packing.

"I meant what I said on Saturday," Roger said. "You're welcome to stay here. I promise not to say anything… untoward." He couldn't help a grin at the archaic term, and she heard the humour in his voice. It helped to soften her attitude.

"Stay for breakfast, at least," he went on. "Make some

phone calls. Have a bath."

She said nothing, wanting to maintain the tension for a few seconds. Without turning, she said, "Are you implying that I smell?"

"No. Oh God, no. I didn't meant to suggest —"

Now she faced him, a broad smile on her face. She'd always been good at fooling him, and his body sagged with relief.

"Bath, and breakfast, and then I'll go."

From her hotel window Alex could see the spot on the beach where she thought her brother had been brought ashore. It troubled her slightly that so many memories had faded. She remembered the wailing of the ambulance but nothing of the crew who had tried in vain to resuscitate him. She remembered Hilda screaming and throwing herself at the crowd around the body, but she couldn't recall who had held her back. Had creepy Uncle Vince been there at this point? The police?

She closed her eyes. All of a sudden she pictured the face of a kindly police sergeant, a luxuriant moustache and wild sandy eyebrows. He had led her away from the frantic activity around the body and sat her on a bench on the promenade. She remembered him offering her a stick of Wrigleys chewing gum, something Hilda had forbidden after a lump of it got stuck in her hair.

He asked her, very gently, what had happened. She smiled now, marvelling at how well she had conjured the necessary shock and incomprehension, teetering on the edge of tears but never quite giving in. Internalising her grief, as today's moronic counsellors would say.

Finally he had gripped her hand in his clumsy paw and told her, "You're a very brave girl. Just don't forget that it's all right to feel sad."

And she had nodded, just as a very brave girl would do. Probably in that moment she had felt a sense of sadness, if not exactly remorse. Billy hadn't been much in the way of company, but now it was just her and Mum, no goofy sweet boy to ease the burden of antagonism and meanness between them. She knew there would be no affection in her life, no lightness, no respite. She could only knuckle down, focus on the pain to keep her strong, and know that one day she would be free.

It's all right to feel sad. So she had. But not for long.

At the window, a mature accomplished woman of forty-five released a long sigh and shut the past away. There were things to be done.

She drained her coffee and cleared the breakfast tray from the dressing table. Then she powered up her laptop and surfed the internet. She quickly located the website for Knight's Accident Repair Centre, and a little more searching on 192.com brought up a good candidate for Roger's home address. At the same time, she had a delicious idea. A way to bring Knight into the picture whilst keeping her attention on Randall.

Before going out she checked a few news sites and also ran through the TV channels. This morning both the BBC and ITV had reported the assault on Howard Franks, but only to say that police were continuing to investigate an incident at the writer's home. There was no mention of the Eddie Randall biography, or of any possible links to Sarah Randall's death. Nothing about Wheeler either, but given the old man's hermit-like existence, it might be days or weeks before the body was found.

The lack of publicity made it easier to return. Not safe, necessarily, but everything she did carried a risk. That was what made her life so exhilarating.

She'd stay another night here, to be sure, and return to Sussex tomorrow, after a quick detour to the flat in Kingston.

She switched off the laptop and felt an urgency about her preparations, even though she had a whole day to fill. Normally she was good at this part – the waiting – but the attacks on Franks and Wheeler had made her hungry for more.

Passing the window, she caught a glimpse of the sea and thought: *thirty-two years.* Where had the time gone?

It's all right to feel sad.

Caitlin made sure she enjoyed what might be her last chance to pamper herself for a while. Her friends, both relatively impoverished actors, lived in a cramped flat in Kemp Town, and they didn't have the kind of bathroom you wanted to linger in.

Lying submerged in hot water for almost an hour left her ready to face the world again. She'd deliberately steered clear of the many awkward questions facing her and settled for the most appealing: was there any prospect of a relationship with Nick Randall? After much internal debate, she decided there was, but it mustn't be hurried. That was OK. Living with friends, dating casually, it would be like her college days all over again.

She dried her hair, dressed in jeans and a t-shirt, and descended the stairs to find the smell of bacon wafting from the kitchen. Roger had obviously been sincere in his effort to make amends: he was spooning fluffy scrambled egg on to a plate that already contained bacon, fried tomato, hash browns and baked beans. There was toast in the toaster, a choice of four fruit juices and a pot of fresh coffee.

They ate in the cosy breakfast room adjoining the kitchen, and for a few minutes there was little conversation. It was Roger who spoke first, selecting what he might have assumed was a neutral topic of conversation. Or perhaps he was still trying to impress her.

"I spoke to Barry Harper yesterday."

Through a mouthful of food, Caitlin said, "Mhnn?"

"We're shutting down. Withdrawing the claims that are still open. Returning cheques that haven't been banked."

"Won't that look suspicious?"

"Barry says they'll be so pleased to get the money back, they won't do anything about it."

"Do you believe that?"

He stared at her, surprised by the question. "I don't see we have any choice."

"No. But if it prompts the very thing you're trying to avoid…"

"Prosecution?" He shrugged. "I got myself into this predicament."

Afterwards she helped him load the dishwasher. He reached out for her arm and she stopped so abruptly that he whipped his hand away.

"Please," he said. "Don't rush off."

"It's best if I go."

"What if Paul and Maria can't put you up?"

"Then I'll stay somewhere else. A B&B if I have to."

"But that's ridiculous when I have all this space here. Why waste your money?"

"Because I need to be independent. We both need that."

He let her walk to the stairs before he spoke again. "Is this so you can feel free to see Nick Randall?"

She had her back to him, which made it easier. "Who knows? Maybe."

"I was right then. You are attracted to him?"

Now she turned. "Please, Roger. Don't interrogate me."

"I'm sorry. I didn't mean to sound churlish."

She climbed another couple of stairs, and he made no move to follow her. Again she paused and said, "What about Lynn? Have you spoken to her?"

He nodded. "I told her I want to come up next week. She didn't seem too unhappy about it."

"Good. I'm glad."

"It doesn't mean anything. For all I know she might have someone."

Caitlin shook her head. "She hasn't."

"How do you know?"

"Firstly, she'd have told you. Secondly, she's still not ready for another relationship."

He looked dubious. "Your psychic powers tell you that?"

"No," said Caitlin simply. "It's clear from the conversations you have with her."

"It's not clear to me."

"No offence, but you're a man."

She left him laughing and went into the spare room, unplugged her phone from the charger and checked for messages. She thought about sending Nick a text but decided against it.

When she was done she sat on the bed and prepared herself for the final act of leaving, which she knew would be the hardest of all. There was a footfall on the landing and she jumped to her feet, quickly wiping her eyes.

"Can I help with the cases?" Roger asked.

"Please."

He insisted on taking them both, leaving Caitlin with only her handbag and a plastic bag containing a few paperbacks and CDs. At the stairs he groaned and pretended to collapse.

"What have you got in here? Lead weights?"

"Quite a lot of shoes," she said. She had already decided to donate most of them to a charity shop.

She took the stairs ahead of him and reached the front door. As she pulled it open she felt a curious pressure against her hand. A shadow occupied the space that should have been filled with sunlight.

Kevin Doyle forced his way inside, wielding a long-bladed knife. Before Caitlin could move or even draw a breath to scream, he had it at her throat. She heard the door slam behind her, a sound more ominous than ever before.

Doyle addressed Roger, helpless with the cases on the stairs.

"Going somewhere, are you?" he said.

26

Roger watched Doyle burst into the house, grab Caitlin and slam the door. He saw the flash of the blade against her neck, tiny beads of blood appearing on her skin. In that moment he believed her throat would be cut in front of him, and he froze completely. He'd never been so terrified in his life.

Then he realised Kevin had spoken. "… are you?"

It was the weight of the suitcases dragging on his arms that broke his paralysis. In a spasm of panic one of the cases slipped from his hand, hitting the stairs and tumbling down.

Kevin reacted as if under attack, brutally twisting Caitlin's body as he shied away from the movement. She screamed and he clamped his free hand over her mouth.

"No!" Roger shouted. He set the other case down and slowly descended the stairs. "Don't hurt her."

"Then listen to me, right? Or I'll fucking kill her." There was spittle bubbling on Kevin's lips, the light of insanity in his eyes.

Roger nodded slowly, palms raised in an effort to placate his former partner. He knew Doyle was more than capable of carrying out his threat, and he meekly obeyed Kevin's order to lie face down on the hall floor.

From this position he caught glimpses of Kevin at work, placing Caitlin at the foot of the stairs, tying her wrists to the newel post with a length of nylon rope. He heard a grunt of satisfaction as Kevin completed this task. Now for me, Roger thought. He wondered if he should try to resist, but lying on his front, knowing Doyle held a knife, he couldn't see what chance he had.

Kevin marched across the hall, saw Roger peering up at him and growled. He leapt into the air and brought all his weight down on Roger's left leg, both feet stamping on the shinbone. There was a sickening crack and Roger let out a heavy guttural cry. Caitlin screamed again and Kevin turned on her.

"Shut your fucking mouth, bitch!"

Roger felt the world go dark. When he opened his eyes Kevin was crouching at his side, gently running the knife blade down his face.

"Thought you'd treat me like shit, didn't you?" he whispered. "Thought I'd just accept what I was given. Fobbing me off with a few lousy quid."

Roger could barely hear him. The agony of his broken leg reverberated in his brain, wiping out every attempt at coherent thought. He knew he had to reply, knew his survival depended on what he said. Had to focus on that. And Caitlin. If only he'd let her go this morning...

"Listen to me!" Kevin bellowed, slicing Roger's cheek from temple to jawline. It wasn't a deep cut, but blood poured down his face, filling his eyes and running into his mouth. He spluttered and tried to reach for the wound, but Kevin leant over and pinned his arms to his back.

"You'll kill him!" Caitlin shouted.

"That's the general fucking idea," Kevin said. "If he doesn't give me what I want." He sat astride Roger and grabbed a fistful of hair, pulling Roger's head back at an unnatural angle. Roger made a gargling noise, blood dribbling from his mouth.

"Now where is it?" Kevin demanded. "The money and the gun."

Roger tried to shake his head. Kevin slammed his face

into the floor.

"Don't… don't have it." Roger sounded like he had a bad case of flu. Blood ran from his mouth and nose, splattering the tiled floor.

"What d'you mean?" A little doubt in Kevin's voice.

"You knew… So I threw it in the river."

Kevin snarled with frustration, and seemed unable to decide on his next move. He glared at Caitlin, who was trying not to cry.

"It's true," she said.

"Yeah," said Kevin, in a defensive *I knew that* tone. "So what about the money? You ain't telling me there's not another stash."

"Gave you… all," Roger gasped. "All I have."

"Fucking liar!" Kevin shouted, and once more he rammed Roger's head into the floor.

Blackness, possibly longer this time. When Roger came round he heard Caitlin whimpering like a wounded animal. He twisted his head an inch and opened one eye. Kevin was kneeling before her, using the knife to toy with her t-shirt. He glanced over his shoulder and made sure Roger was watching, then slit the t-shirt down the front and pulled it apart, exposing her bra.

"You always thought you were too fucking good for me," he spat. "Well, you were wrong. Once I've got the cash I'm gonna give you a taste of the Doyle magic. And boyfriend here's gonna watch."

He prodded the soft, pale skin of her breasts, almost drawing blood. Caitlin winced, but glared defiantly at him.

"Don't go anywhere, darlin'," he said, and sprang to his feet. He looked around the hall, then made for the office. On the way across he aimed a lazy kick at Roger's leg, producing another howl of pain.

When he was done at the police station, Nick drove to his sister's house in Seaford. He had spoken to Diana earlier that morning and briefly explained the reason for his visit. He was surprised when a very glum Patrick answered the door.

"Not at work today?"

"I'm going in late," Pat said. "In view of what Di told me, I thought I'd better hear the rest of it."

Without another word Pat turned and retreated into the house. Nick wondered if he resented the situation they were in, perhaps blaming Nick in some way. He shrugged to himself and went inside.

Diana was in the living room, feeding Chloe from a bottle. "Eight ounces now, greedy guzzler," she said. She addressed Pat, who'd already sat down. "Make some coffee, will you?"

Pat started to rise but Nick raised a hand. "Just had one, thanks."

"I haven't," said Diana frostily.

"Everything OK?" Nick asked, nodding in the direction Pat had taken.

"About the same," Diana said. "No better. No worse."

"Oh." And then he frowned. "Where's Ryan?"

"Asleep. He's come down with a throat infection. He was awake three times in the night." She yawned at the memory. "I dosed him up with Calpol and sent him back to bed."

He tutted. "Poor kid."

"Poor Mum, more like," Di snapped. "I was the one that kept getting up to him."

"Ah." Deciding to dispense with any further small talk, Nick filled her in on this morning's developments: principally the murder of Ted Wheeler and the decision by the police not to put out a public appeal for Alex Jones. Diana didn't look convinced.

"It works with *Crimewatch*, doesn't it?"

"Mm, but they don't have a clear picture." A new search of the CCTV cameras had unearthed various shots of the two women in Eastbourne, the best of which showed Alex browsing women's fashion with Sarah a couple of hours before she died. Perhaps deliberately, Alex turned away just as the camera had its clearest view of her.

"They've put together an e-fit, but I wouldn't have a lot of confidence in it. We know she can change her appearance. Just tying her hair back makes a huge difference."

Pat brought two mugs of coffee into the room and set one down by Diana's chair. "Still worth a try, if you ask me."

"I agree," said Diana. "At least she'd know we were looking for her. It might scare her off."

"Exactly," said Nick. "If she goes into hiding she might never be caught."

"But isn't that better than anyone else dying?"

"Who's to say she won't come back, maybe months or years later?"

Diana shook her head. "This is horrible. It's the kind of thing that happens to other people. I just can't…"

Nick saw tears forming and sensed she wanted to say something about Dad, but the words wouldn't come. They both knew that in his dark exhilarating world, Eddie qualified as one of the 'other people'.

"You see what I mean?" he asked softly. "We have to hope she hasn't gone away, as terrible as that sounds. It also means we have to be very careful."

"Oh, don't worry. She's made me paranoid already."

Pat grunted, and Diana shot him a scornful glance.

"I still can't believe she killed Sarah and then had the

nerve to approach you. The idea that she was inside your house." She shuddered, and Chloe clawed at her bottle, startled by the sudden movement.

"It shows how devious she can be."

Pat said, "You're sure it's the same woman who's done all this?"

Nick shrugged. "We can't be totally sure until she's caught. But all the evidence points to it."

"What about letting us have a copy of the e-fit, so we know who to look out for, at least?"

"I've got copies in the car. I meant to bring one in."

As he stood up, he was aware of his sister's heavy gaze on Pat, and the air was virtually crackling with tension. Glad to escape for a moment, he went outside and checked his phone for messages. Nothing from Caitlin yet.

He took a copy of the e-fit from the back seat, and then on impulse rang her mobile, but there was no answer. Deciding not to leave a message, he sent her a brief text, hoping her meeting with Roger had gone well. While he was cursing the predictive texting, he looked up and saw Diana at the window, her face etched with concern and perhaps something else. Something almost accusatory.

Caitlin tugged on the rope around her wrists, trying to ignore the pain. However much this hurt, it was nothing to what lay in store when Doyle returned. She could hear him trashing the bedrooms, issuing a torrent of obscenities as his search proved fruitless.

She'd been terrified when he was in the office. She listened to him battering the desk, pulling folders from the shelves, smashing the PC. When he came out she half-expected to see him brandishing the gun, but it was obvious he had been unable to find it. He cast a scornful look at Roger, then leered

231

at her.

"Won't be long now, gorgeous."

He clutched his groin and thrust it in her direction, then stomped upstairs.

When he was gone she began to call gently to Roger. He wasn't moving, but thankfully she could hear him breathing. At the same time, she tested the rope and felt movement. Hardly daring to believe there was hope, she worked frantically, using her palm to push the rope over the widest part of her other hand. The skin burned as it was scraped off, and the throbbing agony of it made her nauseous.

There was a moan from Roger, and his head moved slightly.

"Ssshh," she urged him. "He's upstairs. Don't attract his attention."

Another moan, and then his head moved slowly in her direction. One eye was covered in blood, but the other was open, struggling to focus on her. "Cait…"

"Lie still. I might be able to —"

Movement on the landing above her. She heard Doyle muttering and pressed herself against the newel post, praying he wouldn't notice that she'd almost worked one hand free. He jogged down the stairs and approached Roger. Gave him an almost playful kick in the side.

"Where is it? Where's the money, you wanker?"

No response. Another kick, and then he turned away in disgust. Caitlin said nothing. Kevin moved on to the dining room, then the living room, giving them only cursory attention. Caitlin began to work on her restraints and was nearly caught out when he reappeared.

"Garage. The fucking garage." He knelt down and searched Roger's pockets until he found a set of keys. Then he hurried through to the kitchen, sweeping some crockery to the floor on his way, and went outside.

Caitlin took a deep breath and wrenched her hand free, blinking away tears at the pain. This was her chance. Her only chance to save them both.

She turned and pulled the knots apart, freeing her other hand. She'd planned to phone the police, but suddenly understood it would be pointless. A patrol car wouldn't get here for at least ten or fifteen minutes.

Roger stirred again, trying to rise on his elbows. She went to his side and winced at the extent of his injuries. His face was swollen and encrusted with blood.

"Stay still. He's outside."

"Go…" he managed to say. "Go."

She shook her head. "Where's the gun?"

His body gave a violent shudder: the only way he could express his fear for her. "No. Get away."

"I'm not leaving you, Roger, and I don't believe you got rid of it. Now tell me."

There was a crash of breaking glass, and Caitlin let out an involuntary yelp. It came from outside, but sounded too close to be from the garage. Then more commotion in the kitchen.

He was back inside.

"Please, Roger. Where is it?"

"Fucking fucking liar!" Kevin emerged from the kitchen.

"Coat… overcoat…" Roger said.

Caitlin frowned, then saw Roger trying to incline his head towards the front door. There was an old-fashioned hatstand on which three or four coats and jackets hung. One was a full-length cashmere overcoat which Caitlin had ridiculed. Said it made him look like a mafioso.

There wasn't time to question him. Kevin was only a

second or two from the hall. She dashed over and grabbed the coat, lifting it to see if the weight of the gun would reveal itself.

And then a voice behind her: "What the fuck…?"

Roger's heart lurched at the sound of Kevin's exclamation. He wiped at the blood in his eyes, desperate to see if Caitlin had understood. There was a bolt of agony as he shifted some weight on to his left leg. Now he could see her rifling through the coat, but Kevin was already moving fast, raising the knife to shoulder height.

"Cait!" The scream emerged broken and feeble as Kevin skidded to a halt only three or four feet from her, his large body blocking Roger's view.

Then he took a step backwards, and Roger saw Caitlin gripping the gun with both hands, trembling as she raised it level with Kevin's chest.

"You don't know how to use that," he sneered. He advanced slightly, as if testing his proposition.

Roger shut his eyes. This had been a terrible gamble. If Kevin overpowered her, he would kill them both.

But Caitlin sounded remarkably composed. "I'm an actress, remember? I've used replicas just like this." She slipped off the safety catch and cocked the hammer. "Drop the knife."

Kevin held his ground, nervously rolling the knife blade between his fingers while he weighed up the situation.

"I mean it," Caitlin said. There was barely a wobble in her voice, but she needed both hands to keep the gun steady.

Kevin nodded. "All right." He bent his knees and began to crouch, lowering the knife to the floor.

Roger frowned. It wasn't like Doyle to do anything carefully. He opened his mouth to warn Caitlin, but at that moment

Kevin leapt forward, swinging the knife at her face.

Caitlin stumbled backwards, into the hatstand, and went down in a mass of jackets. Before she hit the floor, there was an explosion which punched Kevin across the hall. He landed heavily and gaped in disbelief as his white shirt bloomed red. For a second he didn't move, and Roger feared he would leap up and resume his attack.

But Kevin only blinked like a startled rabbit and peered at the wound in his chest. He looked disbelievingly at Caitlin, still lying in a tangle of coats.

"Fuck it," he said.

And then he died.

Nick was getting worried. He couldn't rid himself of the idea that Caitlin was in trouble.

All morning he had rued the decision to let her return to Roger Knight. He should have offered her the spare room on a more permanent basis and then accompanied her to Knight's to collect her belongings. Putting aside Caitlin's view of Roger, what Nick knew about him was all bad: the nephew of a criminal, a man who was masterminding a large scale fraud and associating with some very violent men.

Diana could tell he was getting restless when he checked his phone for the third time in five minutes. Pat had taken a look at the e-fit and then made his excuses, heading upstairs to get ready for work.

"I take it this is about your new friend," Diana said bitterly. "Caitlin, is it?"

He grunted, which was all the acknowledgement she needed.

"And what do you think people will say, when you suddenly produce a girlfriend only a few weeks after your wife is killed?"

"Who do you mean by people?" he demanded.

"I mean your family, your friends. The police. The media." She was spitting out the words, and it reminded him of their fearsome adolescent conflicts: doors slamming, hateful things said, arguments that sometimes simmered for days or weeks at a time.

He made an effort to keep his voice neutral. "You're jumping to conclusions about Caitlin. But even if we were seeing each other, I couldn't give a toss what *people* think."

"You're just like Dad, that's your trouble. No consideration for anyone else. Ruled by your bloody libido."

"Hey, before you lecture me on relationships, how about giving yours a bit more attention? You and Pat aren't exactly a shining example of wedded bliss."

In the shocked silence that followed they heard noises above them. Diana struggled to her feet, Chloe asleep on her shoulder. "That sounds like Ryan."

"Can't Pat see to him?"

"He'll be off to work in a minute. I think you should go too."

"Di, we can't afford to fall out. Not at a time like this."

She gave him a measured look, and then her expression softened. "No. I'm sorry."

"Me too. Now take care, OK?"

Outside he tried Caitlin again and then, with a certain amount of trepidation, he rang Roger Knight's home number. Supposing Roger answered, he thought. Supposing he and Caitlin were happily reunited?

But after seven rings the answering service kicked in. Trying not to imagine them in bed together, he gave up.

*

The phone rang, and was ignored. With the danger past, it was tempting just to lie on the floor. Despite the pain from his leg and his face, Roger felt he might be able to drift off to sleep, and blissful oblivion.

It was Caitlin who gave him the will to keep going. She crawled to him and they shared an awkward embrace. Then she sat up and regarded him solemnly.

"We have to get you an ambulance. And call the police." Not waiting for a response, she stood up and took a wide detour around Doyle's body, making for the phone in the office.

"No!" he called. "Wait. Come back."

She hesitated, fearful of what he might suggest. "We have to call them, Roger. We have no choice."

"I agree. But not you."

"Why not?"

Instead of answering directly, he heaved himself into a sitting position and reached out for her. "Help me," he said, and gingerly wriggled an inch or two towards the door.

She took as much of his weight as she could bear, while he used his arms and buttocks to shuffle and drag himself over to the fallen hatstand. He picked up the gun where Caitlin had left it and aimed at the wall beyond Kevin's body.

"Cover your ears," he said, and fired a shot into the wall.

"What are you doing?" Caitlin asked, although she was beginning to comprehend.

"Forensics," he said, setting the gun back down. "I need to have fired it."

"Oh, Roger."

"Wipe the newel post and take the rope that he used to tie you. When you get to your friend's, have a bath and destroy everything you're wearing." He chuckled, then winced.

"You'll have to manage the suitcases on your own."

"But what about you?"

"Get the phone. I'll ring for help as soon as you've gone."

Caitlin was distraught. Now she understood only too well.

"They'll arrest you," she said.

"I brought it on myself." He suddenly felt clear-headed and surprisingly cheerful. A complicated situation had been rendered simple. "I don't want you involved. It's not fair."

She took his hand and squeezed it. "You're willing to go to prison for me?"

"Self-defence. I might be lucky."

"You'll need a good lawyer."

He nodded, and they said in unison: "Not Barry Harper."

Feeling wretched, she dragged her suitcases out to the car. Then she got the cordless phone and knelt beside him.

The kiss goodbye was long and deep, and when it ended they were both in tears.

"Thank you," she said.

Roger gestured at the body across the hall. "You saved my life. This is the least I can do."

He listened to the front door closing behind her, the gruff acceleration of her car as she drove away, and then all he could hear was birdsong, the tiny noises of a house at peace, and his own ragged breathing. Into this calm came a renewed throbbing from his leg, and he knew he must decide soon.

He passed the phone into his left hand and picked up the gun with his right. He knew now that he loved Caitlin, but he was glad he had let her go. It felt like the only decent thing he'd done in years. Noble, perhaps.

He hoped one day his children would be proud of him.

27

Nick was passing Stanmer Park on the outskirts of Brighton when his phone rang. He recognised the number and gave a little whoop of delight.

"Caitlin, how's it going?" Hard to appear casual when you're breathless with excitement, he thought.

But her voice quickly changed his mood. "Where are you?"

"On my way home."

"Good. That's where I'm heading. How long will you be?"

"What's happened? Are you OK?"

"I'll tell you when I see you."

That didn't sound good. "I shouldn't be more than ten minutes," he said. Just as he'd feared, Caitlin and Roger must have had an explosive argument, and it was possibly his fault. Again he cursed himself for not going with her.

Her car was parked outside his house, and she got out when she saw him turn into the driveway. As he opened his door she walked towards him, and his mouth dropped open in horror. Beneath her jacket her t-shirt was ripped and splattered with blood.

"Jesus, what's happened to you?"

"I'm fine," she said quietly. "Can we go in?"

"Yeah. Of course." He put his arm around her shoulder and felt her body virtually collapse against him.

As soon as they were inside he pulled her into an embrace and held her tight, not speaking or moving for what seemed like minutes. Then he led her into the living room, sat her down and carefully examined her injuries. There was a scab of dried blood on her neck and some nasty abrasions on her wrists, the skin rubbed raw and weeping.

She refused his offer of first aid, so instead he poured two brandies and sat beside her. She gulped a mouthful, coughed, sipped a little more, and finally she was ready to explain.

She told him everything, from her first argument with Roger in the bedroom, right up to the moment when she closed the front door and left him lying in the hall next to Kevin Doyle's body. Nick could barely comprehend it.

"Roger's going to claim he shot Doyle?"

Caitlin nodded. "He'll tell the police it was just the two of them."

"Do you think they'll believe it?"

"I don't know. He said I should get rid of these clothes, just in case."

"He's right." He shook his head. "That's quite a sacrifice, isn't it?"

"I told you he was a good man at heart. But the police won't see it like that."

"They'll find out about the fraud as well," Nick pointed out.

"He's lost everything, hasn't he? I should have stayed. Even if he claimed to have shot Kevin, I could have corroborated his story, perhaps kept him out of jail."

"No. The police would be bound to spot some inconsistency in your statements. Then you'd really be in trouble."

Caitlin hadn't considered this, and it seemed to offer her some consolation. She thought for a moment, and said, "Is there anything you can do to help him?"

"I was just wondering the same thing. I need to speak to the insurer who instructed me, and then I'll contact the police."

"You could tell them about Kevin breaking in here," Caitlin suggested.

"True." Nick felt a little ashamed of his reluctance: yet more involvement with the police was the last thing he wanted right now, but after what Roger had done to protect Caitlin he could hardly object.

He stood up. "First we should take Roger's advice," he said. "You need to clean up and get changed. I'll sort out your clothes."

Suddenly the enormity of what they were doing hit them both. There was a sombre moment as they considered the situation. They were destroying evidence of a crime. Conspiring to pervert the course of justice.

"Are you sure this is right?" Caitlin asked.

"Not really," said Nick. "But I think we have to do it."

The seconds ticked past, became minutes, and still Roger couldn't decide. With the pain came a light-headed, almost intoxicated sense of unreality. His future boiled down to a simple choice: equally terrible, and yet equally painless, it seemed to him.

The easiest option, the one that ought to have frightened him most, was slowly growing in appeal. He imagined the long hours in an interview room, the prurient media interest, the heartbreak and disgrace of his family, culminating in years of incarceration.

And against that, a forefinger's pressure on a trigger, and then nothing.

He felt tired. It didn't matter that he was giving up, taking the coward's way out. He kept hearing Caitlin's voice in his head, telling him he'd be letting Doyle win. He didn't agree.

He lifted the gun and examined the muzzle. Wondered

how it would feel in his mouth. At the same time the phone grew heavy and he let it slip to the floor.

And then it rang.

"Shit," he said, his voice guttural and unfamiliar. He tried to ignore it but couldn't.

"Yes?"

"Dad! I just wanted to apologise, calling so late last night. I totally forgot the time, but the storm was awesome. And Mum said you might be coming up next week, I really hope you do, you know we're all missing you so much…"

A lull in the torrent of words, and Roger, tears coursing down his cheeks, knew he could never tell his daughter the truth. He cleared his throat, hoping his voice would sound OK. "Wh-what time is it there?"

"Don't tell Mum, but I haven't actually been to bed." Sally giggled. "There's a couple of girls in the hotel and we've been up chatting all night, you know? Listening to music, chilling."

"Drinking?" Roger asked.

Another giggle. "Come on, Dad. I'm fifteen. I'm not a little kid."

It hurt him to smile. "No. OK."

"When I said we're all missing you, I mean Mum as well."

"I doubt that."

"Honestly. She even said it was a shame you weren't here with us."

"She said what?"

"I think she still loves you, Dad."

Her voice choked on the final words. Roger put the gun down and held the phone tightly. "She'd never admit it to me."

"Come and see us. Then you can ask her. Please, Dad."

He found himself running through all manner of

scenarios, a blur of dates and schedules, interviews and court appearances and bail applications. Then he found himself saying, "Yes, darling. Of course I will."

After sending them his love he ended the call and then, before he could change his mind, he dialled 999.

Nick retrieved the garden incinerator from his shed and found an old container of paraffin. While Caitlin had a shower, he burned her clothes and the nylon cord which Kevin Doyle had used to restrain her. Staring at the flames, he couldn't help wondering what DCI Pearce would have to say about this.

He also contemplated the extent to which he'd mis-judged Roger Knight. Then he thought about Diana, bickering with Pat. All their relationships being tested by the malevolent presence of Alex Jones.

And Alex herself. Was it absurd to hope she'd gone away? That she was satisfied with the destruction she had wrought? How long must they wait before it was safe to relax?

When he went inside he found Caitlin in the spare room, unpacking her clothes. She was wearing the robe from this morning.

"Is this OK?" she asked.

"You look great."

She snorted. "I mean putting my clothes away."

"Ah. That." He shrugged, trying to dismiss whatever significance it might have for either of them. "I came to see if you wanted lunch?"

"Lunch?" She pushed her hand through her hair. "To be honest, I'm not really hungry."

"Not surprising after what you've been through."

She grinned. "Actually, I had a huge cooked breakfast

this morning."

"And there was me feeling sorry for you."

Caitlin dropped an armful of underwear into a drawer and stood up. "Cup of tea wouldn't do any harm, though."

"Fine."

"Any biscuits?"

"Now you're getting cheeky."

"That's me, I'm afraid. Lippy." She smiled and stepped towards him. "Take it or leave it."

Reading the challenge, he nodded thoughtfully. "I'll take it."

Then a moment frozen in time, not indecision but preparation, a mental deep breath before the plunge into… the unknown?

No, Nick corrected himself. The future.

They moved slowly, their lips making first contact an instant before their bodies met and pressed together. They kissed for a long time, and for a long time kissing was enough, the urgency tempered by what they had experienced.

And then, when it seemed right, Nick slipped the robe from Caitlin's shoulders and kissed her neck, his hands moving lightly over her small, firm breasts. She gasped as his palms brushed her nipples and pulled him into a hungry kiss, while her hands tugged on his shirt and worked to undo his jeans.

They broke apart again, while Nick undressed and Caitlin slipped off her underwear. For a moment they admired one another, both a little shy, a little scared.

"You're pleased to see me, then?" Caitlin said.

"I'm glad you've noticed."

"I'll need a closer look," she said, and reached out a hand. She stroked him while he kissed and gently nuzzled her breasts. They moved on to the bed, exploring with mouths and fingers, enjoying the growing desperation to be joined until they could bear it no longer. She brought him into her and wordlessly they moved together, managing for a time at least to extinguish the pain and fear of the previous days and weeks.

In her hotel room, Alex was growing restless. This morning she'd had her hair cut short and coloured blonde, a transformation that had drawn compliments from the hotel receptionist, the kind of petite, elfin girl with whom in other circumstances Alex might have tried her luck. The idea of a pleasant distraction was appealing, but she knew she couldn't risk drawing any more attention to herself. Not when her identity and description could be all over the media at any moment.

Now the long afternoon stretched ahead of her. She'd been checking regularly for news updates, and the first reports of Ted Wheeler's murder were dribbling through: *An eighty-three-year-old man has been found dead at his home in Gravesend. Police are treating the death as suspicious.*

She could continue with her planning, but really she knew exactly what she intended to do. She had various alternative strategies lined up, should something go wrong. There were a few technical details to iron out, and certain items to collect from hiding on her way to Sussex, but essentially she was ready to go. All she could do now was wait.

No. There was one thing…

She rummaged in her bag and selected one of the half-dozen mobile phones she was using. Made sure it was the right one, and checked for messages: a text, sent a couple of hours before: *need to c u.*

She smiled. Decided against calling, and sent a text instead: *had 2 shoo bt cmng bac sn. Cnt w8 2 fuK u.*

*

Almost midnight. Nick jerked awake from a disjointed dream and lay startled, trying to assemble the fragments of his day: Caitlin's bloodstained clothes, her part in Kevin Doyle's death, the sensation of her body against his.

He shifted and saw her lying next to him, but still it didn't seem real. They'd spent most of the afternoon in bed, alternately talking and making love. Nick realised it was the first time he'd felt truly alive – and glad to be alive – since DCI Pearce told him that Sarah was dead.

It didn't quite eradicate the guilt, though, and Caitlin was conscious of his feelings.

"You realise this may be a one-off," she'd said while they ate a takeaway Chinese together.

"You think so?"

"Not really. But it's a pretty weird situation, isn't it? With everything we've been through, maybe it's affected our judgement…"

He laughed. "Am I supposed to be offended by that?"

"No. I'm not explaining myself very well. I guess I'm trying to say that when all this is over, you might suddenly feel you made a big mistake."

It was a brave, honourable thing for her to say, and he wanted to let her know he was touched. "If this is a mistake," he said, "it's still the best thing I've ever done."

Now he recalled her words, and one phrase kept repeating in his head: *when all this is over*. But when would that be? Would they ever know?

He remembered a documentary about the Blitz which claimed that illicit affairs were rife in the Underground tunnels and air raid shelters: desperate couplings made all the more thrilling by the proximity of death. Is that what they were experiencing now?

She stirred beside him. "You're frowning even when you

smile."

"I don't mean to. Sorry."

She wriggled closer and placed her arm across his chest. Now she was equally solemn. "What's wrong?"

"I'm not sure. Somehow this feels like the calm before the storm."

"It may be. And you know there's only one thing we can do about it?"

"What?"

She put a finger to his lips. He kissed it.

"Enjoy."

28

Wednesday was glorious, just a few wisps of cirrus in a milky blue sky, a light wind ruffling the police tape around Roger Knight's property. There was now only a single patrol car parked on the driveway, the scenes of crime officers having left late the previous evening.

PC Derek Haynes had greeted his assignment with little enthusiasm: guarding an empty house was hardly the most thrilling of duties. There had been a flurry of media activity yesterday afternoon, when local journalists picked up on the story, but it had quickly died down.

Wasn't much of a story, if you asked him. Dodgy businessman falls out with his colleague, who comes round demanding money. They have a fight, and businessman shoots colleague. The dullest of motives, and nothing particularly interesting about either of the people involved. Now if one of them had been famous...

Nice place though, Derek thought. He'd recently bought an overpriced two-bedroom terraced house in Portslade: dogs barking next door and kids with hundred-watt car stereos screeching past all night. This was just the kind of house he dreamed of owning: detached, large garden, hidden away along the kind of narrow lane where you didn't see a car from one day to the next.

In fact he'd been on duty for three hours and seen only a tractor, a Land Rover and a couple of bicycles. Some nosy neighbours had strolled past, on the pretext of walking their dogs, and a hiker on a route march towards Plumpton had caught his eye: tall, cropped blonde hair, a bit dykey in combats and a baggy sweatshirt, but a good body nevertheless. His practised eye had spotted a very shapely rear.

Obviously all that walking kept her fit, though he had a few better ideas if she fancied some exercise. He wasn't one to boast, but he could have sworn she'd given him the once-over. Perhaps she had a thing about uniforms.

High on the hill above the road, well concealed within a grove of trees, Alex studied the house through a pair of small Zeiss binoculars. The police presence had come as a shock, but of course she'd given no sign of it to the officer stationed outside. She carried on past, aware of his gaze burning into her but confident it was nothing more than primitive male lust.

After watching for ten minutes, she took a cereal bar from her rucksack and considered this unexpected development while she ate. The most obvious theory was that Knight's involvement in some kind of insurance scam had come to light. However, this rarely led to crime scene tape and police guarding the house. That was the kind of reaction you'd expect to a violent crime. Murder, perhaps.

She was disappointed. Leaving Cromer at four am she'd been in high spirits, full of enthusiasm for the long day ahead. After careful reconnaissance she'd returned to the flat in Kingston and gathered the things she needed for several days in Sussex. By nine o'clock she'd found her way to Clayton in a newly rented Renault Clio. To avoid suspicion she parked at the top of the hill and walked back to the road that led past Knight's large country home.

She finished the cereal bar and took up the binoculars again. The policeman was strolling aimlessly up and down the driveway, kicking at the gravel and then smoothing it flat with his boots. At one point he seemed to stare right at her, causing her heart to flutter. Then he stuck a finger in one nostril and performed a thorough excavation.

"Filthy bastard," she muttered.

The grounds occupied several acres, bordered by a mixture of trees, hawthorn hedges and a high wooden fence. There was a tennis court on the west side, some kind of shed or workshop behind the garage, and a grand summerhouse in a slightly elevated position to the north of the house.

Alex thought it over for a while, toying with an audacious idea. She liked a challenge, didn't she? Just because there was something going on down there, it didn't mean she had to disregard Knight altogether.

After all, there was more than one way to create a victim.

"Oh my God! Who is she?"

Nick recoiled. "What?"

"There's a big silly grin on your face. Haven't seen that for a while."

"Not much I can hide from you, is there?"

Morag shook her head. "I can see into the depths of your murky soul," she declared, and then raised her mug of coffee. "Cheers."

He took a sip of his latte, waited a few moments, then said, "Go on, then. Aren't you going to say, 'It's a bit soon'?"

"I wasn't intending to. Do *you* think it's a bit soon?"

"Probably," he admitted.

"Well, that's good. Shows it really means something."

He laughed. "Morag, I should have married you years ago."

"With your wandering eye? I don't think so."

They were in Starbucks in Western Road, a little after midday on a sunny Wednesday. Across the road holiday crowds were plunging in and out of the shops in Churchill

Square. Groups of teenagers loitered on the steps and buskers plied their trade. A procession of buses trundled past, making the windows vibrate.

Nick had told her everything he knew about the fraud, including the revelation that one of the two principals had been killed at the hands of the other. The only important participant still at large was the solicitor, whose involvement had been confirmed by Caitlin.

"We can put the word out," Morag said. "Make life difficult for him, at least."

"With this shooting, the police are bound to find out about the claims," Nick said. "Is that good news for you?"

She pursed her lips. "I'm neutral. Our marketing guys at Head Office might not be too chuffed, but I daresay they'll put a positive spin on it."

"The end result's pretty good for you and the other insurers."

"Oh aye. I'm not denying that."

He winked. "So how much did I save you…?"

"Send me your fee and I'll look kindly on it." She indicated the coffees. "You can stick these on it as well. How's that for generous?"

"Actually, I have another favour."

She frowned. "Oh yes?"

"If the police decide to charge Roger with fraud, will CBA support them?"

"Why shouldn't we?"

Now he looked sheepish. "It would do me a big favour if you found a reason not to."

She thought about it carefully. "Anything to do with your new girlfriend?"

"Morag, you're frightening."

"Not frightening enough, or you wouldn't ask." She

tutted. "I'm not promising. Depends what pressure they bring to bear."

"OK. I just happen to know he's a pretty good guy, despite what you'd think."

She reacted with alarm. "Is this you going soft in your old age?"

Nick smiled. "Would I ever?"

While Nick was in Brighton, Caitlin finished off a few household chores that she'd insisted on doing. "It helps me feel I belong here," she told Nick. "And it takes my mind off everything else." Then she rang her agent and learnt there was still nothing promising in the pipeline other than a TV commercial for margarine: she was shortlisted to play Perfect Mum to a couple of glossy stage school brats.

After that she went for a walk, first up and down a couple of the avenues that bisected New Church Road, wanting to get a feel for the area; then she dashed across the busy seafront road, walked through the Lagoon and on to the promenade. She was sitting on the steps overlooking the beach when her mobile rang: a London number, unfamiliar.

It turned out to be Roger's solicitor, Nigel de-something, who sounded like Hugh Grant and was very jolly and reassuring. He told her that Roger was in good spirits, despite a broken tibia and various other injuries. The police had accompanied him to hospital and would be conducting their interviews as soon as he was discharged. Most importantly, Nigel would be doing his utmost to get his client freed on bail.

"Soon as I know more, he or I will give you a bell," he said, as though they were arranging a game of tennis. "Chin up and all that. Super to talk to you."

"Super," Caitlin echoed, wondering how much Roger

had told him.

Heartened by the call, she walked as far as the King Alfred leisure complex and bought an ice cream. The horror of the business with Doyle was starting to recede, and now she knew Roger would pull through, she didn't feel so concerned about her developing relationship with Nick. It was still in it's infancy, of course, but she had a good vibe about it, an intuition. It felt right.

Nick was preparing a pasta salad when the phone rang. Caitlin answered and handed it to him. "DCI Clements."

The London detective sounded apologetic from the start, and Nick felt his good mood ebbing away. "Can't hold off any longer, I'm afraid," he said. "Too much pressure from on high. And a couple of the papers have got wind of a connection between Franks and Wheeler's murder."

"How is Howard?"

"Stable. Conscious. Arrogant." Clements grunted. "And pissing through a tube, of course."

Nick shuddered. "So when will it break?"

"Tomorrow. The big guns have decided to get Alex's description all over the media. I just thought you should have some warning."

"Thanks."

"Don't thank me. We both know this could be disastrous. We have no idea how she'll react, so just take care."

The warning was ringing in his head as he sat down to eat. What should have been a relaxed meal was consumed in morose silence. At some point the journalists were bound to uncover Eddie Randall's part in provoking the wave of revenge killings, and he knew it would be regarded as a sensational story.

It occurred to him that he should warn Diana, since her

doorstep was just as likely to be besieged as his own. From the way she sounded when she picked up the phone, Nick assumed she already knew.

"Have Clements or Pearce been in touch?"

"No. Why?"

"The media are on to the story. The police intend to splash Alex's face all over the TV tomorrow."

He heard her snuffling, and a couple of times she tried to speak. He realised Chloe was bawling in the background.

"Di, what is it?"

"Pat's gone," she said. "I kicked him out. He'd been… sleeping around."

"What?"

"One of his clients. Said it was only a couple of times. Meaningless sex, he said. And yet the bitch rang him here. Left a…" She choked up. "Left a message on the fucking answerphone."

Nick didn't know what to say. Pat had never struck him as the type. "Where's he gone?" he said. "You need to talk to him. Perhaps there's an explan—"

"Oh, trust you to stick up for him," she shouted.

"Di, I'm trying to…"

"I don't want to hear it, Nick. It's bullshit. He's gone and that's that."

He sighed. Caitlin was watching him anxiously. "Should I come over?" he asked Diana.

"Not a good idea. Not today."

"What about the kids?"

She made a noise in her throat. "They'll be all right. They're with me."

He knew he'd achieve nothing by arguing. He said, "I'll see you in the morning. We need to talk about this… other stuff."

"Whatever." She put the phone down.

Caitlin had guessed most of it. Nick told her the rest and she shook her head. "Why was she so abrupt with you?"

"I was unfaithful to Sarah," he confessed. "Diana takes fidelity very seriously. Now that she's experienced what Sarah went through, I imagine she resents me all the more."

Caitlin held out her hand and he clasped it, drawing her into an embrace. "You and me," he said sadly. "Feels like the only good thing in my life. Everything else is just…"

"Darkness?"

He held her tight. "Darkness," he agreed.

29

After sunset the air rapidly grew cold. Alex turned the ignition and pressed the button to close her window. The whir of the motor was the only sound in the deserted street, lit by the sodium lights in Hallowe'en orange. She was wearing a navy suit from Karen Millen with a crisp white blouse, a briefcase on the seat beside her and a cardboard folder resting on the steering wheel. To passers-by – and there had been only a few – she looked like a financial consultant catching up on paperwork between evening appointments. She even had a little stack of leaflets she'd taken from a bank, just in case she was confronted.

She'd had the house under observation for most of the day. This morning she had watched Diana load the children into the car and followed her as far as the local supermarket. When Diana turned into the car park beneath the store, Alex quickly drove back to the house and prepared stage one. It took little more than ten minutes and went without a hitch.

The next stage involved a phone call, which she made from the car. Then she waited, skimming a *Telegraph* with little interest: carnage in Iraq, corruption in Europe, Blair and Bush slated for something or other.

In a day or two they'll be writing about me, she thought.

Diana soon returned, ushered the children into the house and came out to unload the shopping. In the paper Alex discovered a grudging tribute to Howard Franks by a writer who clearly resented his success. The gist of the story was that Franks, although a talentless prick, didn't quite deserve what had happened to him.

Perhaps I went too easy there, she thought. Nick's intervention had thwarted the agonising death she'd planned for Franks, and she considered whether one day she might have to finish the job.

She had also begun to contemplate the next stage of her life. This project was nearly complete, and if it all went to plan she would have no further need of killing. And yet... could she really give up such an intoxicating sense of power?

There was another potential outcome, of course – that in this final most hazardous stage she might be captured or even killed. But she found it impossible to give either possibility any serious consideration.

It took fifty minutes for Pat to get home. After less than half an hour inside he emerged, crestfallen and distraught, clutching a sports bag. An item of clothing, possibly a sock, fell from the bag as he tossed it on to the back seat of his Volvo. He kicked it angrily into a flowerbed and sped away, almost colliding with a skip lorry turning into the road.

Alex saw the flash of brake lights in her wing mirror and shook her head in mock disapproval. Life was full of setbacks. Reckless driving wasn't the answer.

Now, hours later, she continued to wait. The growing darkness comforted her, offering the promise of concealment and what felt like a guarantee of success. She held a key in her hand, which she flipped and twisted from palm to palm, passing it between her fingers with a magician's dexterity. In the briefcase at her side the rest of her props awaited: the carefully crafted letter, the surgical gloves, the syringe.

It promised to be quite a show.

The conversation with his sister did nothing for Nick's mood. Even Caitlin found herself admitting defeat in the end.

"Bed with a book for me," she said, tutting as she bent to kiss him goodnight.

"Sorry." He pulled her into a long, passionate kiss and held her on his lap. Just when it might have led to something, he tickled her under the arms and she leapt free with a yelp.

"Hey! That was sneaky."

"Couldn't resist. I promise I'll be less miserable tomorrow."

"I hope so."

He fetched a beer and spent some time channel-hopping, then switched the TV off and noted how the silence didn't have the same lonely quality now Caitlin was here. He heard her turn off the bedroom light at eleven and told himself he ought to go up, but by then he was lying on the sofa, eyes shut, feeling relaxed but not sleepy.

And yet he must have dozed off, for around midnight a noise caused him to jerk upright. Someone hammering on the door. He had a terrible flashback to the night DCI Pearce told him about Sarah's death.

He reeled into the hall, concerned not to wake Caitlin. Who would have the nerve to disturb him at this hour? He remembered with relief that Kevin Doyle was dead, then wondered about Alex Jones. His sister was probably a better bet, given what had happened earlier…

But it was Pat: drunk, dishevelled, and clutching an empty Kronenberg bottle. He moved forward, tripped on the step and lurched into the hall. Nick managed to grab him, then debated whether he should have let him fall.

"Sorry, mate. Pissed out of my head."

"Don't tell me you drove here?"

"Nah. Car's…" He frowned. "In town somewhere."

Nick helped him upright and took the bottle from his hand. Pat was suddenly crestfallen, as if he'd only just realised who he was with.

"Got so much to tell you, mate. So sorry."

"You stink," Nick said, recoiling.

"Started smoking again."

"Worse than that."

Pat followed Nick's gaze to the front of his shirt, which was stained with something unpleasant. "Oh shit." He rested his head back against the wall and moaned. "What a bloody disaster."

There was a noise on the stairs and Nick turned to see Caitlin on her way down, her eyes wide and worried. Pat peered round and did a comical double take.

"This is Caitlin," Nick said, and then, "Caitlin, meet my brother-in-law."

"Pleased to meet you," said Pat. He pushed himself upright, stepped forward and promptly fell over. This time Nick didn't catch him.

Alex followed Diana's progress to bed by the procession of lights throughout the house, as she religiously checked every door and window. Eventually only a single light remained, on the landing, no doubt in case one of the children woke in the night.

Or perhaps Diana, so recently separated from her husband, needed the reassurance.

Alex gave it another hour, until midnight. She put on gloves and a black bomber jacket. Her faithful woollen hat covered her short blonde hair. She opened the briefcase and took out the items she would need.

She had switched off the car's interior light, and the opening and closing of the door made hardly a sound.

Leaving the car unlocked, she hurried up the driveway to the front door, where she was hidden from view by a large rhododendron.

Now she waited another five minutes, alert for any movement within the house. Nothing.

She eased the key into the lock, knowing from this morning's reconnaissance that it fitted perfectly. Turned it fully and waited, taking deep breaths. The next stage was crucial.

The alarm's control unit was by the front door. It started bleeping as soon as the magnetic contact between the door and the frame was broken. This morning she'd estimated that someone asleep in the main bedroom was unlikely to be disturbed for the few seconds – three, as it turned out – that she needed to step inside and enter the code.

Leaving the front door ajar, she moved to the foot of the stairs and waited again. Then she climbed the stairs, keeping her feet to the outside of the treads, avoiding those which had squeaked on her previous visit.

She knew the baby still slept in a crib in the main bedroom. The second bedroom was a spare, while Ryan's room was at the end of the landing. It meant she had to pass Diana's room, and the door was half open. She spotted the glow of the bedside clock: 12:13.

There was a squeaky floorboard right outside, which she avoided by flattening herself against the wall and edging past, crab-like. She had to remember to do the same on the way back.

Now into the bedroom, easing open a door which had creaked until this morning, when she sprayed a little WD40 on it. Ryan was in a bed shaped like a racing car. A spaceship mobile kept watch over the sleeping child, and a nightlight provided an eerie glow.

Closing the door was a gamble, but one she felt she must take, in case he made some noise. She took the syringe from her pocket and removed the protective cap from the needle. It contained a dose of ketamine, a sedative she'd acquired while working in a Surrey hospital on a short-term contract – in fact she'd vanished after less than a week. The drug was fast-acting and should keep the boy quiet while she took him from the house.

Scanning the room, she spotted a small cushion with his name embroidered on it. She pressed it over his face to muffle any sound as the needle went in. He flinched, and she held the cushion firm, slowly injecting the ketamine into his arm. Then she felt him relax again.

Dropping the cushion, she put the syringe away and opened the door. As she turned back towards the bed there was a rushing, gurgling noise and she realised Diana had just flushed the ensuite toilet. She cursed and waited behind the door.

A moment later the floorboard protested as Diana came out on to the landing. Alex tensed. At worst she'd have to kill Diana right now, throwing all her plans into disarray.

Then silence, as if Diana had stopped in the doorway.

She's seen me through the gap in the door, Alex thought. But she couldn't risk turning to check. Any movement now would betray her presence.

The door began to swing open. Alex slowly retrieved the syringe and gripped it like a dagger. Providing she retained the element of surprise, she could plunge it into Diana's neck before the woman had a chance to react.

A weary sigh from inches away. Then Diana stepped into the room.

It took both of them to help Pat upstairs and into the

bathroom, whereupon Caitlin diplomatically returned to bed, leaving Nick with the unenviable task of undressing his brother-in-law. He had to step back sharply when Pat suddenly dropped to his knees and vomited into the toilet. The sour smell of regurgitated beer filled the room.

Pat stood under the shower for ten minutes and emerged looking slightly more human. Nick threw him a towel and went downstairs to make coffee.

When Pat joined him, the towel tied round his waist, Nick handed over a glass of orange juice and two paracetamol.

"Feel a bit better now," Pat said, gulping down the tablets.

The kettle boiled and Nick spooned coffee into a couple of mugs. He had his back to Pat. "I spoke to Diana earlier."

"Oh?"

"You bloody idiot," Nick said, and before Pat could respond, he turned to face him. "And I'm talking as someone who knows."

"Yeah." Pat nodded towards the ceiling. "Who's she?"

"Long story. Too long for tonight."

"Seems nice."

"She is."

Nick handed him a coffee and they went through to the living room. To ease the silence, Nick put the TV on and they both stared at a poker game for a while.

"I used to play poker a bit, at uni," Pat said, and snorted wistfully. Nick took it as a signal that he was ready to talk.

"So what happened?"

Pat shrugged. His eyes lost focus and he shivered, as though he'd looked inside himself and didn't like what he saw.

"Emma Slade. She was a potential client, wanting a place in Sussex. Half a million to spend. Great looking, professional woman. Divorced. Available. Seemed to be offering it on a plate."

"And you took it?" Nick tried to sound harsh, but he knew what a hypocrite it made him.

"I didn't mean to hurt Diana. But we've got Chloe sleeping in our room, Ryan playing up during the day… Our sex life is bloody non-existent." He gave Nick a pleading look. "Honestly, mate. I thought it was just a fling."

"How many times did you see her?"

"Maybe half a dozen. Couple of meals out. Usually just a drink in her hotel and then, wham!"

"So why ring you at home and leave a message?"

"I don't know. The last time we talked about how dangerous it was becoming. Sending texts, all that silly stuff. I knew I was being drawn in deeper, and it was time to get out while I could."

"Did you suggest that to her?"

"Not in so many words."

"But that was her interpretation?"

"Could be. I don't know." Pat cupped his hands around his face and blew through his fingers. Then he drew in a breath, opened his mouth to speak but evidently thought better of it.

Nick yawned and said, "Why don't you get off to bed?"

"The couch is fine."

"Don't be silly. There's a spare bed." Thereby confirming the status of his relationship with Caitlin, he thought.

Pat nodded sheepishly but didn't refuse the offer. He finished his coffee and tramped upstairs. Nick followed him, feeling like he was running a boarding house. Diana would no doubt view his hospitality towards Pat as the worst kind of betrayal. He still intended to visit her in the morning, but maybe he wouldn't mention where Pat had spent the night.

He got into bed, turning away from Caitlin so as not to disturb her, and fretted that he'd be unable to sleep for hours. In fact he was out within seconds.

It was twelve-twenty-five.

Diana stood on the threshold of her son's room and peered sleepily into the gloom. Behind the door, Alex held her breath and kept absolutely still, poised to strike the instant Diana came into view.

After a few seconds Diana shuffled round and went back to bed, satisfied that Ryan was sound asleep. It was another five minutes before a low, throaty snore came from the bedroom, and Alex judged it safe to move. She lifted the unconscious child from his bed and carried him against her shoulder on to the landing.

The stairs were a challenge; at one point she nearly lost her balance, almost dropping Ryan in the process. As it was she stepped off the bottom stair with an audible thump. She took the envelope from her pocket and propped it on a narrow shelf by the front door.

She had to make a noise to shut the door behind her, but by then she didn't much care if Diana woke. A minute later she was driving through Seaford, Ryan concealed under a blanket on the back seat.

It was done. She was flying now, soaring above the world, all her plans drawing towards a beautiful conclusion.

She glanced at the clock on the dashboard: 12:30.

The last day had begun.

30

Later, Diana would say she knew something was wrong the moment she woke, at exactly six in the morning. At the time she put it down to Pat's absence, the memories of yesterday's events flooding back. He was an early riser, eager to get on with the day, while she tended to struggle against sleep for a while.

She checked the clock again. Usually Ryan came running in around now, and one of them would take him down-stairs to stop him waking Chloe. Maybe he'd sleep late this morning. After Pat left yesterday he'd been grouchy and difficult, and last night it had taken her nearly an hour to settle him. She had been tempted to let him share her bed, but decided she couldn't jeopardise the long months they'd spent coaxing him to stay in his own room.

She lay back, listening to the tiny noises that Chloe made in her sleep, and thought about dozing off again. After a couple of minutes she knew she couldn't, but she didn't exactly know why.

The first thing she noticed was that Ryan's door was nearly shut. She remembered checking on him during the night and was sure she'd left the door open. Maybe a draught had caused it to swing.

When she saw the empty bed, her initial reaction was to laugh. He must have heard her coming and decided to hide. And yet a part of her knew this wasn't the case. Four-year-olds tend not to conceal themselves very well: usually you saw a foot poking out or heard a muffled giggle. This room *felt* empty.

She searched it nonetheless, preparing the delighted

smile for the moment he leapt out with a shout of "Boo!", all the while trying to ignore the growing anxiety.

Next she looked in the spare bedroom, the big airing cupboard on the landing, and then the bathroom. Maybe he's sneaked into my room, she thought. She noticed her hand was shaking as it rose to push the door open.

He wasn't in the bedroom. Chloe was still asleep, but stirring, her face twitching as she dreamed of milk and cuddles. It was irrational, but Diana suddenly knew she couldn't leave her here while she searched downstairs. She lifted the baby into her arms and rocked her a few times. Better if she stayed asleep.

The real fear kicked in when she reached the bottom of the stairs and the alarm failed to bleep. The system was always set at night, and Ryan understood that he couldn't come down without waking Mummy or Daddy.

She hadn't forgotten to set it. Not with Pat gone. She *knew* she hadn't forgotten.

"Ryan!" she cried, her voice breaking with panic. "Ryan, come out! Please, darling."

But the words seemed to echo back at her.

Then two things happened: Chloe woke up and started to cry, and Diana spotted the envelope by the front door.

The bedside phone dragged Nick awake. He felt like he'd been asleep for about five minutes. Beside him, Caitlin groaned and turned over.

It was ten past six. He swung his legs out of bed and sat up, grabbing the phone midway through the second ring.

"Nick he's gone Ryan's gone she's taken him *she's taken him!*" It wasn't so much speech as a hysterical scream.

He recoiled from the blast, jumping to his feet and almost dropping the phone. The noise woke Caitlin, whose mouth opened in a wordless question. Nick shook his head, trying to concentrate on Diana, trying to make sense of what she'd said.

He had to shout to be heard. "Diana, calm down! Breathe. Breathe. That's it."

She made a huge effort, still speaking in gasps, and with a longer pause between each word he just about got it.

"Ryan. He's gone. She took him. That woman. Alex."

"Oh Jesus, she can't. She can't have." He was willing himself not to panic, not to go the same way.

"Left. A note. I can't… I can't…"

"Di, have you called the police? Have you called Melanie Pearce?"

More gasps. "No."

"Right, I'm going to ring her, and then I'm going to call you straight back."

"No," Caitlin said, reaching for the phone. "Use your mobile to call the police. I'll talk to her."

He thought about it and saw she was right. This way Diana wouldn't be left alone.

Caitlin took the phone and immediately began making the kind of soothing noises that Nick would have found impossible. His phone was in the kitchen and he was taking the stairs three at a time when he remembered his other houseguest.

Pat.

He grabbed the mobile, rang Pearce and woke her. His explanation was a garbled rush, but she agreed to go round immediately.

Pat was standing in the doorway, rubbing at a smear of dried saliva on his cheek. "You always get up this early?" he asked irritably.

"Sit down," Nick said.

"What? Why?" Pat's eyes were still glassy, inebriated. "I feel lousy."

"Listen to me, Pat. Diana's rung. She says Ryan is missing. She's saying that Alex Jones has taken him."

It was as if he'd hit Pat with a sledgehammer. He didn't say anything for ten seconds, then he started flailing. "What? Taken…? But why?"

"I don't know, but Caitlin's still got her on the phone. I think you need to speak to her."

Pat balked at the suggestion, and something else crept into his expression, not just fear and confusion, something darker and meaner, something more personal.

Guilt.

And suddenly Nick listened to the questions running through his head. How did she take Ryan? For Diana to ring now it must have happened during the night, but his sister would have made sure the house was secure, especially without Pat there. He'd warned her to be careful, hadn't he? There was a burglar alarm. *How did Alex do it?*

Pat said, "Fucking hell," and buried his face in his hands. "What?"

"No, it can't be," he whined. "This can't be happening."

"Tell me. Quickly."

Pat raised his head and said plaintively, "I was going to mention it last night. It just seemed so ridiculous…"

In his helpless silence, Nick found the answer. "The woman you slept with?"

"When you gave Diana the e-fit the other day, I thought… it looks a bit like Emma. But it seemed a mad idea."

"And it meant you'd have to admit to the affair."

Pat was distraught. "If I'd known Ryan was in danger, or any of them, I'd have owned up. I put it down to coincidence. I mean, why would she sleep with me?"

"Because this is what she does, Pat," Nick said quietly. "This is how she hurts us."

"Oh God, if anything happens to him…" Tears rolled down his face and dropped unchecked on to his lap.

"We have to stay calm," Nick said. "However difficult, we mustn't panic. That's what she wants."

Pat nodded, but Nick wasn't sure if his advice would be heeded. He could feel valuable seconds ticking past.

He said, "How did she get into the house? Did she take anything from you?"

Another sledgehammer moment. "One time I left my keys at the hotel. She rang me when I was back at the office. Said they must have fallen out of my trousers."

"What about the alarm? Diana would have set it."

"I keep… I have so many damn codes to remember, I keep them on a card in my wallet."

Nick said nothing. He couldn't add to the punishment Pat was meting out to himself.

"Talk to Diana," he said at last. "Talk to your wife."

Alex spent the night dozing fitfully in the back of the Renault, Ryan lying next to her, both of them covered by the blanket she'd bought for the occasion. She'd driven what she judged was a safe distance and finally decided on a quiet spot next to some parkland on the coast between Worthing and Ferring. She was just off the main road, less than a hundred yards from the shore.

In the grey dawn she woke and checked on the child, who appeared to be sleeping soundly. Her legs had gone numb and she shifted, trying to stretch out. Ryan made a snuffling noise and reached for her, throwing an arm across her waist. Alex was momentarily horrified, then she gently lifted the boy's arm free and tucked the blanket around him.

She got out of the car, shivering despite her jacket. The grass was thick with dew and the light was softened by a misty layer of cloud. Crows drowned out the sweeter bird-song in the trees around her, but she could hear the cry of gulls far out at sea. She locked the car and walked the short distance to the beach.

For half an hour she stared at the water, watching it turn placidly from grey to blue as the sun rose and burned away the cloud. She thought about the long day ahead, the day in which months of planning would be brought to fruition. The day in which Ryan would, in all likelihood, become an orphan.

It was getting on for seven o'clock when she returned to the car. Ryan was still lying on the back seat, but now his eyes were open. He seemed to have suffered no ill effects from the sedative, and he studied her curiously, without fear.

"Hello Ryan," she said. "Did you sleep well?"

He thought about it, and shook his head. "I feel poorly," he said.

"I'll see if I can get you some medicine later. My name's Auntie Alex. Your mummy wants me to look after you today."

Again he digested this information. "Where is she?"

"She and your daddy have some important things to do."

"They had a big fight." His bottom lip quivered at the memory.

"I know, but don't worry. Would you like a drink?"

He nodded, and she helped him sit up. He'd been wearing short-sleeved pyjamas and his arms felt cold, so she arranged the blanket around his shoulders, reminding herself that she was simply protecting a valuable asset.

There was a rucksack on the front passenger seat containing some cartons of fruit juice and a bar of Galaxy. She gave Ryan a juice and showed him the chocolate.

"Do you want some of this?"

"I'm not allowed that for breakfast," he told her. "I have to have something healthy."

She snorted. "Today's a special day. Today you can." She broke off a strip and handed it to him, then ate a couple of squares herself. "Later we can go to McDonald's, if you're a good boy."

Ryan nodded, but not as gratefully as Alex expected. She fought an urge to slap him.

"Do you know how old I am?" he said, dribbling a little chocolate on to his chin.

"Four," she said, and then realised he'd wanted to tell her himself.

"I'm going to big school in September."

"Very nice. Now eat your chocolate."

He did as he was told, but without wiping the dribble from his chin. Alex shuddered. The next few hours would be a huge test of her self-control.

Diana was too upset to speak to Pat, so Nick suggested they drive straight over there. While Pat threw on some of Nick's clothes, Caitlin asked if Nick wanted her to come.

"I'll spare you this one."

"Are you sure?"

"Yeah. Thanks, though."

A couple of minutes later Nick was driving fast along the seafront in light early traffic. Pat kept wiping his face with his hands and muttering to himself.

Nick's phone rang as he was touching eighty on the dual-carriageway past Roedean school. Melanie Pearce.

"I'm at your sister's," she said. "Where are you?"

"On my way," said Nick, adding, "with Diana's husband, Patrick," in case there was anything he shouldn't hear.

"OK. Diana's very upset. I've seen the letter from Alex and it warns against calling in the police. But I came alone, in an unmarked car."

"Oh Christ, we can't risk…"

"Don't fret," Pearce told him. "She won't know we're involved."

It took another fifteen minutes to get to Seaford. He screeched to a halt behind the detective's car and ran to the front door. It was opened by Pearce, who offered them a grave smile. "She's in here," she said.

Diana was pacing up and down, Chloe on her shoulder. She stopped when Pat entered the room, Nick and Pearce hanging back. They eyed each other cautiously, and then Pat opened his arms.

"I'm so sorry," he said.

They embraced, both in tears, with Chloe between them. Nick nodded at Pearce and said, "We'll give you a few minutes."

They headed into the kitchen and stood like guests at a party nobody wanted to attend. Nick told her about Pat's affair, and its implications. "Alex probably has a copy of the door key, as well as the alarm code."

"She's really been planning this, hasn't she?"

"Diana and Pat haven't been getting on lately, but I just put it down to stress. It never occurred to me that she'd target him."

"Is he explaining all this to your sister?"

Nick nodded. "I don't envy him."

"Look at this," said Pearce. The letter was carefully laid out on the table. "We'll need to run some tests on it, so don't touch."

He quickly read the letter.

Ryan is with me. He'll be perfectly safe, as long as you obey my instructions.

FIRSTLY, no police! Any sign of them and you'll never see your son again.

SECONDLY, I intend to leave you alone very soon, but only when my demands have been met. This will include a financial settlement, the rightful compensation for my father's murder.

THIRDLY, I will need to speak to you, Diana, and your brother. Make sure you are both here at your home by 4.00 pm today. I'll explain what you should do next.

LASTLY, a message for Nick: I know you're trying to track me down, but you were too late with Franks, too late with Wheeler, and you'll be too late with Ryan. Be patient. Wait for my call at 4.00pm.

Ryan is well-hidden but safe. No harm will come to him, but you must follow instructions.

Alex.

Nick collapsed into a chair, his shoulders slumping. He'd been completely outwitted at every turn, and now she was taunting him for his failure to anticipate her next move. Ryan's life was at stake and there was nothing he could do about it.

He thumped the table in frustration and turned to Pearce, who looked almost as angry. "What do you suggest?"

"That you involve the police, for a start. I don't think she'd risk keeping a watch on the house, but plainclothes officers can check the area. We need to set up a trace on the phone, and get the helicopter and armed response on standby." She checked the time. "There's a lot to do. I need a go-ahead pretty quickly if I'm to get this authorised."

"OK." He launched himself to his feet. "I'll talk to Pat and Diana."

The waiting felt unbearable to Caitlin, so she could barely imagine what Nick's sister was going through. She checked her phone every couple of minutes, willing it to ring.

When it finally did, a little after nine, it wasn't Nick but Roger. He sounded in remarkably good spirits, and for a moment she forgot he was probably still in custody.

"How are you?"

"Patched up. Leg in plaster. They kept me in hospital Tuesday night for observation." He chuckled. "With a policeman sitting at my bedside. They're just setting up a hearing at the Magistrates' Court."

"And then what?"

"If I get bail, I'm going to fly up to Scotland and explain what a total bloody idiot I've been."

Caitlin couldn't help smiling. "I mean, what will they charge you with?"

"Who knows? Nigel thinks the CPS might go for manslaughter on grounds of self-defence. Then there's illegal possession of a firearm, and the fraud, of course. A custodial sentence, probably, but maybe not a long one."

"How do you feel about that?"

"I did it, didn't I?" he said flatly. "I'm going to take my punishment and then get on with my life."

There was a moment's silence. He sighed. "I'd better go…"

"Thanks, Roger," she said quickly. "I'll never forget, you know."

"I just wish things had been different."

"Me too."

She was still pondering on the call when she heard the front door open and Nick came in, his face pale and gaunt. She immediately rushed to all kinds of terrible conclusions, and Nick must have read it in her face.

"There's no news," he said. "I was going crazy waiting there. I wanted to see you."

She hugged him until her arms ached. "How's your sister?"

"She's coping, just about. I think she appreciates that Alex was determined to seduce Pat." He shook his head. "They're both sick with fear for Ryan."

"You don't think Alex would hurt him, do you?"

"I'm praying she won't."

He produced a sheet of paper on which he'd copied out Alex's letter. Caitlin read it and said, "So she's holding him to ransom?"

"That bothers me," Nick said. "Up till now it's just been about revenge, pure and simple. Why suddenly go for money?"

"Because she's seen an opportunity?"

"I don't know." He sighed. "I thought if I got away for a couple of hours, something might…" He jabbed the side of his head angrily. "…shake loose."

She watched him brooding for a minute, then said, "Come on. Let's get some air."

31

"Put it together."

"What?"

Ryan thrust the box at Alex and rattled it annoyingly. "You need to put it together."

Alex sighed and grabbed the box from his tiny hand. She'd given in to his constant whining and bought him a toy, a robotic action figure called a Bionicle. She'd assumed it came fully formed, but now discovered it had to be assembled from lots of small parts.

They were sitting at a picnic table in the park on the edge of Worthing. They'd spent nearly three hours in the town centre, killing time in various shops and cafes. Although she had collected clothes and shoes for him when she went into the house yesterday morning, it turned out the trainers no longer fitted. She'd had to buy him a new pair in Clarks, where he charged around the shop, refusing to stand still while his feet were measured.

Without the option of violence she found herself buying his good behaviour with the constant promise of treats. In the course of the morning he'd eaten a doughnut, a gingerbread man and a packet of crisps. Then in McDonald's he'd thrown a minor tantrum when his Happy Meal failed to contain the toy he wanted.

It was to pacify him that she'd gone to Woolworths and bought him the Bionicle. He spent ten minutes deliberating, only to change his mind again when they were at the till. She was heartily sick of him, and knew if she'd ever had a child of her own she would have strangled it within a year.

While Alex dutifully clipped the bits of plastic into

place, Ryan ran off to play in the sandpit. It must have been a school holiday, for the playground was packed with children.

For a while Alex was able to tune out the shouts and screams, her mind drifting away to what would happen at four o'clock. She became aware of a woman at her shoulder: one of the mothers, short, heavy-set, with cheap blonde highlights and a small tattoo of a rose on her flabby upper arm.

"Is that your boy?" she said, and pointed towards the roundabout, where Ryan was kneeling on the ground, his head flopping forward. "He's just been sick," the woman added, in a tone that seemed to suggest it was Alex's fault.

Belatedly remembering to show concern, Alex hurried to Ryan and stood him up. There was a small pile of vomit on the rubbery tarmac, and more on his t-shirt. He was crying the kind of self-indulgent tears that made her itch to inflict real pain on him. She pulled him close and he tried to wriggle out of her grasp. It took all her willpower not to smack him off his feet.

"You sure he's all right?" the woman said, still loitering close by.

"He'll be fine." She took Ryan's hand and began to lead him away. He was sobbing loudly, drawing looks from everyone around her.

"I'd take him straight home," the woman chipped in. "Let him have a lie down."

Alex turned on her with a vicious glare. "I said, he'll be fine."

The woman recoiled and stomped away, muttering angrily. Alex grabbed up the partly-completed Bionicle, shoved it into Ryan's hand and started towards the car.

"Back to sleep for you," she said. "A nice long sleep."

Without intending to, Nick and Caitlin walked for miles along the seafront, past the skeletal storm-lashed remains of the West Pier, past the noisy hive of tourism that was Brighton Pier, along the slightly forlorn stretch of beach bordered by Madeira Drive and finally to the Marina. They threaded their way through the grim concrete ramps and took refuge in the Katarina pub. Nick bought two Cokes and they carried them to a table outside.

All the way along the front they'd talked about Alex, but neither of them felt they were any closer to anticipating her next move.

"Something's not right," Nick kept saying. "I know there's some part of this that should be making sense to me."

At Diana's he had listened to the phone message and confirmed that the voice almost certainly belonged to the woman who had posed as Howard Franks's researcher.

You said you loved me, Pat! she had exclaimed. *You promised me you'd leave the fat bitch! So where are you?*

"I'm sure she intended to leave that message rather than actually speak to Diana. It provided evidence of the affair, something my sister could confront Pat with. But that means Alex had to be watching the house, to make sure Di was out."

Caitlin went with it. "And then Diana called Pat, I suppose?"

"Yep. Demanding an explanation. Pat comes home, they have a big fight and he gets kicked out."

"Leaving Diana on her own when Alex broke in."

"It's perfect, isn't it? She's treating us like rats in a maze, and at the centre of the maze there's poison."

Something did make sense then, but so deep in his subconscious that he couldn't reach it. The more he dug, the deeper it fell.

It was Caitlin's idea to change the subject for a while, and he was more than happy to oblige. They spent some time discussing the films showing at the nearby cinema, and then moved on to other forms of entertainment: theatre, clubs. When they reached music Nick suddenly froze.

Someone's Got It In For Me…

"Nick?"

Just like last time. Nothing's changed. Her objectives are the same. Not money.

Revenge.

"She was watching the house," he said, hearing his own voice as if from far away. "We know she had keys and the alarm code. That means she could have gone inside at any time."

Caitlin was frowning. "When the house was empty?"

"Precisely."

"What, you think she stole something?"

"Maybe. Maybe the opposite."

"I don't get you."

He dug in his pocket for the copy of the ransom note. "The answer's in here," he said, his confidence growing. "Look at this. *Make sure you are* both *here at your home by 4.00 pm today. Be patient. Wait for my call at 4.00 pm. You* must *follow instructions.* She's desperate that we do as she says."

Caitlin continued to look perplexed. "Yeah. I get that bit."

"Don't you see? She's using Ryan as bait. What she really wants is me and Diana together in the house at four o'clock."

"But why?"

"Maybe because she's left something there?"

He let the idea sink in. She gaped at him, not believing,

or maybe not wanting to believe.

"You don't really mean…?"

He was already reaching for his phone.

It was eleven o'clock.

Alex kept to the speed limit on the dual carriageway. She couldn't risk being stopped by the police with Ryan unconscious in the boot. At least, he'd been unconscious when she put him in there. She didn't much care if he was dead when she took him out.

There was another tantrum back at the car when she tried to clean him up. This time, away from prying strangers, she slapped him hard across the face. For a moment he was winded, mouth open in astonishment while his lungs struggled for air. Before he could start bawling she clamped a hand over his mouth and threw him on to the back seat. With the door shut and the radio on, he could make all the noise he liked while she found the other syringe.

He saw the needle and instinctively knew it meant him harm. For ten seconds she let him writhe and scream and lash out with his puny limbs. Then she slapped his face again, held him down with her knee and thrust the needle into his arm. He was out by the time she reached the A27.

Last night's *Argus* had contained an explanation for the police presence at Roger Knight's home. A brief report stated that a man had been found dead at a house near Clayton. The householder, a forty-eight-year-old businessman, had been arrested and was being questioned by police.

So Knight would be out of circulation for a while. She'd had to consider whether to alter her plans in the light of this situation, but decided it only added to the challenge.

Descending towards Waterhall, she moved across into the slip road for the A23 northbound and happened to notice Ryan's Bionicle lying crippled on the passenger seat. At the point where the lane separated from the A27 she opened her window and tossed it into the weeds by the side of the road.

Nick finished the call to DCI Pearce on the run, heading for a taxi parked across the road. Ten minutes later they were home, and he managed to speak to Diana on her mobile. She was a lot calmer than he expected.

"They brought a doctor round, but I refused to take anything. I want to be clear for this, Nick."

"Good. How's Pat?"

She made a noise, a kind of sorrowful groan. "I don't know if I can forgive him."

"He was tricked, Di. You can't blame him for what's happened."

"I don't want to talk about it now. I want Ryan back. That's all."

"I know. And we'll get him." He hesitated. "Did they... has Melanie Pearce spoken to you yet?"

"Not really. They sent us away. They won't tell us what's happening."

"OK. Don't worry. I'm coming back now."

This time Caitlin was with him, and she insisted on driving. He joked that she just wanted a chance to use his car. It was the best he could do to lighten the atmosphere.

"Get in," she said, "and don't criticise if I crunch the gears."

On the way he kept trying Pearce's phone, but it was constantly busy. Finally she called him back. They were in

Saltdean, passing the Art Deco open air pool.

"First, a bit of good news," she said before he could get his question in. "DCI Clements managed to delay the media splash. Says he had to twist a few arms to do it. I gave him a bit of background here, told him what you'd suggested."

"What did he say?"

"Thought I was taking the mickey, and if it turns out to be nothing he'll look a right twat. His words exactly."

"And will he look a right twat?"

A pause. Pearce swallowed, and said, "No."

"Bloody hell."

"I don't know how you worked it out, but thank God you did."

"So what happens now?"

"I work my little arse off and perform miracles." She laughed, a burst of gallows humour.

"You know you're swearing a lot at the moment?"

"I do swear under pressure." She put on a bad American accent: "You gotta problem with that?"

He laughed and said, "Where do we meet you?"

"Look for a white van on the corner."

She was going to cut off when he stopped her. "You know this is a perfect opportunity?"

"Go on."

"How sure are you that she's not watching the house?"

"Pretty sure. We've swept the neighbourhood a couple of times."

"So this is our chance to go on the offensive. Lay a trap for her."

When Pearce spoke, he could hear the broad smile in her voice. "Nicholas, I'm actually ahead of you there for once."

32

By one o'clock Alex was back in Brighton, the boy successfully stowed away. She selected a restaurant at random in the Lanes and ordered risotto with a single glass of red wine. She felt calm and untroubled by what lay ahead. All the hard work had been done, and now she could simply let it unfold. Savour every moment.

At two o'clock she returned to her car, parked beneath the Churchill Square shopping centre. She took the bag containing her disguise and used the centre's lavatory to change. The woman who emerged ten minutes later was in her sixties, bulky in a tweed skirt and green Barbour jacket, tall but stooped, with grey hair and large unfashionable glasses. She looked like a colonel's daughter, stalwart of the golf club and keen hunt supporter.

She'd considered adding a limp and walking with a stick, but decided against it. At the back of her mind it niggled her that she needed some kind of prop, and as she drove into Peacehaven she had a wonderful stroke of luck.

Slewing into a short lay-by outside a little parade of shops, she left the engine running and hurried towards a newsagents. A small Pekinese was tied to a railing outside. She crouched down and let it sniff her hand before untying the lead. The dog yelped as she picked it up, then started yapping at her. She opened the back door and put the dog inside, securing the lead around one of the seatbelt clasps.

As she pulled back into the traffic she checked her mirror and saw a middle-aged woman emerge from the shop and look round in confusion. Probably thought the lead worked loose and the dog ran away.

After all, who would steal such a horrible little animal?

Three o'clock. Eight people in Diana's front room, waiting.

DCI Pearce, fresh from performing miracles, rested her head against the back of an armchair. "Thinking," she'd snapped when someone whispered, "Is she asleep?"

Her colleague – "Call me Doug" – was Team Leader of the Tactical Firearms unit. He sported a Tom Selleck moustache and the gentle bedside manner of a kindly GP, at odds with his black overalls, body armour and Sig Sauer pistol. He was monitoring developments on a tiny earpiece, occasionally asking for reports and giving orders, never raising his voice.

A man and a woman from the Telecoms Unit sat at the dining room table with laptops and headphones. They'd barely spoken a word to anyone else.

Diana and Pat clung together like shipwreck victims, living an agony that no one else present could comprehend. Next to them on the sofa, Caitlin flicked through an old copy of *Hello*, trying not to feel like an intruder.

Nick was unable to keep still, his body humming with an almost uncontainable mixture of anticipation and fear. He tapped out anxious little drum rolls on the window ledge until Caitlin pointed out how irritating it was.

All of them counting on Nick, who knew more about Alex than any of them. And all of them harbouring the same dreadful thought, which finally, unable to contain it any longer, Diana voiced.

"What if she doesn't come?"

"She will," Nick reassured her.

"But if she doesn't, we've lost her. And then we've lost Ryan." She clamped a hand over her mouth. Pat hugged her tighter than ever.

"She'll be here," said Nick.

For half an hour Alex waited on Seaford seafront, parked in a quiet spot near the Martello tower. She worked on befriending the dog, stroking it, feeding it chocolate. For a furry rat it made a more amenable companion than the child.

She took it for a walk on the beach, practising her old lady persona. There was a bitter wind off the sea, and she was glad of the thick coat. She watched a tiny speck on the horizon transform into the ferry from Dieppe, and decided that when it slid out of sight into Newhaven harbour it would be time to go.

The endgame.

She drove cautiously on the main road through Seaford, as befitted her character, and parked in the street parallel to Diana and Pat's. Yesterday she'd scouted the area carefully and worked out a couple of escape routes.

It was three-forty-five when she set off along the pavement, the dog now trotting happily at her side, stopping every few yards to sniff at the grass verge. She watched for unfamiliar cars or signs of anything out of place, but it seemed quiet. At the far end of the street a couple of young women were sitting on a garden wall, bags of shopping at their feet.

There were builders working on the house opposite Diana's, putting rubble into a skip parked on the road. She remembered how Pat had nearly collided with the skip lorry the day before. As she walked past one of the men looked her over and turned away: far too old to merit a wolfwhistle.

A little further on there was a side street. She turned into it and stopped, letting the dog probe a fascinating collection of scents around a road sign.

After ensuring that she couldn't be seen by the women

on the wall, she produced a mobile phone and made the call.

Two minutes to four.

The landline rang, and everyone seemed startled. Pearce checked the time.

"A bit early."

"She can't wait," Nick said.

All eyes were on Diana, who stood up and smiled bravely. Nick winked at her, and for a moment it was like they were kids again, offering encouragement before a big exam.

Diana took a deep breath and then snatched up the phone. "Hello?"

"I hope you've been sensible and followed my instructions so far."

Nick saw his sister's face darken. "I have."

"Good. But because I don't trust you, I won't be staying on the line for long enough to be traced. Put Nick on."

Nick, who'd been instructed to keep Alex talking for as long as possible, took the phone and cleared his throat.

"Hello, Alex."

"Nick. Nice to speak to you again."

"A pleasure to speak to you, too. Why don't you pop in for a coffee?" He saw Pearce grinning and knew he'd produced the right tone of relaxed affability.

"I'm afraid that's not feasible," Alex said, sounding slightly rattled.

"Oh, I'm sure you could find the time," Nick said.

"Unfortunately, Nick, time's just run out." And she terminated the call before he could say anything else. Nick frowned and turned to the phone techs. They had taken a chance that Alex would use the same mobile as the day before, and they were already in contact with the service provider. There was an agonising wait while the male officer listened intently; finally he nodded.

"Seaford," he said. "The eastern side of Seaford. That's as close as we can get."

Nick turned to Pearce with savage jubilation. "I knew it."

She held his gaze for a long moment, and nodded decisively. She turned to Doug. "Let's do it."

Alex slipped the phone back in her pocket and waited for the blast that would kill Nick and his sister.

Nothing.

She stared at her watch for a full ten seconds. Yesterday she had synchronised it with the timer linked to two pipe bombs, which she had placed in the loft. Following instructions she'd obtained on the internet, the bombs had been ridiculously simple to construct, fuelled by explosives taken from a box of fireworks. Ignited via a timer and a flash bulb, they should have destroyed the house and everyone in it.

But it was now a minute past four, and nothing had happened. Annoyed rather than angry – and certainly not afraid – she tugged on the dog's lead and walked back to the corner. The two women were still gossiping. The builders were still at work. Diana's house remained stubbornly intact.

Suddenly the front door opened and a man emerged: a policeman, carrying a gun. The instant he appeared, one of the builders ran over and they began to confer. They were quickly joined by more people from the house, some of them police but also Diana and Patrick.

And then Nick. Looking up and down the street.

She spun away and heard the squawk of a radio, horribly close. Tried to glance casually over her shoulder and saw one of the young women dip into her shopping bag and bring out a heavy police radio.

Alex yanked the lead and began to walk, almost forgetting she was supposed to be an elderly woman. She forced herself to slow down.

Nick stood with one foot on the low boundary wall, convinced that if he just looked carefully enough he would see Alex hiding somewhere in the empty street. One of the firearms team who had posed as a builder was talking to Doug, while DCI Pearce was speaking urgently on her radio.

"Any sign of her?" This from Doug.

"Nope."

"OK. Get everyone roaming the streets. Are the cars ready to seal the junctions?"

"Just waiting for the word."

"What about Karen and Jenny?" Doug asked Pearce.

"Nothing to report."

Nick spun round, bunching his hands into fists. He briefly caught Diana's eye, and felt the burden of her faith in him. "Has anyone been past?"

The officer glanced resentfully at Doug before answering with a shrug. "Just an old dear walking her dog."

"A woman?"

"Yeah." The policeman scowled. "Sixty, seventy-odd. Had one of those ratty little dogs."

"When?"

"Few minutes ago."

"Which way?"

The policeman pointed, and Nick leapt over the wall, hitting the pavement at a sprint. "Get a car!" he shouted.

*

It took him less than twenty seconds to reach the side street. He saw the old woman about to disappear around the next corner, and his movement must have caused her to turn towards him.

He was too far away to see her face, but instinct told him it was Alex. For a fraction of a second she slowed, and something in her body language acknowledged that recognition.

And then she was gone.

He screamed her name and ran on.

He'd worked it out. Nick had worked it out.

The words resounded in her skull. Somehow he'd found the bombs, had them disarmed, filled the area with police and waited for her to walk into a trap.

And she had.

She got to the corner, sensed movement in her peripheral vision and turned for just long enough to see Nick Randall staring straight at her. The women on the wall were crossing the road to join him.

She dropped the lead and ran. The car was less than fifty yards away and the one advantage of her sensible old-lady shoes was that they enabled her to move fast. She reached the car in a few seconds, opened the driver's door and risked a look back just as Nick came dashing around the corner.

She fumbled with the ignition key, then saw Nick weaving on the pavement and guessed that the dog had gone for him. It only delayed him a second, but it was long enough for her to gun the engine and take off.

Nick saw the car door open and judged that he might just make it. Then from nowhere he heard barking and looked down to see a small dog leaping across his path. He broke his stride and moved sideways, but the dog went with him, nipping his ankle. Nick muttered, "Fuck," and kicked the dog out of his way.

He was less than three or four yards from the Renault when it sped away. He ran on a bit further, but knew it was useless.

There was a sudden squeal of tyres and he spun round, saw Pearce's Vectra taking the corner almost on two wheels. It screeched to a halt alongside him and he jumped in.

"Starsky and Hutch or what?" she said, and hit the accelerator.

Alex was doing fifty in third gear, heading for the junction with the main A259 when a patrol car appeared at the end of the road. Luckily for her, it turned in and then realised too late that it should have blocked the junction. She caught it with only a glancing blow and it swerved away from her, mounted the pavement and hit a postbox.

She stamped on the brake, shifted to second gear and risked making the turn into the main road without checking for traffic. A bus was pulling out of the stop a few yards away and she made it just in time: another second and she would have hit it side on.

The road ahead was clear. She pressed the accelerator to the floor and watched the speedometer needle flicker upwards: fifty, sixty, seventy. Then she was out of Seaford, the magnificent panorama of the Cuckmere Valley opening up before her. Suddenly she saw everything with a startling clarity: the dark carpet of Friston Forest, cloud shadows gliding across the Downs, the glassy sheen of the meandering river. At a remove from this detached appreciation of natural beauty, the cold rational part of her brain understood that it was all over.

She became aware of a noise, above the sound of the straining engine, above the roaring of blood in her ears. Recognised it, seconds before it swooped overhead, as a helicopter.

Nick Randall. Nick Randall had done all this, and she hated him with a vengeance greater than anything she'd ever known.

There was no escape now, but at least she had a chance to mete out one final devastating punishment.

She thought of Ryan, and the slow death to which Nick would condemn him.

DCI Pearce passed the damaged patrol car and skidded to a halt as a bus rumbled across the junction. It took them valuable seconds to break out on to the main road and over-take the bus. When they reached the long descent into the valley Alex's Renault was about a quarter of a mile ahead. Behind them a stream of vehicles joined the pursuit.

Suddenly the police helicopter dipped into view from the south, banking towards the river.

"She won't get away," Pearce said.

"She mustn't. Ryan's life depends on it."

"OK. We'll ease off. The chopper can track her."

She slowed a little, and Nick felt an irrational sense of disappointment. He knew they couldn't risk an accident, in case Ryan was in the car, but at the same time he didn't want to let Alex out of his sight. There was always a chance she had some other plan, some way of turning the tables on them.

At the bottom of the hill the road curved to the right. The Renault took it at speed and disappeared from view behind a hedgerow.

"Don't lose her," Nick said, jittery now.

"It's all right. She's got to slow down for Exceat."

Pearce sped up, then braked for the bend. Coming round, they saw the Renault heading for the narrow Exceat bridge, which required a sharp left turn. Both of them saw instantly that she would never make it.

Alex didn't know the road well, but vaguely recalled a bridge just round the bend that wasn't quite wide enough for two cars. Pushing seventy there wasn't a chance in hell she'd do it.

But by then she didn't care.

By then she'd made up her mind.

The Renault tore across the opposite lane, struck the raised concrete kerb and flipped into the air. In that moment she found herself thinking of Billy, and the perfect wretched irony that she was about to die as he had died, under the water.

The impact killed her instantly, which is to say that she felt nothing: not the eruption of metal and plastic, not the crushing obliteration, not the swirl of icy water around her body.

And yet in another sense, that same instant stretched almost to infinity. Rather than the fabled rush of memories there was but a single idea, an awareness that of all her tragedies, the greatest was not the loss of her father, but the fact that she had sacrificed her brother for no better reason than that she could, and in doing so she had condemned herself to a life utterly devoid of love.

33

Within seconds the road was in chaos: traffic at a standstill on both sides of the bridge, police cars screaming down the hill in the wrong lane, the helicopter clattering overhead. DCI Pearce turned into the car park of the Golden Galleon pub and stopped as close to the riverbank as she could. Nick was out of the car before she had engaged the handbrake.

The noise of the helicopter assaulted his ears, and he gestured angrily for it to back off. Air pressure from the rotor blades was disturbing the surface of the river, making it harder to see anything. From the water level Nick judged it was approaching high tide, the brown water flowing swiftly upstream.

More cars joined them. He saw Caitlin, closely followed by Diana and Patrick. His sister was distraught, quickly putting together what had happened and even quicker to comprehend what it meant. Her mouth fell open as she saw Nick, and he made a tiny movement of his head, indicating that he understood.

Was Ryan in the car?

Before he could be talked out of it, he slipped off his shoes and dived in, dimly aware of Pearce's protest as he hit the water.

It was freezing: that much he had expected. The shock was that he could see no more than a few inches in front of him. All he could do was swim blindly towards the car.

Though his mouth was clamped shut, he was sure he could taste the oil and fuel leaking from the vehicle. Within two or three strokes his hand made contact with a smooth metal surface, which he guessed was the car's roof. He grabbed the doorframe with one hand and felt broken glass pressing into his skin. Praying for some luck, he managed to reach down and grab the door handle. He was already disorientated by the darkness, but felt sure the car had landed on its side.

A sudden terror gripped him, the stuff of horror movies: Alex's cold dead embrace waiting for him in the car.

Or could she still be alive, and ready to attack?

He pushed the thoughts aside. Couldn't give in to the fear. Finding Ryan was all that mattered.

He'd been under less than twenty seconds but already he could feel his lungs protesting. He peered into the car, one hand groping to make sense of the dim shapes in front of him. He realised he was touching a mangled steering wheel, which had been compressed almost into the driver's seat. His fingers touched something soft and yielding and he recoiled, almost losing his grip on the car.

He was certain there'd been no one in the back seat, which left only the boot to check. He felt his way round to the rear, and again something that might once have been alive brushed his face as the current flushed out the hideous contents of the car.

His lungs were bursting now, black spots firing on his retinas as he ran his hand up from the bumper and located the line of the hatchback frame. He knew that if it hadn't popped open in the crash, he'd never get the boot release to work.

His fingers slipped into a space where the frame had buckled, and he tried to wrench the hatch up, but it didn't budge. It was stuck. If Ryan was in the boot, he would drown before Nick could fetch the tools he needed.

And then someone grabbed his shoulder.

His heart lurched with horror, and he almost sucked the filthy water into his lungs. Another strong hand moved across his vision and he just made out a familiar chunky signet ring.

Pat.

At the same time he realised his stupidity. The rear screen had shattered, and he could get to the boot space that way.

He pulled Pat alongside him, and they each gripped a corner of the hatch frame and reached inside, frantically tugging at the parcel shelf. After a few seconds Pat punched right through it and wrenched it out of the car. Nick pushed himself into the space, not trusting his vision when Ryan's life was at stake.

The two of them ran their hands around the boot, Pat even pulling up the carpet and checking the compartment housing the spare wheel. Then Nick put his face against Pat's and shook his head.

The boot was empty.

On the bank Caitlin, Diana and Melanie Pearce stood together, arms interlinked in a gesture of solidarity. Beside them, a couple of the firearms team were stripping off their body armour ready to join the rescue.

It felt like whole minutes had passed since first Nick and then Pat had disappeared beneath the water, but in fact it was less than forty seconds. Suddenly Diana made a low keening sound and her legs gave way. Only the instinctive movement of the other women prevented her from collapsing.

Then a head burst into view, followed by a second, both men gasping and choking as they swam towards the bank. Four or five officers scrambled down to help them.

"They're OK. They're OK," Pearce was saying, but Diana

didn't seem to hear her. It was only when she raised her head and saw Nick flopping on to the grass that she seemed to regain some strength.

Nick tried to speak, retched, then met his sister's eye.

"Not there," he said.

After Nick and Pat had been checked over by paramedics, they were taken back to the house to clean up. The firearms team were stood down and their place in the car park taken by police frogmen and a civilian vehicle recovery unit, alongside the CID, forensic and traffic officers already present.

"Half of Sussex police here," Nick said as Pearce drove them up the hill. "And we still have no idea what she did with him."

By six o'clock the media had picked up not just on the fatal accident, but on the whole complicated saga of revenge killings, complete with the one ingredient that any really juicy story needs: celebrity. News teams began to congregate at Exceat and in Seaford, while other journalists set up camp outside Nick's home in Hove, the hospital where Howard Franks was still recovering and various police stations in London, Kent and Sussex.

"Fucking bedlam," said Pearce. "Excuse my French."

Pat had switched on the TV, caught an aerial shot of the Cuckmere Valley on News 24, and promptly turned it off again.

The adrenalin of the chase had been replaced by a level of exhaustion and despair that no warm words or cups of sweet tea could alleviate. They sat together but mourned separately.

*

At six-fifteen Diana said, "He's going to die. He's alive, but he'll die if we don't find him." She tried to move, but her eyes rolled up in her head and she slumped back on the sofa. A doctor was called and recommended sedation, but finally compromised with bed rest.

While Pat sat with her, Nick and Caitlin went into the back garden, which so far had not been invaded by journalists.

"You know, I almost think this was part of her plan," Nick said.

"She killed herself on purpose?"

"Why not? She knew she'd never get away. And if we caught her there would be huge pressure to give up Ryan. Her lawyers would use that to get a reduced sentence."

"Whereas this way the agony continues."

"Yeah. She's won, hasn't she?"

Caitlin was standing behind him. She threaded her arms around his waist and rested her head against his shoulders. "Don't say that."

"She must have put him somewhere safe, where he couldn't escape or call for help. Maybe a rented garage, or a house, an apartment. Even just locked in the boot of another car. Without water he's got… what, a day or two at most?"

His voice choked, and he shook his head in disgust.

Neither of them spoke for a minute. They could hear traffic and voices in the street as local people congregated to discuss the drama unfolding on their doorstep, and the distant buzz of a helicopter filming the site of the crash. Even the throaty call of wood pigeons in the trees around them seemed urgent and concerned.

Nick said, "Where's the letter?"

∗

They read it at the kitchen table, alone except for DCI Pearce. She should have gone off duty hours ago, but she said she couldn't leave them now.

Nick stared at the letter, trying to put himself into the mind of the woman who wrote it. At the same time there was another thought nagging away, something that had been troubling him for the past two days.

"Ted Wheeler," he muttered, almost to himself. "Why did she torture him?"

Caitlin and Pearce exchanged a mystified glance. "To find out more about her father's killers?" the detective suggested.

"That's what we assumed. But hadn't she got all that from Franks? Wheeler was the only one she couldn't trace. The actual killers were long dead. So was Mickey Leach."

"And Ray McPherson," Caitlin said.

He nodded. There was a pause, and then they said in unison: "Roger."

"Hold on," said Pearce. "I'm trying to catch up here."

"Remember when she came to see me, calling herself Lindsay," Nick said to Caitlin. "She overheard us discussing Roger. She knew he was linked to Ted Wheeler. That's why she tortured him. She wanted to know about Roger."

"You think he was a target?" Pearce asked.

"He was Ray McPherson's nephew. I'm sure that was good enough for her."

"But Roger's been in custody since Tuesday," Caitlin said. "What could she do to hurt him?"

Nick was still working it out. A bitter smile appeared on his lips. "How about implicating him in her own crimes?" he said.

There was silence. Neither seemed entirely persuaded, but they weren't shouting him down either.

"Can you get us out of here without being followed?" he asked the detective.

DCI Pearce called her husband Trevor, who agreed to come immediately. Nick and Caitlin were helped over the back fence and through the house opposite, where Trevor collected them in his Daewoo. At the same time Pearce left the house, stopping to exchange a little banter with the waiting reporters, and then drove to the small police station in Seaford. A couple of cars pursued her, but she paid them no attention.

At the station she parked outside, waved to the journalists, hurried through to the staff car park and gave Trevor a peck on the cheek before climbing into his car. A couple of uniforms went out to the reporters with an offer of refreshments, providing cover while Pearce drove out with Nick and Caitlin crouching down in the back seat.

A mile down the road they were joined by two police motorcyclists. One of them gave a thumbs up as he sped past, clearing their path through the traffic.

"Lovely lads," said Pearce, accelerating up to ninety. "But the favours I'm gonna owe after this…"

It was seven-fifteen when they reached Clayton, a mellow evening with a cool wind and patchy cloud obscuring the sun as it sank behind the Downs. Nick had a shock when he saw the officer guarding Knight's home, and for the first time he felt glad he hadn't mentioned his idea to Diana or Pat. Suddenly it seemed absurd.

"Has someone been here since Tuesday?"

Pearce confirmed it was likely. "Can't risk anyone tampering with the scene."

"Shit." Nick exhaled slowly, seeming to lose some of his

spirit in the process. He looked at Caitlin, whose shrug only seemed to confirm his doubts. And if he was wrong about this, he was out of ideas. Ryan would die a terrible death, and he would always blame himself.

Exactly what Alex wanted.

They parked on the drive and Pearce quickly spoke to the officer on duty, PC Haynes. He confirmed there had been no unauthorised visitors.

"None at all?" Nick asked, his desperation sounding almost rude.

"All I've seen is tractors, jeeps and a few ramblers."

"Any women?" Nick said. "Tall, athletic physique? Or possibly disguised as an old lady?"

Haynes chuckled, then stopped abruptly when he caught Pearce's glare. "Sorry, ma'am. Actually, there was one went past yesterday morning. Hiking." Again he smiled, as at a fond memory. "I suppose she was rather shapely."

Nick was chewing his lip as he thought about it. "She'd have needed vehicle access," he said, gesturing at the driveway. "And if someone's been guarding this area…"

Caitlin gasped, turning towards PC Haynes. "You know about the lane, don't you?"

Haynes looked blank, squirming a little as all eyes turned on him.

"What lane?" said Nick.

Caitlin pointed to the way they'd just come. "About half a mile back there's a private access road leading to a farm. It runs past the rear of this property."

Caitlin and Pearce made for the house while Nick took the shed. Weaving between a sit-on mower and a motley collection of garden implements, his heart nearly stopped when he spotted a suspicious lump covered by empty rubbish sacks. He lifted them off to reveal a bag of chipped bark.

As he emerged, he saw Caitlin waving from the back door. "The summerhouse," she shouted. "I saw something from upstairs."

They dashed across the long expanse of lawn, and as they got closer Nick saw the double doors were slightly ajar. The padlock had been forced and lay broken on the ground.

"Oh Christ," he whispered, adding to himself: *Let him be alive...*

The summerhouse was constructed of redwood timber and measured ten feet by twelve. Inside there was a suite of wicker furniture, covered by dustsheets, and various bikes and garden toys lying around: beach balls, cricket bats, water pistols. In the far corner there was an old fridge, next to four large packing crates stacked against the rear wall. A faded Barbie doll sat drunkenly against one of the crates.

"Roger barely uses this any more," said Caitlin. "Not since the kids left."

Nick went straight to the fridge, fearing a gruesome discovery, but it was empty. "What's in the crates?" he asked.

Caitlin wasn't sure. "More toys, I think."

Nick pushed against one of them. It felt heavy. Then he noticed a thin line of the floor was free of dust. They'd been moved recently.

"Here," he said, pulling the top one towards him. Caitlin and Pearce helped him peel off the packing tape and they discovered a treasure trove of dolls, model cars and books.

The crate below had no packing tape. They found Ryan inside, curled in a foetal position and partly covered by a blanket. He seemed to be asleep, but none of them could breathe until they saw his eyelids flicker. He had his thumb in his mouth.

"Oh, thank God," said Caitlin, and she fell against Nick. He hugged her. Then he hugged Pearce. They all had tears in their eyes.

"I can't thank you enough," he said to Pearce.

"Don't be silly. Let's get him out, make sure he's OK. Then you can ring your sister."

He leaned over and gently touched Ryan's cheek. The boy stirred and turned away. Nick managed to reach under his arms and lift him up, and as he rose out of the crate Ryan opened his eyes and blinked sleepily. He smiled at Nick.

"Where's my Bionicle?" he said.

Epilogue

Two weeks later, when the tabloids finally decreed the story had run its course, Nick drove to London on a warm Saturday morning and parked in Wood Lane. The visit had been arranged two days earlier, at Franks's instigation, and as he approached the house Nick wasn't sure what to expect.

The door was answered by a shy young Indonesian nurse, who led him into a generously-proportioned living room, where Franks was sitting in a wheelchair. He had lost a lot of weight and his skin had a yellowy hospital pallor, but there was plenty of vitality in his blue eyes. His hair was neatly trimmed, and Nick saw his nails had been manicured: appearance was still important to him.

"Thought we'd go for a stroll," he said. The bossy manner was unchanged as well. "I'm under instructions to get plenty of fresh air."

"Fine with me," said Nick.

He led the way as the nurse expertly manoeuvred the wheelchair out of the house and down the drive, and at Franks's suggestion they made for Queens Wood.

For a while they kept to small talk, Franks asking after Diana and Ryan. The media onslaught had been ferocious, but the sheer joy of recovering her son unharmed had made the whole experience bearable.

"Actually, I think she could get a taste for this celebrity stuff," Nick told him. "She loved being on *Richard & Judy*."

"It's dangerously addictive," Franks said, and his rueful tone suggested he was ready to talk about what had happened.

They headed towards the old keeper's lodge, an attractive redbrick villa that had been converted into a café, and Nick helped the nurse back the wheelchair up the steps on to the veranda. There was a small play area adjoining the café, where half a dozen children were happily negotiating a rope bridge. Nick went inside and fetched coffee and cake for them all.

Franks toyed with his chocolate sponge for a while, and then said, "I wanted a chance to thank you. I understand you uncovered Lindsay's real identity and alerted the police. If not for that, I would have died."

"I wish I'd worked it out sooner."

"Well, I'm grateful." He sighed, met Nick's eye briefly and looked away. "Though I can honestly say there have been days when death seemed preferable."

"I'm sure."

Now Franks took a deep breath, gearing up for a revelation. "I also wanted to inform you that I've decided to abandon the book."

Nick was taken aback. Discussing it with Caitlin, he'd felt it was likely to be the opposite decision, with Franks pressing ahead and incorporating a lurid account of Alex's murderous spree. *That* book would make him a fortune.

His reaction was clear enough for Franks to look defensive. "I don't intend to claim my motives are entirely honourable. I'm sure you're well aware that I'm a laughing stock. The jumped-up hack whose manhood was hacked off."

Nick grinned in spite of himself. That was a pretty fair summary of the tabloids' position.

"The bastards are jealous, of course. I've made lots of money and lots of enemies. This is their chance to knock me down, and like all good journos they're relishing the opportunity."

"A taste of your own medicine."

"Quite. And I admit it's made me see things in a different light. If I go ahead with this book, I'm just putting myself back in the firing line."

"What will your publishers say?"

"I don't give a damn, to be honest. I'm comfortable enough financially. Rattling around in that silly big house. I might sell up and move to Florida. Swim. Play golf."

"Write a novel?"

Franks cracked a smile. "Of course."

They drank their coffee, watched the children on the rope bridge, and then it was time to go back. As they ascended the steep incline out of the wood Nick tried to engage the nurse in conversation, but Franks interjected.

"Wasting your time. Doesn't speak a word of English." He made a huffing noise. "The agency sends a different one every few days. Costing me a bloody fortune, but what the hell." Then his tone softened. "Quite a beauty, isn't she? In the old days I'd have fancied my chances."

Nick glanced at the nurse, who caught his eye and quite emphatically shook her head. He concealed his laugh with a cough.

He was still debating whether to ask when Franks said, "Sex life has gone for a burton, if that's what you're wondering. They managed to re-attach it, but there were some… complications." He looked up at Nick. "Everyone winces when I say that."

"I bet they do," said Nick, wincing.

They trudged up Muswell Hill Road, passing the cottage where Peter Sellers had once lived. Franks was gazing sadly at the pavement.

"I suppose I had my fair share over the years. Same as your dad."

Nick felt uncomfortable. This was the first mention of Eddie Randall.

"You know, after eighteen months' research and writing, I expect I know him nearly as well as you did, if not better."

It wasn't said as a boast, and Nick couldn't disagree. "Perhaps," he said. "There are lots of things I wish I didn't know."

Franks shook his head. "Disregard anything that came from that evil woman. The fact is, nobody knows for sure what happened, and no one can prove your father did anything wrong. That's why the papers have had to be so careful."

"Maybe," said Nick, aware of how much he wanted to be persuaded. "It poisons his memory, though. Losing him at nine, he was always a pretty distant figure, but he was still a hero to me." He smiled fondly. "And I had the films. Any time I wanted I could watch him being funny, or clumsy, cheeky or tough."

They reached Nick's car and stopped. He dug in his pocket for his keys, glad of the distraction.

"I liked him," Franks said abruptly. "I don't know if that means anything, but I liked him. Ignore the rumours. It's the man you see on screen that counts."

Nick held his gaze for a few seconds, and then nodded solemnly. They shook hands and he wished Franks a speedy recovery.

For twenty minutes he drove with tears streaming down his face, and afterwards he felt better than he had in weeks. A couple of times he caught himself glancing at the passenger seat, certain he would spot a familiar face: cheeky and tough, warm brown eyes and a smile full of charm.

Are you ready, Nicky lad?

Alone in the car, he nodded. It was time to move on.

COMING SOON
from Crème de la Crime:

Baby Love
Maureen Carter

Third in Carter's hugely popular Bev Morriss series.

Rape, baby-snatching, murder: all in a day's work for Birmingham's finest – but when the removal men have only just left your new house, your lover's attention is elsewhere and your last case left you not too popular in the squad room, it's sure to end in tears. Detective Sergeant Bev finds herself in serious trouble when her eye slips momentarily off the ball.

Published June 2006
Price £7.99
ISBN: 0-9551589-0-7

No Sleep for the Dead
Adrian Magson

Another outing for crimebusters Riley Gavin and Frank Palmer.

Investigative journalist Riley has problems. Palmer disappears after a disturbing chance encounter, her love affair seems set to stay long-distance and she's being followed by a mysterious dreadlocked man.

Frank's determination to pursue justice for an old friend puts him and Riley in deadly danger from art thieves, gangstas, British Intelligence – and a bitter old woman out for revenge.

Published August 2006
Price £7.99
ISBN: 0-9551589-1-5

Behind You!

Linda Regan

Crackling debut novel by popular actress turned crime writer.

Christmas: a time of peace and goodwill.

Oh no it isn't, thinks Detective Inspector Paul Banham. Was the suspicious death at the pantomime an accident – or murder? Banham finds the theatrical glamour tarnished by rivalries, grudges and illicit liaisons; and then there's a second death. But the panto is sold out and the show must go on.

Published September 2006
Price £7.99
ISBN: 0-9551589-2-3

ALREADY AVAILABLE
from Crème de la Crime:

WORKING GIRLS   MAUREEN CARTER
Dark and gritty… an exciting debut novel…
Reviewing the Evidence
ISBN: 0-9547634-0-8   £7.99

A KIND OF PURITAN   PENNY DEACON
A subtle, clever thriller…
Daily Mail
ISBN: 0-9547634-1-6   £7.99

NO PEACE FOR THE WICKED   ADRIAN MAGSON
…the excitement carries right through to the last page…
Ron Ellis
ISBN: 0-9547634-2-4   £7.99

IF IT BLEEDS   BERNIE CROSTHWAITE
Pacy, eventful… an excellent debut. Mystery Women
ISBN: 0-9547634-3-2   £7.99

A CERTAIN MALICE   FELICITY YOUNG
a beautifully written book… Felicity draws you into the life in Australia…
you may not want to leave.
Natasha Boyce, Ottakar's crime buyer
ISBN: 0-9547634-4-0   £7.99

PERSONAL PROTECTION   TRACEY SHELLITO
a powerful, edgy story… I didn't want to put down…
Reviewing the Evidence
ISBN: 0-9547634-5-9   £7.99

DEAD OLD   MAUREEN CARTER
confirms Carter among the new generation of crime writers.
J. Wallis Martin
ISBN: 0-9547634-6-7   £7.99

NO HELP FOR THE DYING   ADRIAN MAGSON
Gritty and fast-paced detecting of the traditional kind, with a welcome injection of realism.
Maxim Jakubowski, The Guardian
ISBN: 0-9547634-7-5   £7.99

A THANKLESS CHILD   PENNY DEACON
… moves at a fast slick pace… a lot of colourful characters… a good page-turner… very readable.
Ann Bell, newbooks
ISBN: 0-9547634-8-3   £7.99